The Bleecker Street Bodies

Aaron S Gallagher

This book is dedicated to Cara

My wife
My friend
My book widow

The Bleecker Street Bodies

Chapter One

They set on him at the corner of Bleecker and Mott. Because the wind whipped snow into his eyes, he didn't see anything until they were on him. There were three of them in the dim twilight, one of which he thought he recognized, but before he could speak, they dragged him into a dark side alley. A fist slammed into his gut and he lost his wind in an explosive gasp.

A second punch caught him just behind his jaw. He made a squeaking noise and dropped to his knees in the grimy slush of the alley floor. Rough hands pawed at his pants and his wallet vanished. His attackers started to run when one skidded to a halt. He pulled out the wallet and ID, looked back at the lump on the floor of the alley.

"Come on, Keen," one of the others said. "Let's go, man, go!"

Keen shook his head, heaved a sigh, and trudged back to their victim. He put an arm under the man's shoulder and hauled him to his feet. He held their victim up as the older man tried to catch his breath.

"Keen, what-"

"Shut up, Deit. It's DeMarko," Keen said. Deit swore under his breath. The third punk laughed, "What's the big deal? Come on, man!"

"Naah," Deit said. "Keen's right. He's not a mark. We know him."

They pulled Harry out of the snow and helped him over to the side of the alley where he leaned against the dirty brick catching his breath. His ragged breathing slowed and finally he could speak. "Jesus, guys. You could have *asked*."

Keen handed the scuffed Lord Buxton wallet back to Harry.

"Sorry, Harry," Keen said. Harry examined Keen's face. There were new bruises as well as the old scars over his eyes. Once upon a time, Keen had been a boxer. That was before the detached retinas, and well before the drugs.

"I mean, for God's sake, guys, I *live* here, you know?"

"I said I'm sorry," Keen said. "We just- we just thought-"

"You *didn't* think, man," Harry said. He straightened up with an audible popping from his spine. He turned his head each way and got further snaps. "Jesus, you hit me in the *neck*."

He rubbed the red spot.

"Hurts to swallow, Keen."

Keen looked abashed. "I'm sorry, Harry-"

"Food, booze, or crack, Keen?" Harry asked.

"What?"

"Which were you gonna buy? Huh? Speak up."

Keen scratched his arms, digging through his thin coat at the sallow flesh with dirty, broken nails. "Uh… food. We haven't- we-"

Harry dug out his wallet, produced two grubby bills, and handed them to Keen. The junkie grabbed them, but Harry didn't let go. "Keen, look at me. Look me in the eyes."

Keen tore his gaze away from the fives and looked DeMarko in the face.

"You go right now and buy food. Don't go to a restaurant or a street cart. Go to the corner, to

Dahli's, and buy some *food*. Get some bread. Some cold meat. Get something that'll last you a while. Get some cans of something. This is all I have, understand? It's all you get, because it's all I have."

Keen nodded. Harry kept his grip on the money.

"Say it, Keen."

Keen cast his eyes down and stammered, "G-go to Dahli's grocery. Get some food that'll last a while. No junk. Good food."

"All right. Go on. And stop hassling locals, Keen. You're gonna catch a bullet," Harry said.

Keen hesitated, said, "Thanks," in a low voice, and walked away. Deit and Teddy followed along behind him. Harry watched them go with a bemused look. He stuck his hands in the pockets of his old overcoat, gripping the .38. Someday those punks would roll someone who wouldn't be nice. And that would be that.

He took a step and grabbed for the wall, and took another, forcing himself to stay upright. The shot to the belly had hurt more than it should have. He'd been neglecting the old exercise routine of late. Not long, only three or four years. Or six or seven. Eight at the outside.

He gained momentum as he hit Bleecker and continued east. At the corner he glanced into the window of Dahli's Grocery, through the myriad of stickers and ads and homemade notices, to see his three would-be muggers buying supplies. *Sure*, he thought. *I'm not a mark*.

Dahli's didn't stock the hard stuff so he didn't go in. He turned the corner and walked half a block down before he came to Brandt's Discount Liquor. The door chime sounded desolate in the empty store.

Sandy Redmay slouched behind the counter reading a magazine, her dark skin shining under the fluorescents.

"You look beat," she said. "More than usual."

"Yeah, yeah. Had an accident. Slipped," Harry said. He showed Sandy where his knees and the back of his coat were dark with the damp and smeared dirt. "It's getting bad out there."

"Gotta stay warm," Sandy said. "You'll catch your death."

"I wouldn't be so lucky. Who's here?"

Sandy grinned at him and put a hand on her chubby hip. "You and me, Porter and Cathy. Just waiting on Mitch and Mikey."

"All right. Is there food?"

"Yep. Grabbed cold cuts and cheese from the deli. Grab a bottle you like," Sandy said. "I'm gonna lock up."

"You got it." Harry walked down the bourbon aisle and grabbed a bottle of Wild Turkey. He opened the green and scarred Employees Only door that led into the storage room. In the middle of all the boxes sat a faded green felt-topped card table. Two other people sat talking. They had six tumblers on the table, but no drinks in them.

"Hey, Harry," Cathy called. She looked like her sister Sandy, only thinner.

"Cathy. Porter," Harry said. He set the bottle on the table and shucked his coat.

"You have such exquisite taste in liquor when you're not buying, Harry," Cathy said. She unscrewed the cap and poured a measure in each of the six glasses. She swigged a nip out of the bottle before capping it. Harry went to the smaller side table and began making sandwiches for the crowd. He kept going until he ran out of bread.

The door opened and three more people filed in. Sandy, followed by a lanky beanpole of a man named Mitch Abso, and the owner of the liquor store, Michael Brandt. Brandt raised his hand to them and Harry said, "The founder of the feast. How's it hanging, Mikey?"

"Left, Harry, as usual. How've you been?" Mike called to him.

The bi-weekly poker tradition started when Harry had broken up a robbery back when he was a rookie. He hadn't been looking for anything wrong, he'd actually come in for a bottle. Two punks with knock-off .32s trying to rob the place interrupted his night. He and Mikey had drawn down simultaneously. After calling it in and giving a statement, Mikey asked him if he played cards. At first it was he and Mike, Sandy and Cathy. One night not too long after, Harry'd been spending some quality time not talking in a bar near the station house with Porter Rockwell, one of the homicide detectives. They'd just finished a case together- a murdered cabbie. They hadn't made a collar. The perp had gone down in a blaze of glory and taken another rookie with him.

After drinking themselves into a less angry mood, Harry off-handedly asked Porter if he wanted to come get his ass kicked at cards. Mitch started playing because Porter had invited him one night when Harry worked late. Going on ten years later, they still met twice a week to play cards, get drunk, and shoot the shit. When Harry retired in seventy-six they threw him a party and wanted to invite half his precinct, but Harry told them if they did, he wouldn't show up. His retirement party had consisted of sandwiches, cards, and Wild Turkey.

Harry passed around the sandwiches. Sandy passed him the deck.

"Your deal, Harry," she said.

He shuffled and dealt them around.

"So how you been, Harry?" Porter asked through a mouthful of roast beef.

"Cold," Harry told Porter. "How's work?"

Porter shrugged. "Mostly frozen winos the last couple of days. Pretty slow."

"That's a damned shame," Mikey said. He ran a hand through his thinning hair. "Those winos are some of my best customers."

Cathy said, "That's profiteering, Mikey."

"That's capitalism," he said. "See a weakness, exploit it."

They all chuckled.

"Doesn't it bother you, Mikey?" Harry asked.

Mike shrugged. "I didn't make them drunks. I didn't screw up their lives. You know, I had a woman in here yesterday trying to buy wine with food stamps. Food stamps! Tell me that isn't all kinds of screwed up. I didn't invent that system. I didn't take the stamps."

"Would you have?" Porter asked.

"If I could," Mikey said. "But the city won't reimburse me."

Sandy slapped his arm. "You're terrible."

"Hey, I'm just trying to make it in this harsh world. No one looks out for you. You gotta look out for yourself. I have mouths to feed."

"Whose?" Cathy asked.

"I don't know, someone's," Mike said with a wry smile.

Harry watched each of them while he casually laid his cards down. When everyone begun to pay attention to the table again, he was sipping his drink. He fanned open his cards.

"Bastard," Cathy said, chucking her cards in. Mike sucked his teeth and folded. Mitch tossed his into the middle and they landed face-up. He had nothing.

"That's a nice hand, Harry," Porter said. "Small straight. Pretty unbeatable. I mean, unless you have a *real* hand."

"And you have a real hand?" Harry asked.

He and Porter locked eyes. "Of course I have a real hand. I wouldn't bullshit you."

"You'd *of course* bullshit me, Porter," Harry said. "It's what you do instead of actually playing."

Porter narrowed his eyes. Harry just smiled. Porter laughed and threw his cards down. Fives and sevens. "I need dumber friends," he said.

"I get raising on a busted flush," Mike said, "but what the hell do you get out of trying to bluff on a busted *call*? That doesn't even make sense."

"I'll tell you after we finish this bottle," Porter said, holding up the Wild Turkey. "I guarantee it'll make more sense then."

They laughed.

"Whose deal?" Harry asked.

"I got it," Sandy said. She shuffled them quickly and dealt them out.

They began the rituals and dance.

Chapter Two

They finally knocked off after one. Harry stumbled and tripped his way down the worsening street. The slush and snow had built up into frozen ridges and the drinks didn't help his balance. There were no other people dumb enough to be out and he walked alone through the silence. The street lights showed the flakes in the air in freeze-frame distinct shapes, blowing on the breeze, but still somehow illuminated and individual.

He turned down Elizabeth Street. Halfway down the narrow side street he stepped around a bum slumped in front of an old closed-up shop. The bum had cleared away the snow from his little spot and lay shivering, balled up around a pint bottle. The wide front window of the former Chinese restaurant had been soaped from the inside, and the outside bore no markings save grime and frost. Some comedian had scratched 'for a good tim call yur mom' in the dirty glaze. Glued to the front of the door was a neat wooden placard labeled 'Investigations' and his phone number.

"Harry?"

He turned at the tentative, familiar voice. Toni emerged from the gathered darkness of an alcove. She wasn't dressed for the weather, clad in a cheap plastic skirt, a halter top, five-inch bright red heels, and fishnets. She had a thin coat wrapped around her shoulders. There were layers of makeup on her face and her hair had been teased into a crown of reckless brown curls and dangling streamers. She had glitter on one cheek and a bruise on the other. He sighed, slumping his shoulders and standing aside for her. She slipped inside and he followed.

Once upon a time Ming's Chinese Restaurant had been a single large room with a modest kitchen behind flimsy partitions. Now it was Harry's office and home. In a fit of energy and handiness he'd yet to match, he had taken one week to divide the large room into two smaller rooms. A sturdy wall cut across the width of the restaurant, separating the office in front from the living quarters in back, complete with a nice door. The front office had a scarred desk, a relatively clean couch, and a coffee machine bequeathed to him by the owners of the restaurant that was so old he suspected the building had probably been built around it. He poured the remaining coffee, still hot from the burner, into a paper cup. He stepped out and handed it to the bum curled up against the dirty stone face of the building.

"Thanks, Chief," the bum whispered. His weathered face stretched into a gapped grin. "You're a real humin bein."

"Don't tell anyone," Harry said. "I've got an image to maintain."

He went back inside. His answering machine, easily the most expensive piece of equipment in his office, wasn't blinking, but he checked it anyhow, expecting nothing and getting it. The mail basket next to the door stood empty too. Well, no news is good news sometimes, right? Sure.

He followed Toni into the living area. He'd long since plumbed in the necessary details. It wasn't the Hilton but it worked fine for just him. He heard the shower running, and he sighed. If *only* it was just him.

"Hey, save me some hot water, Toni!" he called through the bathroom door.

"Come join me!" she yelled back. "It's more efficient!"

"Screw that," he muttered.

She heard him, though, and responded. "No, screw *me!*"

He pulled off his overcoat. Before he tossed it carelessly onto the rack in the corner, he pulled his gun from the pocket. The coat went on the rack, the .38 went in the cheap pasteboard nightstand next to his huge bed.

The apartment was roomy enough, but sparsely-decorated. A bed, a second couch matching the one in the office, another smaller desk, a couple chairs and a table, an old television. The walls were some grungy wood paneling he'd gotten remaindered and cheaply. A myriad of rugs covered the floor, none of which matched but all of which had one virtue: they were cheap. He stripped and stood in front of the full-length mirror nailed to the back of his bathroom door.

Nothing much to look at, he thought. Sandy brown hair, balding. Thick dark eyebrows. He scrubbed at his chin and cheeks. Four days of stubble. Skinny chest but a flat belly, more or less. Wide, boat-like size thirteens stuck on the bottom of unremarkable legs. No, nothing much to look at, except for the scar. *The only really interesting thing about me,* he thought, *tried to kill me.*

It blossomed on his left breast like an exotic and dangerous tropical flower, just where his shoulder and clavicle met. It was ragged and star-shaped and the hole in the center wasn't perfect, but a little oblong.

They'd had to open him up wide to get all the shrapnel out. He'd gotten lucky. That's what they said. Lucky. Lucky he was a righty. It had screwed up his left arm pretty good. He still couldn't curl much with it. Maybe fifteen, twenty pounds. Couldn't pull the trigger quickly. And it hurt like a sonovabitch when it was cold. A career-ending wound. Goodbye, NYPD Officer DeMarko, hello civilian Harry DeMarko. Hello partial disability. Hello shitty twenty-year half-pay retirement. Goodbye uniform.

Okay, it wasn't *all* bad.

He'd never wear the blues again. Or the horrible shoes. No standing in the freezing snow for hours directing traffic with those goddamned white cotton gloves that never stay clean and don't keep your hands warm for jack.

The powers-that-were let him add some years so he could have a meager twenty-year pension. It was enough to live on if you didn't actually need a real place to live or enjoy hot food. Partial disability picked up the slack a little. Sometimes he even got to have steak.

Fine, fine. Money isn't an issue if you've got low taste, like Harry did. He wasn't given to expensive suits or gourmet restaurants and the museums were free most of the time, just like the library. But what do you *do* with all your time? Suddenly, your life's not measured out by five eight-hour shifts (if you're lucky). Suddenly you don't have to go anywhere, or do anything. No paperwork keeping you chained to a desk in the middle of the night. No babysitting some crime scene at three in the morning with the snow building up on your shoulders, or the rain soaking you until you're shivering and blue. No canvassing some neighborhood where no one saw anything, no one heard anything, and theft, rape, and murder were just another day. Suddenly there are no brothers and sisters at your back, suffering the crap along with you. Suddenly, you're all alone when you were part of a great big family. What then?

Well, you figure it out or you go crazy. He had, at least sort of. He had a taste for carrying a gun. He liked being on the right side of the law. So he applied and took the test and got his private investigator's license, a permit to carry concealed, and made a plaque for his door. The rest, as they say, was history. He was wildly successful-

He looked around his dim little handmade apartment that smelled like fried rice no matter what he did, and snorted laughter.

He had the adoration of scores of beautiful women-

He heard Toni switch off the shower. He sighed. Yeah.

He had the respect and awe of his peers-

Half his friends from the force didn't talk to him anymore. Not because they didn't like him, but because he wasn't blue any longer. Nothing personal. That was the easy part. The hard part was dealing with the rest, the ones who threw him a bone now and then but were quietly contemptuous of his meager living, scraped from snoop jobs and the occasional missing person case. He shrugged to himself. They were contemptuous out of fear, he knew. He could be them. But they gave him the occasional tip and it allowed him to keep playing detective, something he'd never been able to do as a cop. He'd always assumed he would get the gold shield in due time. He never rushed to take the advancement tests. He wanted as much street experience as he could get. All the good detectives had ten, fifteen years of street behind them. Now he was a detective, chasing cats and wayward husbands.

It was a living. Sort of. It was also a way to keep one hand on the past. Like a former soldier hanging around the base bar. Not pitiful, exactly, but... wistful.

He was still staring at his naked body when the bathroom door opened and Toni stepped out naked and clean, surrounded by steam. She'd have been an enticing sight except everything about her, Harry thought, was a little *too*.

She had big eyes and high cheekbones, but her mouth was a little too wide. She had perky breasts, but they were a little too small for him to consider voluptuous. She was thin, but a little too thin, and her ribs stood out like slats in a tenement apartment wall. She had too little pubic hair. Claimed the johns liked it better that way. She looked prepubescent to him. She had legs a little too narrow to be curvy, and she had feet that were a little too small. She looked odd to him with those tiny feet. Like she melted into the floor.

His cynicism had noted all of these details and he had summed her up. That was Toni. Just a girl who was a little *too*. Girl, hell. He didn't know how old she was, but he wouldn't bet on her being more than seventeen or eighteen, and that was being generous. He turned away from her.

"It's about damned time," she said while sliding her arms around him. One hand dipped low. She toyed with him for a second before he slapped it away. He studiously ignored her pout.

"Put some clothes on," he said. "It's cold in here."

"So come warm me up," she grinned at him.

"You know the answer to that."

She grimaced. "You know, none of the girls believe you're not screwing me. They can't believe you'd let me stay here for free, charging no pussy tax. They all keep offering theirs to stay here, too. Could have yourself quite a party, Harry. Two, three, four at a time. Maybe more."

"I only take one charity case at a time. You better have left me some hot water," he threatened.

"Probably," Toni said as she slipped into one of his old tee shirts and a pair of terry shorts. She curled up on his bed, smiling as the springs squeaked and creaked. She hopped up and down a little, making them sing. He poked his head out the bathroom door.

"What are you doing?" he asked.

"Fantasies are better with sound effects," she said. She continued making raucous noises on the bed until he closed the door on her.

After his shower he slipped into his fuzzy robe. When he came out she had the TV on, trying to get it to show anything but static. He grabbed some beer from the walk-in fridge left over from the restaurant days, and a couple of cold hamburgers in a paper sack. He tossed one on the bed and chewed on the other.

"Jiggle the aerial," he instructed. She grabbed the rabbit ears and waved them. The picture faded in and out and finally she found the sweet spot. The snow-speckled   rebroadcast   of   the   dolorous pronouncements of Walter Cronkite solidified into view.

"…the electoral count now looks like thirty-five for Carter, and some two hundred and thirty-eight for Ronald Reagan. As you can see, Ronald Reagan is very close to the two-seventy he needs to win."

The picture jumped to an anchor who wasn't important enough to work regular hours. "That was the turning point this evening. Our predictions of the election were borne out by the polls. To repeat for those of you just tuning in, California Governor Ronald Reagan has been elected president of the United States by a virtual landslide and is our fortieth president. This was the scene earlier at Reagan campaign headquarters-"

Another jump cut and a crowd of enthusiastic Reagan supporters cheered as the handsome, affable Reagan addressed his admirers. "-family. I'm so grateful to them, for the love, for the support, and for the hard work, because some of them were out on the campaign trail easily as much as Nancy and I were. And speaking of Nancy, she's going to have a new title in a couple of months. And it isn't really new because she's been the first lady in my life for a long time. Now-"

Toni plopped on the bed and picked up her hamburger. She wolfed it down. Harry shook his head at the television. "That poor peanut farmer never stood a chance."

Toni watched the screen with disinterest. "What do you mean?"

Harry shrugged and handed her a beer. "This was pretty one-sided. It looks like people wanted a cowboy in the White House."

"Cowboy?"

Harry smiled at her. "Reagan's an actor. Was. Maybe still is. He gives good speech and he looks good on the tube. But he used to be a movie actor. Westerns and comedies and the like. Death Valley Days, Bedtime for Bonzo. Like that."

"I never saw those, I guess."

"Before your time." Harry rolled his head back and forth, grunting. He palpated his belly. "Ow, damn it."

"What happened?" Toni asked.

Harry said, "Got rolled on the way home. Keen and his pals. Didn't know it was me. Got in a couple punches before we straightened it out."

"Straightened it out?" Toni asked. She said disgustedly, "You mean you gave them your cash."

Harry shrugged. "Doesn't matter."

"Why'd you wanna go and do that?" she asked. "You'll never see it again. They're not going to repay you. None of them ever do, Harry."

Harry frowned and blew air through his ballooned cheeks and pursed lips. "Not the point. I had it. They needed it."

"*You* need it. It's not like… wait. Is that why I'm here? Because *I* needed it? Or because *you* did?" she asked him.

Harry didn't say anything. Toni reached out to touch his arm, but he got up. He grabbed a blanket off the foot of the bed and went to the couch. Sipping his beer he lay back on the couch and covered up with the blanket. Toni popped the top on her own beer.

"Why don't you sleep here?" she asked, as she always did. "Plenty of room. Warmer, too."

"I'm good," he mumbled.

Toni growled at him. "I don't understand you, Harry. Is it me? Or is it girls?"

"It's not you. And it's not girls. It just *is*. Leave me alone," he said. He rolled over and put his back to her.

"Come on, Harry," Toni said. The tone of her voice made him look over at her. She looked young and lost. "Come on. Just sleep here. Okay? Please?"

He sighed. "No."

"Why not?" she asked. "Why not?"

"It wouldn't be right. I don't let you sleep here because I want something from you," he told her.

"Not even if I'm offering?" she asked.

"You're not offering it freely. You want to repay me," he said.

Toni said impatiently, "Just like you're repaying me by letting me sleep here. Letting me *live* here. All because I-"

"I know what you did!" he snapped. She flinched away from his anger and he regretted it. She didn't say anything. He thrashed back and forth on the couch and finally sat up.

"I know what you did," he said more softly. "And you're right. I let you stay here to repay you. I owe you. But that's not the same as-as…"

"As me wanting to show *you* how grateful I am," she said with a dour look.

"You don't *need* to show me. Just say it, if you want to. Or don't. The point is, you don't have to. You don't owe me. I don't have any claim on you. So just-just let it alone," he said, and turned away again.

She got up and turned off the television. He listened to her, keeping his eyes closed, as she moved around the space. She turned off the bathroom light and then the standing lamp that served as the main light in the room because he hated the fluorescent lighting the restaurant had used. In the dark he listened to her sitting on the edge of the bed. She got up again and went to the couch. She bent down and kissed his cheek, resting a hand on his shoulder. He pressed the back of her hand briefly, and she went back to the bed. The springs creaked as she climbed into it. In the darkness, he said, "Toni?"

"Yes?"

"How'd you get the bruise?" he asked her.

She was quiet for a moment. "Mr. Jay. I was short today. He slapped me around to remind me who I work for."

Harry was silent for so long that she thought he'd fallen asleep. And then he said in a dead voice, "Do you want me to talk to him?"

"I-I don't want him to hurt you, Harry," she said.

He laughed bitterly. "I wouldn't talk to him alone, Toni. I'm not an idiot. I'd bring a couple of my friends. From Vice."

"That'd be nice… right up until he took it out of *my* ass for dropping the cops on him. I'd get more than a slap for that," she told him.

Harry exhaled. "Yeah, probably. But I could persuade him to stop running you. I could get you free."

She said with a wry smile, "You keep offering and I keep telling you, Harry. If it's not John it's someone else."

"You could stop peddling ass, Toni," Harry said. "You don't *like* what you do, do you?"

She sounded honestly baffled as she told him, "Why not? It's not hard. I get to keep some of the money and I don't pay taxes. Make more than a waitress or secretary. What's not to like?"

Harry didn't say anything.

"Come on, Harry. What am I supposed to do? It's not like I have a lot of skills. I'm not smart, I don't have a high school diploma, but I *do* know how to suck-"

"Stop it!" Harry snarled. "Would you just quit?"

She laughed at him. "Jesus, you think you'd never had sex, the way you go on about it."

"Just shut up and let me sleep," he muttered.

"Whatever you say, Harry," Toni said. "Come on, Harry. Don't you want me?"

"Shut up, Toni," he said.

"Whatever you say, Harry," she said.

Chapter Three

Toni was already gone when Harry dragged himself off the couch in the morning. He only knew it was morning because of the clock; no windows in the apartment. He flicked on the elderly TV and waited for the picture to warm up.

He ran the shower and flicked on the stove while waiting. After breakfast and another hot shower he pulled on his pants and shirt and went into the office. He poured himself a cup of fresh coffee. They might bicker and squabble, but Toni always made sure he had coffee when he woke up. He sipped and grimaced at the bitter taste, but it reassured him after the previous night's bickering. She made it stronger when she was in a good mood. The message machine blinked at him. He kept the ringer off because of cranks and incessant calls for Chinese takeout, so he never heard it when people called him. He pressed the button.

"Hey, Harry, it's Porter. It's nine, more or less. Gimme a call when you get this. They'll patch you through. Later."

Huh. He looked at the clock. Ten minutes, maybe fifteen since Porter called. Maybe it was a tip on a job. He called the stationhouse and had them put his call through to the rover in Porter's car. The connection was terrible, but he could hear the false joviality in Porter's voice anyhow.

"Hey, Harry, how's it hanging?" Porter called.

"Porter."

"Listen, Harry, I caught a case this morning that I could use your help on," Rockwell said. "It's on your beat and you're more clued in around here than I am."

"Oh, yeah?" Harry asked. "What've you got?"

"You got any lowlifes around here good with a blade?" Rockwell asked.

"Most all the junkies and bums around here carry knives, Porter. You know that."

"Yeah. Listen, you busy right now?" Porter asked.

Harry grimaced. Porter knew damned well Harry probably didn't have anything going. He'd finished his last job, a snoop piece. Chasing around after a Mr. for a Mrs. who wanted to know where he was putting it to good use. Harry reminded himself he needed to drop the film off at Dahli's.

"You say this happened last night?" he asked.

"Yeah. Couple hours ago, about four blocks from your place. You know the alley between Bleecker and Bond?" Porter asked.

"Yeah, I know that one. Secluded. Guys like to take the hookers there."

"Come on over, if you've a mind. Let me know what you think," Porter said, and his tone made Harry think it wasn't so much a request.

"Yeah, all right. I'll be there in a few," Harry told him.

"Want me to send a car?" Porter asked.

"No," Harry said. "The walk'll do me good. I'll see you in a while."

"Sure, sure. See ya." Porter hung up.

Harry grabbed his overcoat and stuck the .38 in his pocket. He took the camera out of his other pocket and pulled the film, putting the camera back into the drawer. He'd drop the film off today. He refilled his cup and a second one as well. Balancing them awkwardly, he levered open the front door. It wasn't locked because he wouldn't give Toni a key. He liked her well enough but he didn't trust her, not with a key to his house. He was afraid he'd come home to a house full of hookers, or worse. He was a sucker, but he wasn't an all-day sucker.

He stepped into a freezing wind. November was gearing up and gaining momentum, and when December hit he'd wish he was a bear and could just pull his hole in behind him for the winter. Jasper was covered with a dusting of snow. Harry nudged him with a foot. Jasper looked up and Harry handed him the steaming cup of coffee.

"Thanks, Chief. You're a real humin bein," the bum muttered.

"Keep warm," Harry told him.

"Don't worry about me, Chief. I'm part polar bear. The rest is penguin," the gap-toothed grin said.

Harry chuckled. "I'd love to have seen that wedding night."

He started up the street with Jasper's rusty cackle following him in the crisp morning air. He trudged through the fresh snow, making the first path of the day. Around the corner and up Bleecker he could see the crowd of police cruisers in the distance. He lowered his head against the wind and sipped his coffee as he walked.

The stores that lined Bleecker weren't open because of the weather. With the way the snow was piling up they might not open today at all. He tugged his coat closer and crossed to the far side of the street, wishing he'd picked up some gloves. Traffic wasn't a worry. That was the best thing about a New York winter; it cut traffic practically in half. Made it almost nice to be out, even with the cold.

He came up to the cordon, lined with gawkers even in the weather, everyone hoping to see blood or a body. He waved over a patrolman. "I'm DeMarko. Rockwell's waiting for me," he said. He didn't bother flashing the consultant's ID the city had given him for such times. The patrolman confirmed it with a quick question into his walkie.

"All right. Come on." The rookie lifted the tape and Harry squirmed under. The crowd wanted to come with him, but the rookie planted himself and held up his hands, exerting excellent command authority, especially for a rookie. The crowd was trying to bait him as they always did, and he was having none of it. The rookie had some stones. Harry remembered when he was learning crowd control.

Harry went into the mouth of the alley, staying close to the wall. He slipped past the crowd of cops standing around not looking busy. The ME bent over the body of slim woman face-down in the slush. Rockwell stood to one side watching. Porter was wide-faced second-generation German peasant stock, broad through the shoulders and quicker than he looked. He liked letting people misjudge his intelligence. He looked up and saw Harry. He raised a hand.

"Hey, Harry," he said.

"Morning, Porter. Eugene," Harry said, addressing the ME.

The medical examiner looked up over the top of his spectacles. Kaminski seemed surprised, but a grin appeared out of his bushy grey beard. "Why, Harry

DeMarko. Haven't seen you in a long time. You back?"

"No, I'm a consultant. Whatcha got, Gene?" Harry asked.

"Oh, a stabbing. Nothing spectacular." Gene looked down and waved a hand. "Cause of death is easy. One to the heart. Pretty instantaneous, lucky her."

"Weapon?" Harry asked.

"Nothing we've found," Eugene said. He looked up at Porter. "I'm done. Want to roll her again?"

"May as well. Give old Harry here a look," Porter told him.

Eugene nodded at one of his assistants, and the two men took hold of the limp body. Harry noticed that the body wasn't stiff and the snow had melted around her. Her silk shirt was flashy yellow, soaked, and had pulled out of the cheap skirt. "Limp body, melted snow. Feels recent to me," Harry remarked.

Eugene nodded. "I'm betting two, three hours, maybe. Just before dawn."

"Got any id? Wallet? Anything?" Harry asked.

Porter watched Harry running it in his mind. Sure, a lot of the guys had written him off as a medical casualty, and sure, he'd never gotten his shield, but Porter had known Harry for years and he knew Harry had it where it counted. He had the kind of dogged, suspicious mind that made a good detective, even if he was just playing part-time PI.

"No, she wasn't carrying anything at all. Typical if she was robbed," Eugene said.

"Who called it in?" Harry asked.

Porter said, "Some news hack cutting across the alley spotted her. Anonymous call. Why? Whatcha feel?"

Harry shrugged. Something was nibbling at his hindbrain, but he couldn't get it out in the open.

"What about tracks?" he asked.

"Snow killed any tracks. Very little blood, too. It was a good shot, as that goes," Eugene said. "Stopped her heart instantly."

Porter watched Harry's face. "You recognize her, Harry?"

Harry looked at the slack-faced girl and frowned. "I do, actually."

"Well?"

"Her name's Bebe, I think. Bebe something. She's a hooker," Harry said. "Was, I mean."

Porter nodded. "I figured. Hooker, junkie, something. She's got that look about her. Cheap snatch in cheap clothes. She's got tattoos, some scratches. Greasy look about her. Unsavory."

"Yeah. She's not too local. I know most of the workers here. But she'd worked near here, I think," Harry said. He didn't bother chastising Porter about his manner. It was the way he was.

Porter grinned. "Tell me how you know that?"

"I know one or two of the girls around here, in a talking sort of way. She's from around. Maybe uptown a bit, but she's not big time," Harry said.

"You know one or two of the girls, huh?" Porter asked.

"Yeah." Harry ignored Porter's leer.

"Gimme names?" Porter asked.

Harry pursed his lips. "I don't know last names. I know a Taneesha. There's an Angie. And… uh… a

25

Tina, I think. They come into Dahli's sometimes, you know?"

"You a frequent flyer, Harry?" Porter grinned. Eugene looked up with an interested gleam in his eye.

"Nah. Just I live here, you know? I know people," Harry said dismissively.

Porter nodded. "All right. I'll run Bebe here through the system. I'm sure she'll ring cherries somewhere. That'll give me a last name and a list of known associates. And then we'll see."

"All right. Anything else you need from me?" Harry asked.

"No. I just wanted to see if she was a mover and shaker around here. See if she belonged to someone I should be worried has retaliation plans, or anything," Porter said.

"I don't think so. She didn't have a posse I know about," Harry said, "and the girls working around here aren't too well protected. I'll ask around, see if I can get a name for you of her pimp."

"Yeah. Well, I'll run it up the pole, but I don't think anyone's gonna salute," Porter said. "I do what they tell me until five, but I gotta tell you, I'm not terribly worried about some hooker gets rolled. It's not high on the list of good uses of our time and presence. So spake the Masters, and further affiant sayeth naught."

Harry rolled his eyes, half at Porter's snotty tone and half in grim acceptance of the knowledge that hookers were pretty low on the list of importance to the city, and nodded.

Porter pointed his pen at the body. "You guys can zip. Get her out of here. She's messing up my streets."

Eugene laughed. "Just we're here to clean up the trash, eh?"

"Hey, that's why they give you the big car, right?" Porter said. Eugene's assistants unfurled a rubber body bag. Porter jerked his head at Harry and they walked back up to the mouth of the alley.

"I'll go write it up. That'll give me a chance to get out of the cold. You going to be around today?" Porter asked.

"Sure. I get anything about her I'll give you a ring. But it could be a couple of days. The weather the way it is, I bet they're going to be scarce on the streets. Double that if one of them knows who did do this," Harry said.

"Right. Well, have a good one," Porter said.

Harry ducked his chin against the cold and said, "You too, Porter. I'll send you a bill."

Porter snorted. "I'll send you a pizza. That should square us."

"See yas." Harry turned away and walked back down Bleecker. The curtains of snow had parted as the sun rolled up its sleeves and got to work in earnest. He could see all the way to the corner now. A couple of businesses had opened while he'd been in the alley. A struggling art gallery, a Mexican cantina, and an optimistic dry cleaner. But for the most part, both sides of the street were still deserted. The wind blew harder, spreading the snow evenly. The air was filled with big, fat, wet flakes the size of Jersey mosquitoes. He followed the street until he was in front of Dahli's Grocery. The lights were all on and the 'Open' sign was lit. Dahli's had never been closed so far as Harry knew.

Malik Dahli stood behind his counter as usual. In fact, as Harry thought about it, Malik had been behind that counter every time Harry had ever come in. Open to close, every day. He nodded at the man. "Mr. Dahli."

"Good morning, Mr. Harry. What can I get you?" Malik's voice was deep, dark, and smooth. He was a terribly skinny man, almost cadaverous. The red dot between his eyebrows was bright on his dark brown skin and his Adam's apple stuck out like a knob of rock along a cliff face. The sparse hair on his chin was black, as Harry assumed the hair on his head had been, when he had it. He was bald as a newborn.

"Oh, the usual. A new car, a new life, and a bottle of Dom Perignon, Mr. Dahli," Harry said ruefully. He pulled the film out of his pocket. "Or you could send this out for me."

Dahli nodded. "Of course. Two days."

Harry smiled. "Good enough."

Harry wandered down the aisle and grabbed a couple six-packs of Miller from the cooler. He pulled out his wallet and realized he had given all of his money to Keen and his pals the day before. "Shit."

Dahli waved his hand. "It is no problem, Mr. Harry. Do you know when you will be able to pay?"

Harry smiled gratefully. "Thanks, Mr. Dahli. I'll get you back with the film. That okay?"

The Indian man nodded. "Absolutely." He put the beer in a paper bag.

"Stay warm, Mr. Dahli," Harry said.

"I grew up in Bombay, Mr. Harry. I moved here because I never want to be warm again," the man said with a smile. Harry laughed.

"Careful what you wish for," he said. The cold chilled him instantly as he stepped out and he shivered. A thought struck him, and he poked his head back inside.

"Mr. Harry?"

"Question, Mr. Dahli. Have you seen Toni B. lately? This morning?" Harry asked.

Dahli shook his head. "No. Miss B. hasn't been in for several days."

Harry nodded. "All right. Thanks anyhow. See you."

Back in the office, Harry poured another cup of coffee for Jasper and carried it out to him. The bum took the coffee without his customary reply. Harry said, "Jasper. Wanna come inside for a while? Get warm?"

Jasper shook his head. "No thanks, Chief. Can't stand closed places, me. I'm fine. Got me a good coat. Hot coffee. This'll blow over. Supposed to be warmer tomorrow, I hear."

Harry didn't argue. "Okay, Jasper. Say… you seen Toni leave this morning?"

Jasper nodded. "Heard her. Too dark to see her."

"Thanks, Jasper." Harry went inside. He sat at the desk and brooded.

Chapter Four

He was asleep in the chair when she rapped on the door just past midnight. He made her wait until he grabbed a cup of coffee. He opened the door and she hurried past him. He handed Jasper the cup and patted him on the arm. Jasper nodded to him. Harry followed Toni into the apartment.

Toni was in the bed, huddled under the covers. Her face was blue and she shuddered uncontrollably. He sighed and went for a second cup of coffee. He handed it to her and slid next to her on the bed, scooting close so she could leech his body heat. He tugged the blanket up over her shoulders.

"What the hell's wrong with you?" he asked. "Trying to work in this weather? You're not gonna make any money if you freeze to some guy's prick."

She giggled. "You're f-f-f-fucking hilarious. J-jesus *Christ* I've never been so c-c-cold."

He pulled the blankets tighter around her and held her while she rolled the cup back and forth in her hands.

"I'll run a shower for you," he said.

"No thanks," she shook her head. "I don't want to get wet right now. It's too damned cold. I'll just sit here."

"Okay."

"You know, I read somewhere that with hypothermia, the best thing to do is strip and get close, skin to skin. That's the best way to warm someone up," she said, a teasing lilt in her voice.

"Look like this is the end for you," he said mournfully.

"You're a shit, Harry."

"Nah. If you were really in trouble I'd be worried. You're not hard and white. No frostbite."

She craned her face up to look at him. "What about *you*? Are you hard and white?"

He shook his head. "You're a brat."

"Yeah," she agreed. Her face brightened, and she said, "You should spank me."

"No, you shouldn't enjoy a punishment. Listen," he said. "I have to ask you something."

"Oh, my God, yes, I'll marry you! But you have to take my last name," she told him primly. "I'm old-fashioned."

"Yeah yeah," he muttered. "Be serious. You know a girl I think she's called Bebe?"

Toni's eyes darkened. "That bitch. You been fucking around behind my back?"

"Come on, be serious for a minute," Harry said. "You seen her lately?"

"Nope. She's been off our streets for a couple weeks. Mr. Jay put her to work on the other side on account of she can't get along with anyone. Why?" Toni asked.

"You're sure?"

"I said so, didn't I?" she said. "Why are you asking? She get busted and call for bail money or something?"

Harry shook his head. "If we're talking about the same girl, I have some bad news."

Her face went a shade whiter, and she asked him, "What happened?"

Harry pursed his lips. "Well, I got a call this morning. Had to run over and see a body. Turns out it was her."

Toni went still in his arms.

"You're sure you didn't hear anything? I know the grapevine. It's probably all over town by now," Harry said.

Toni shook her head. "I swear I didn't, Harry. She… was it a john? Or-"

"We don't have any ideas yet, Toni. But it wasn't nice. She was stabbed. Once in the chest. She went quick," he offered.

Toni sipped the coffee again. In a small voice she said, "Oh."

Harry held her tightly and a tear slid down Toni's cheek. "She was a bitch," Toni said, "but there's a limit, you know?"

"Yeah," Harry said. "You know of anyone that had a grudge? I mean a real, permanent-type beef?"

"No," she told him. "No one liked her, but she was just, like, annoying. A pain in the ass. She stole customers, low-balled us. Like that. You'd get a face full of nails, or your hair ripped out, but nothing like what you said. Besides, if one of us did *that*, we'd have to face Mr. Jay. That's not a story with a happy ending."

Harry nodded. "All right. You know what her last name was?"

"No. But her real name was Beulah," Toni said.

"Beulah. Huh. But no last name?" he asked.

"None I ever heard. It's not like we have to fill out an application," she said.

"Yeah."

They sat in companionable silence for a while. She snuggled against him and for a change, he let her. Half an hour went by, until he heard her stomach growl.

"What do you want for food?" he asked.

"How about Chinese?" she asked playfully.

"Smartass," he groused. He squeezed her once and got up to start rummaging around in the walk-in cooler. "Hey... I got some old steaks back here. And I think there's some salad left. What do you think?"

"I'm game if you are. We gonna cook 'em or just tackle them to the ground and chew them to death?" she asked.

He pulled out the meat and set it on the prep table next to the stove. "I got it. Go get warmed up."

She nodded. She tossed the empty coffee cup into the garbage on her way to the bathroom. She paused to strip off her tank top and skirt. She was bare underneath. "Sure you don't wanna join me this time?"

"Thanks, but I have to concentrate or I'll burn 'em," he said. He didn't turn to look. She screwed up her face and stuck out her tongue.

"Jerk," she said.

"Yeah, yeah," Harry replied, and hunted for the pepper. By the time she got out of the shower, he had the steaks done about medium and the salad mixed. She wore a tank top and a pair of terrycloth shorts, and he tried hard not to notice her legs. They ate in companionable silence at the small table.

"Harry?"

"Yeah?" he asked.

"Did she... did Bebe suffer?" Toni asked with a wince.

Harry chewed thoughtfully. "I don't think so. She went fast. Whoever did it either surprised her or she knew them. It was a single wound, stab to the heart, and it wasn't messy. She didn't linger."

Toni nodded. "That's good."

"It's something, anyhow," Harry said. He popped a tomato into his mouth. "I want you off the streets a couple days, Toni."

"I can't do that. You know I can't," she said. He read fear in her eyes.

"I'm just telling you what I want from you," he said soothingly. "I want you off the streets. The weather's too bad for you to be making any money anyhow. You're gonna freeze your moneymaker right off."

She said with trepidation, "But Mr. Jay-"

"He'll sit still for it. I'll make sure of it, if you want. You're liable to freeze to death. Besides, I'm hoping we find this sicko that killed Bebe soon. That's another reason to keep off the streets. You never know. Huh... do you think," Harry said thoughtfully, "that Mr. Jay is the one who killed her? Is he like that?"

Toni looked torn. "I'd love to say he is... but it'd be a lie. He's more likely to beat you to a pulp. Maybe cut up your face a bunch. Dead girls can't earn, Harry. Ugly girls, they still have a moneymaker."

He nodded. "Yeah, it seemed like a long shot. Even if she was stiffing him? Holding back on money?"

"Naah. It's not worth the heat. You know that. Unless she ripped him off for, like, thousands. And even Bebe's not that popular."

"Huh," Harry grunted. A thought occurred and popped out of his mouth before he thought it through. "How much do you make in a day?"

Toni eyed him. "Depends on how busy I get. You really want to know?"

Harry shook his head, coloring. "Forget I asked."

"Come on, you must be curious or you wouldn't have brought it up," she said with a smile. It grew as she saw him blush more deeply. "You devil, you! If you had a thing, you should have-"

Harry said, "Will you shut up? I'm trying to-"

"Trying to what?" Toni barked, startling him. "Run my life? Ruin my reputation with the guy who'll dice me if I screw up? It's got to be *one* of those two, because it sure as hell's not because you want to wedge yourself into my panties."

"Hey, that's-"

"So tell me, Harry," she leaned over the table and took one of his tomatoes. "What *are* you trying to do?"

He looked at the table as she put the tomato into her mouth and chewed. "I don't know."

"I know," she said. "You say that a lot."

"Yeah, well, shut up." Harry finished his beer.

"No."

"Yes," he said.

"Make me, baby," Toni said with a grin.

"I will literally toss you out of this place ass-first into the snow and lock the damned door on it," Harry got up and tossed his empty can. He opened the walk-in. "Shit. I'm out of beer again."

"Well, run over to Dahli's. Or I'll do it, if you want," she said.

Harry shook his head. "Can't. No cash. I already owe him."

"I can get it, Harry." Toni reached over and picked up her purse. "I've got-"

"No." Harry grabbed the purse from her and dropped it back on the bed. "You're not paying for anything."

"Are we just going to keep interrupting each other all night? And why the hell not?" she demanded.

Harry stared evenly at her for a long moment. She just stared back. Finally, he opened his mouth. "I-"

"Well?" she cut him off and smiled.

"Asshole," he said. He tried to fight it but he grinned at her, and she laughed.

"That's better," she said. "You're too serious all the time."

"Yeah, yeah," he said as he pulled out a half bottle of bourbon and held it up. "How about this? Too early?"

"Hell no. You want to get some cups or are we just gonna tag-team this thing?" Toni grabbed the bottle from him and pulled the cork.

"Whatever works," Harry said. "Give me that."

He took the bottle back and swigged. He handed it to her, and she followed suit.

"Ugh. Why do you like the ones that taste like dirt?" she asked, grimacing.

"A, it's peat, and B, in three shots you won't care," he said loftily, taking the bottle from her. He took a second pull.

"Don't hog it," she said. He handed her the bottle and threw himself on the bed. He loosened his tie and tugged it off. Toni swigged and set the bottle on the table before crawling over to him.

"What's on your mind, Harry?" she asked. She unbuttoned his shirt and helped him pull it off.

"I don't know. I'm just... I think I'm *pissed*, more than anything else." He balled up his shirt and flung it across the room. Toni slipped his belt open and tugged it out of the loops of his trousers.

"Pissed about what?" she asked while unbuttoning his pants.

"Too far, Toni," he said, slapping her hand away. "Knock it off."

She pouted. "I knew I should have waited until you finished the bottle."

"Wouldn't help."

"You're a dick," she said. "But whatever. Why are you pissed at me?"

"I'm not pissed at *you*, Toni. I'm pissed at whatever son of a bitch is feeling cocky enough to kill someone on my turf. This is horseshit. This is my *home*, for Christ's sake. There's *rules*," Harry said. "They better find the son of a bitch before I do."

"The cops?" Toni said.

"Of course the... what the hell, Toni?" Harry muttered. "Who do you think?"

Toni sat back and crossed her arms. "You don't have to be a dick, Harry."

He sighed. "No, I guess not. Sorry."

"That's better. But you can make it up to me. Strip," she commanded.

Harry smiled tiredly. "Nice try. Hand me the bottle."

Toni did so. Harry took another drink. He offered it back to her and she drained the last two inches. She threw it on the table. It rolled off onto the chair and bounced to the floor. "I killed it," she said.

"Ha," Harry said, and struggled to his feet. His head swam and he swayed in place. He'd intended to go to the bathroom, but forgot his mission because a question had popped into his head. He stared at Toni for a long moment. He said, "You're a nice girl. You're too nice. Why are you on the street, anyhow?"

She arched a shaggy eyebrow at him and said, "Did you *really* just 'what's-a-nice-girl-like-you' me?"

He shrugged. "Yeah, I guess I did."

She snickered. "You're chatting me up."

Color darkened his cheeks. He growled, "Shut up."

Toni flopped over and crawled to his side of the bed. Harry stepped back a little out of her reach.

"Come on, Harry. You've done everything right. You got me liquored up, you're making me laugh, hell, I'm in your *bed* already. Come on and *do* it. Make your move. Just between you and me," she whispered, "I bet I'll fall to your charms, you sly dog, you."

He sighed and picked up the bottle. He squinted at the trash until it resolved into a single object, and threw the bottle into the basket. "Good to know."

She reached out and snagged the waistband of his pants, pulling him off-balance. He tumbled onto the bed with a yelp and a squeal of springs. She climbed on top of him, straddling him, and leaned in to kiss him.

"Come off it, Harry," she said. "You *want* me."

"Get off me, Toni," he said, grabbing at her arms. She ground her hips against him.

She whispered, "I can feel you. Can't hide *that*. And unlike you, *it* doesn't lie. I *know* you want me. And I'm free, white, eighteen, and willing. What's stopping you?"

He rolled her off with concerted effort and clambered back off the bed. "I told you: no."

She pouted. "A girl could get her feelings hurt, listening to you. To your words, anyhow. The rest of you isn't playing along with your stupid game."

He adjusted his pants awkwardly. "Too bad. I said no."

"I heard you. I just don't understand why," she said. She got up and stripped off her shirt and shorts. She lay back on the bed naked, one hand behind her head, the other cupping her left breast. She drew one knee up and parted her thighs.

He looked away uncomfortably and said, "You don't need to understand. Just respect my wishes, okay?"

"What about *my* wishes, Harry? You don't respect them," she said, and her tone seemed to command him to look at her. Her eyes were darker with desire, and burned into his.

Her question seemed serious, and he gave it real consideration. He said, "Look… I can't. And I can't tell you why because I don't *know*. I don't know why, but I don't *feel* it, Toni. Period."

She swallowed hard and looked away. "Fine."

"It's not you, Toni. It's me. Believe me. You're very…" he trailed off helplessly.

"Cute? Adorable? Gorgeous? Hot? Fuckable?" she asked. "What?"

"Yes," he said distractedly. He fell onto the couch. "All of the above. But I… I can't. And believe me, I know it's not because of *you*."

"Yeah, well, hard to believe. There isn't another man on the planet would turn down what you keep turning down, Harry," Toni said. She traced a finger along her curves, over her breasts and down her belly. He looked away before she got to the bottom.

"Probably not," he muttered, and pulled the blanket over his shoulders.

"Definitely not," Toni said. The bed made suggestive noises as her hips moved. "Are you *sure* you don't want to join me?"

Harry gritted his teeth. He was tempted. But... it still felt wrong to him. He said, "Whether or not I am, I'm not. Get the light, would you?"

"In a minute," she said breathlessly as her hand moved faster. "I like to watch. Do *you* want to watch?"

He stubbornly refused to roll over. He didn't answer her. He tried hard to ignore her until she was done. He didn't succeed as well as he'd have liked to.

Chapter Five

The next morning he discovered that despite the snow, the mail had come. It was good to know that their motto meant something in an uncertain world. Harry grabbed the envelopes as they slid through the slot, snagging them before they hit the floor. Two checks, no bills. *Glory be*, he thought. *Everything's going my way.*

He dressed, filled two cups of coffee, and wound an old scarf around his neck. Toni had been gone again when he got up. Woman couldn't take a hint. Stubborn. He grinned to himself, allowing the scene from the previous night to play through his head. Stubborn to the end. *Wonder what that's like?* he thought wryly. He handed Jasper one of the steaming cups and walked the six blocks to his bank. He paid some bills, deposited some money, and stuffed some cash in his pocket. He had a positive balance in his account. It was even two digits for a change.

He whistled as he trudged through the fresh snowfall. He could pay off at least one favor today. And then he'd see where the fresh, new day would take him.

He headed up the steps to Dahli's and opened the door to find chaos.

Chapter Six

Dahli had a huge pistol in his shaking hands. It looked like a .44 and Harry would bet Mr. Dahli had bought it precisely because it looked intimidating and scary. Harry could have told him, had he asked, that a hand cannon of that magnitude only frightened people unused to guns. Anyone who knew guns knew the really scary ones were smaller, easier to control, and a lot more accurate in the hands of an experienced shooter.

Dahli waved the enormous gun frantically to and fro in an effort to cover the group of people in front of his counter. His eyes were so wide the whites were showing all around his pupils. Three women and two men were scuffling, or attempting to, and Toni was one of them. The two men were in the process of slapping the girls around, but the girls were waving their hands and clenching their eyes shut, trying to block the slaps.

Harry recognized one of the men, having seen him on the streets once or twice. He was Toni's pimp, Mr. Jay. The other man wasn't someone Harry knew, but he knew an enforcer when he saw one. Where Jay was slim and unintimidating, the other guy was wider, bulkier, and had fighters' eyes.

He stood there for a second. Dahli whipped his head around to stare at him and blinked as though not sure he was seeing Harry at all. Harry stood in the doorway with his hands stuck deep in his pockets. He raised his eyebrows. For a moment, nobody moved.

"Mr. Dahli. How's it going?" Harry asked laconically.

Dahli stuttered, "Mr. Harry… these… these-"

"Who the fuck are you?" the enforcer growled. He had a nice, low voice, and flavored his words with a hint of menace. Harry imagined the man sounded angry asking for someone to pass the salt.

"I the fuck am Harry," Harry said. "I the fuck am a customer. Who the fuck are *you*?"

"None of your business," the man growled. He seemed to lean into his words, pushing them out at Harry. "Get the fuck outta here. Place is closed."

Toni's eyes found Harry's. They were wide and scared and she seemed to hold her breath, waiting to see if he'd do as ordered. He smiled a little at her and shook his head. No, he wouldn't abandon her. Relief showed on her face and her shoulders relaxed.

"Doesn't look closed. Door's not locked," Harry pointed out. "That's the universal sign for 'open' on this planet."

The enforcer doubled down, and snarled, "I told you-"

"Whatcha doing, fellas?" Harry asked.

"I told you, it's none of your business," the enforcer snapped. Harry dismissed the man, his eyes roving to Mr. Jay's serenely calm face.

"Wasn't talking to the help. I was asking management," Harry said as he pointed at Mr. Jay. "You. What are you doing?"

"Dealing with an personal matter, asshole. What's it to you?" Jay asked, and he seemed on the verge of laughter. He had eyes that danced and he looked like he was having fun. Harry bristled at that look. He didn't like Jay on principle. Having met him, he didn't like him one bit.

"To me, nothing. But I like this place. I like this guy," Harry said as he hooked a thumb at Dahli. "And I don't like trouble in here."

"Oh, yeah?" Jay said.

"Yeah," Harry said. "And he's got a gun. You didn't see that? Or are you just stupid?"

"He uses that, we better be *dead* when he's done, man," Jay said.

"Oh," Harry said.

"Do yourself a favor and turn around," Jay said. "Just walk away."

Harry sighed. "Mr. Dahli, what happened?"

"They were hitting those girls! I do not allow such behavior here! I warned them. I would call the authorities!" Dahli seemed near tears. The dignified Indian man's lower lip trembled. "They told me they would break up my store! That they would hurt me and burn up my store."

Harry's melancholy eyes settled on Jay and his companion. He said remotely, "It that true? Did you threaten my friend?"

"What's it to you, Samaritan?" the enforcer sneered. "You gonna cry about it?"

Harry sighed. He had met a hundred punks like Jay's enforcer, and it was depressingly familiar. They were all dangerous, they were all wide, and strong, and intimidating. And they were all about as intelligent as your average cocker spaniel. Harry could tell it wouldn't take but one or two gentle pushes to wind up this one. He said as condescendingly as he could, "Right now we're just talking. And I asked you a question. Do you need me to repeat the question? Did you not hear me, or didn't you understand it?"

"I'm tired of you, asshole," the enforcer said. He shoved the girl he'd been clutching aside and started for Harry. "You're leaving, pal, feet first."

Harry waited until the lunk grabbed the lapels of his jacket. As the enforcer's hands clutched him he brought his gun out of his pocket and up, looping it across the enforcer's face. The man's nose crunched and blood squirted out. The barrel of the gun dug into the side of his face and ripped a trench into his pasty flesh. The enforcer squealed and hit the floor like he was sliding for home. In the shocked silence left by the overloud thud of his gun on the man's skull, Harry settled his eyes on Jay. The pimp's own eyes were wide and no longer dancing. Jay seemed dangerous to Harry in a way that his muscle had not. Harry studied Jay intently, paying particular attention to the way he held his shoulders. He needed to know if Jay was a lefty or a righty. It might be very important.

"What's your name, pal?" he asked. His voice didn't change from that conversational tone, and Harry could see this shook Jay. Jay stared in disbelief. He eyed his muscle, but his enforcer didn't move. The man was out cold. Blood oozed around the cheek pressed to the floor.

"I asked you your name. First, last, and middle. Speak, boy," Harry said, and again his voice was playfully taunting. Jay tore his eyes from the unconscious muscle at Harry's feet and looked into his eyes. Harry saw fear, anger, and a fierce, burning hatred there. Harry didn't raise the gun.

"My name's Jay. *Mistah* Jay to you, asshole," the pimp snarled in a Bronx broadside.

"How nice for you," Harry said. He didn't raise the gun, but he did cock the .38 for effect. "First, last, middle. Now."

"Name's John. John Dean Leslie," the skinny, sneering pimp told him. Harry could see him trying to get his street armor back on.

"Leslie. Heh. Nice to meet you, Leslie. I'm Harry Philip DeMarko," he told the pimp.

Jay shrugged. "So what?"

"So this is my neighborhood, that's what. I live around the corner. I've been here a couple years now. I don't recall seeing you on my blocks, but I'll *remember* you now. You want to walk out of here right now, go ahead, I'll let you. But you have to get gone. I don't want to see you on Bleecker again," Harry said. He didn't add anything to the speech, no emphasis, no anger, no threat. Jay's eyes narrowed.

"So who the fuck do you think you are?" Jay demanded. "You the law around here? I don't see a badge, asshole. If you're a cop, prove it."

"Oh," Harry said with a smile that didn't reach his eyes. "I'm not a cop. Now ask yourself this: you think that makes me less dangerous or more dangerous?"

"I've had enough of you," Jay snarled. "You-"

Harry held up a hand. Now he sounded bored. "Feeling's mutual, I'm sure. Turn around and walk away, Leslie. This is the one shot you get. Take your free pass."

"What about my man?" Jay demanded.

Harry looked down at the enforcer. He looked up at Jay and raised the pistol for the first time. "Back against that cooler over there or I'll put one in your leg."

Jay blinked in confusion. "What the hell's your damage, man?"

"Do as you're told, Leslie," Harry said quietly. He didn't need to wave the gun. The man backed away from the girls and his back thumped against the Pepsi cooler. The bottles inside rattled.

"Mr. Dahli?" Harry asked.

"Yes, sir, Mr. Harry?" Dahli said.

"Put your gun away- I mean *away*- and call the police, please. Tell them you've had an altercation on your property, the perps are still on the scene, and you need assistance," Harry told him.

Dahli did as asked. Jay's lip curled and he almost looked fierce. Harry bent to the enforcer. He began slapping the man lightly. "Hey, Leslie. What's this guy's name?"

"Fuck you," Jay spat. Harry shrugged and smacked the thug again.

"Hey. *Hey*. Wake up, idiot," he said.

The man's eyes cleared a little and he looked up at Harry. He started to rise but the gun pressed against his forehead and he settled back down with a faint thump.

"Can you understand me?" Harry asked.

"Yeah," the man muttered.

"What's your name, pal?"

"Marvin," the enforcer stuttered. "M-Marvin Salano."

"What's the matter, not smart enough to join the mob, Marvin?" Harry asked.

"What?" Marvin asked, blinking.

Harry shook his head. "Nothing. Listen to me closely, Marvin. I'm going to tell you something important. You need to pay attention. Ready?"

"Yeah, man," Marvin told him, a little bravado creeping back into his uneven voice.

Harry leaned in and said, "I don't know you. But I don't like you. And I have no desire to get to know you and change that opinion. So what you're gonna do is, you're gonna stay the hell away from me. Ten blocks around this store just became a no-fly zone for you. Get me? I see you within ten blocks of Dahli's Market and I'm just going to have to shoot you. And I'm *not* a good shot. I'll tell you, I'm gonna try like hell to make it non-lethal, but like I said, I'm not a good shot. I might aim for your leg and shoot you in the fucking face. Or I might aim for your arm and shoot you in the fucking face. Or I might try to just put one in your ass, but shoot you in the fucking face. All I'm saying is, I'm not great at not killing someone I don't like when I shoot at them. So you're gonna want to steer clear of me if you don't wanna get shot in the fucking face. Got it?"

Marvin stared up at him. He didn't answer.

"That nose looks bad. Is it broken, do you think?" Harry asked.

Marvin reached up and touched his nose gingerly. He looked confused. "No, man. I don't think it's broken."

Harry looked over at Jay. "Pay attention, Leslie. Watch what happens next."

Leslie grimaced. He knew what was about to happen, even if the hapless Marvin did not. Harry looked back at Marvin. "So, I'm sorry about this," he said.

Marvin asked, "What?"

Harry slammed his gun down on the bridge of Marvin's nose again and the crunch of shattering cartilage was louder than the howls. Harry stood back, examined the gun, and leaned down to wipe the blood off the barrel onto Marvin's shirt. He looked at Jay. "So, Leslie. Have I made my point?"

Jay's eyes were burning pools filled to the brim with a noxious mixture of hatred, fear, and, indignation, but he said, "Yeah, man. I take your point. Can we go now?"

Harry looked at the girls. Toni looked all right, but one of the other girls, a surely absolutely genuine platinum blonde, had a freshly-slapped mouth. Blood trickled from her lip. Harry's vision sharpened and pulsed faintly. He shook his head and said, "Nope. Just stand there."

"What the fuck, man? The cops are on their way! You're gonna get busted, too. What *is* this to you?" Jay demanded.

Harry said, "I don't like guys who hit girls."

Jay growled, "They ain't girls, man. They're *my* girls."

"I don't see collars and id tags. They're people, asshole. They don't belong to you," Harry told him.

"They *work* for me."

"Yeah, well, you shouldn't be hitting employees," Harry said. "It's bad for your-"

The sirens clawed at the air a second before a cruiser squealed to a stop outside. Harry put the gun in his pocket and raised his hands. He looked over at Jay and smiled. He said, "Better reach. They're all riled up. Anything could happen to a punk-ass."

Jay stuck his hands in the air as the door burst open. Two uniforms came in, guns high.

"Nobody fucking move," the first one growled. The second hung back and covered his partner. Jay had a smirk on his face, right up until the first officer dropped his gun and said, "Oh, hey, Harry."

"Lawrence," Harry said genially. "Ralph."

Ralph Matisse nodded at Harry. Lawrence Bender looked at Dahli. "You're the one who called it in?"

"Yes, sir. I made the call," Dahli told the officer.

"What happened?" Bender asked.

Dahli looked fearfully from Jay to Harry. Harry rolled his palm at the man with a smile.

"The two men were fighting with the women. That one," Dahli pointed to Marvin, "hit that one," he pointed to the platinum blonde.

Bender looked at the man on the floor, holding his nose and swearing softly as tears rolled down to mix with the blood. Bender looked at the girl. "Did you do that to his nose, ma'am?" he asked.

The girl shook her head, clearly terrified. She started to raise a hand, but stopped. She glanced at Harry. He nodded to her with a smile and she pointed her finger at him.

"H-he did it, officer," she stammered. "H-he stopped M- the man there from hitting me again."

Jay scowled at her, but his eyes were on Harry. Bender turned to Harry. "Harry… you hit him, huh?"

"Yeah, a little," Harry admitted.

Bender examined Marvin's cuts and broken nose. "A little?" he asked.

"Well, twice," Harry amended.

"With what? A truck?" Bender asked.

"Naah," Harry said. "My .38."

Both cops looked at Harry. Jay's grin was wide enough to stretch ear to ear, but it didn't last long.

"Your service pistol?" Bender asked. Jay's smile faded and he stared at Harry.

"Yeah."

"So," Bender said, "you got a permit then."

"Conceal carry," Harry affirmed. "In my wallet."

"All righty," Bender said. "So what's your side?"

"Walked in, saw the fracas. Had to step in. He made the first move, I made the last two. You know how it is," Harry told him.

Bender nodded thoughtfully. He cocked a thumb at the seething pimp. "And him?"

Harry pointed to the prostrate form of Marvin. "Brawn." He gestured to Jay. "Brain. Such as it is. Mr. Jay here is an enterprising local entrepreneur. He specializes in horizontal refreshment, priced to move. He was in the middle of a board meeting when I came in. I'm afraid I interrupted a crucial discussion about the direction of the company."

Ralph snorted. Bender looked at the girls and said, "You pressing charges?"

They looked at each other and at Jay, whose jaw was set and rippling. "N-no, sir," the platinum blonde said for the group.

"Figures. All right," Bender swung his notebook shut. "Clear out before I run you all in on a disorderly charge."

"What about him?" Jay demanded, pointing a finger at Harry. "You ain't gonna ask if *we're* pressing charges?"

"For *what?*" Bender asked.

"For-" Jay shook his head. He pointed to Marvin. "For my friend's fucking *face*, man!"

Bender squatted and examined the unfortunate Marvin's face. "Huh. Hey, Mr. what's-your-name? Owner."

Dahli spoke up. "Yes, sir. Dahli, sir."

"Did this unfortunate-looking gentleman come into your shop looking like he'd gone to funky town with Ali?" Bender asked.

Dahli looked blank. "Pardon?"

"Did he look like *this* when he came in?" Bender clarified.

Mr. Dahli frowned for a second, and then the light dawned. "Oh. Uh, yes, sir. Yes he did. He did look that way."

Bender looked at Jay. "You were saying?"

"Fucking pigs," Jay snarled. He pointed at the girls. "Get back to work, damn it." He brushed past Harry and helped Marvin to his feet.

"Better get him to a hospital," Harry told him. "There's a couple good ones about ten blocks from here. Right?"

Jay sneered at him and didn't say anything else. He helped Marvin out the door. The cops looked at Harry. Ralph said, "Okay, DeMarko. Fun time's over. What the *hell* was that about, Harry?"

He shrugged. "Just what it looked like. They were slapping the girls around. I didn't like it. We got into it."

"So you pistol-whipped him?" Ralph asked.

"Eh," Harry shrugged, "it was faster than getting down to fists."

"What if they'd pulled a gun too?" Bender asked.

Harry looked at Dahli, who probably didn't have a permit for his. He winked at the man and smiled. "They didn't. I had the only gun in the room."

"Lucky bastard," Bender said.

Harry nodded. "Look… I know it's a little weird, but thanks for letting this slide. I can't *stand* that asshole."

"You know him?" Ralph asked.

"Nope. Never met him before today, but I have a pretty good idea that I don't like him. Call it a hunch," Harry said with a grin.

The officers laughed. Ralph looked at the trio of women. "You want me to clear the shop?"

"No, leave it to me. I wanna have a little chat with them before they go," Harry said.

"All right. You have a good night. Be safe," Bender said.

"You two do the same. See you later." Harry shook with each of them. They left the store and got back in the cruiser. Harry waited until they had pulled away before settling his eyes on the girls.

"Okay," he said, "let's chat."

Chapter Seven

He led them to the booth near the lunch counter in back and sat down. Toni and the other two girls squeezed into the bench opposite him.

"I'm Harry. Who're you?"

The girls looked at each other. Toni said, "Uh-"

"Come on, come on, I haven't got all day."

Toni snorted and looked away, trying not to laugh.. The other two girls just smiled. Harry sighed. "So, you know who I am."

"Harry, this is Annette," Toni gestured to the blonde, and then at the other girl, "and that's Cherry."

Cherry's name was descriptive. Her hair was dyed a bright, maraschino red. She raised a hand to Harry.

"And you're Toni's boyfriend," Annette said. "Thank you for what you did."

"You're- hey. I'm not... forget it. She's my *friend*," Harry protested.

"Whateva," Cherry said in a Brooklyn-flecked voice. "Ya livin together."

"She's *staying* with me. It's not the same," Harry insisted.

Toni snorted and stared off into the distance.

"Look... do either of you know anything about what happened to Bebe?" Harry asked.

The girls looked at each other. Toni said, "It's okay. You can trust him."

"Trust him to royally screw us," Annette said. "Mr. Jay's already gonna tan someone's ass for what happened today."

Harry said, "You come to *me* if that happens. I'll make sure he never does it again."

"Yeah, right," Cherry said. "'Cause you're onna street twenty-four seven. Or are you puttin together a string?"

Harry blinked and shot a startled look at Toni, who grinned at him. She said, "Yeah, Harry. You making a move? Trying to put together a pussy posse?"

Harry blushed. "I'm not-"

"Because I don't think I'd mind so much, working for you," Toni said. "We'd be real good to you, right, girls?"

Cherry and Annette both nodded. "I could see it," Cherry said. "After what you did to Mahvin, word'll be out not to fuck witcha. We could work in peace. We're good workers, Harry."

"I'm not a pimp," Harry said darkly.

"Why not?" Toni asked. "There's good money in it. And you're the kind of guy keeps his girls loyal. Some guys have to hit. All *you'd* have to do is smile."

"What the hell? Does- look. I'm not trying to… you know what? Forget it. I give up. I'm done," Harry said, and started to rise.

Toni pouted. "Come on, Harry. It's just a joke. Listen, girls, seriously, do you know anything about what happened?"

Cherry shook her head. "I dint find out until this morning. Couldn't say I care a whole lot. I mean, not for nothin, but who cares?"

"*I* care," Harry said. His jaw rippled.

"Why?" Cherry asked. "No one else does. You think the cops are gonna throw a lotta effort at a dead hoor? Do they eva? They ask a couple questions, then go get donuts. They never help out."

"*I'm* helping out," Harry said.

"What makes you any different?" Annette asked. "You're just another cop."

"I'm not a cop anymore," Harry said. "That means no one tells me to give it a rest, and no one reassigns me the second a senator or the mayor's kid gets a jaywalking ticket. No one buries me under busywork instead of doing something about an asshole killing girls on *my* streets."

Harry suddenly realized he was angry, truly and deeply *angry*. How many times had they done just that? How many times had he been 'prioritized'? Sent to help out on higher-profile cases, sent to direct traffic when the Giants played, or Sinatra came to town? How many cases got short shrift while the hot-topic crimes got all the attention, press, and manpower? He realized for the first time how *powerful* it made him, not wearing a badge anymore. He'd never considered that. He grinned to himself, but Annette didn't look convinced. Cherry just looked glum. Toni patted Harry's arm. "Look, girls, no matter what else you think, you can count on Harry. He's never let me down."

The other two still didn't look convinced. Cherry said, "Well, like I said, I didn't know nothin until this morning. And Mr. Jay was beating on us because he thought we *did*. He don't know either. He *wants* to. He thinks it's another manager moving in on him."

Harry said, "It could be. You know of anyone around making a move for his streets?"

"There's a guy a couple blocks over who's been recruiting for a while. I don't know his name, but his

56

girls are really creepy. Like, they look sticky," Annette said. "Low-rent bitches."

Harry snickered. "Okay, I'm sure that'll help."

"Whatever," Annette said. "Anyhow, they work over on Third and Fourth."

"Got a name?" Harry asked.

"Name of what?" Annette asked.

"Of one of the girls. The pimp. Anyone. A lead of *some* kind. Or do you expect me to just wander around asking random girls if they're hookers, and if so, who do they work for, and if so, is he muscling in on another pimp's turf, which resulted in the murder of one of his girls." Harry said all of this patiently, trying to keep his temper in check. All his time on the street came back in a rush. How many times had he pried information out of reluctant witnesses? "I'm trying to help, but you're not exactly making it easy."

Annette sighed. "Well, until you actually *do* something, you're not helping. You're just talking."

Harry looked at Toni. "I give up."

"No, don't. Come on. You have to understand, Harry. No one gives a shit about us. We're used to it," Toni told him.

"Yeah, well, I'm not everyone," Harry told her. He got up. "Toni, if you hear anything, let me know."

"Where are you going?" she asked.

Harry smirked at her. "Apparently I'm going to go wander Third Street asking stupid questions until someone shoots me, knifes me, or arrests me for solicitation."

He made it most of the way to the door when Annette said, "Cassandra."

He turned back impatiently. "What?"

"There's a girl named Cassandra. She can put you onto someone," Annette said, staring at the table. She looked up at Harry. "If you really want to help."

"I really do," he said. "Thank you."

"Yeah well," Annette mumbled. Toni beamed at Harry.

"Thanks, Harry. Thank you very much. I'll see you tonight, right?" she asked. Annette and Cherry looked at them in turn. Harry's face grew hot.

"Uh, yeah. I'll be around." He turned to leave and snapped his fingers. He went to the counter and pulled out his wallet. "I owe you for those pictures, Mr. Dahli. And that beer. How much-"

Dahli shook his head. "Mr. Harry, I believe we will call that even. I'm very grateful for what you have done today."

"I didn't do it for you," Harry said. "And I don't-"

"Nevertheless, do not think I do not count myself lucky," the gentleman said with dignity. "Please accept this small gesture as a token of my thankfulness."

Dahli handed over an envelope thick with pictures. Harry took them. "All right, all right. Thank you. And you're welcome, I guess. I'll see you later."

"Have a good day, Mr. Harry."

"You too, Mr. Dahli. Let me know if you have any more trouble, okay?"

Harry walked out into the cold and shivered. It didn't feel any better outside. He walked back to his place. At the desk he shook out the pictures. They were just as he had shot them- through two windows and a snowstorm. Despite the amateurish pictures, the distance, and the snow, the husband he'd tailed to the cheap motel was clearly illuminated along with the woman that wasn't his wife. He rotated one of the pictures to get a better view of the festivities. Huh. That didn't look at all comfortable. Harry shoved them back in the envelope and picked up his phone. He dialed. After four rings someone answered.

"Hello," a distracted, faraway voice said.

"Mrs. Angelo? Harry DeMarko," he said.

The woman on the other end of the line inhaled sharply. "Yes, Mr. DeMarko?"

"Do you have some time this afternoon? I... I have the pictures you wanted," he said.

Her voice sounded distant. "I see."

"I can deliver them any time you want," he said. She didn't respond, and for a moment he thought she'd hung up.

"Could you... come by at five this evening?" she asked.

Harry said, "I suppose I can do that. Don't forget there's the second half of the fee-"

"I haven't forgotten, Mr. DeMarko. I'll have a check for you," she said with frost in her voice.

"All right. See you at five, Mrs. Angelo. Have a-"

She hung up on him. He grunted and set the phone in the cradle. Suppose it would be too much to expect her to be *happy* to hear he'd succeeded in proving her husband a cheat. He drummed his fingers on the desk. The clock lied to him about how late it was; it read only eleven. He sighed, heaved himself to his feet and put on his coat and scarf. What the hell. He had nothing else to do. The snow was worsening outside, his afternoon had just been shot to shit, and he couldn't think of a single constructive thing to do. It was a perfect day to go talk to hookers on Fourth Street.

Chapter Eight

He trudged through the snow that plows had been piling onto the sidewalk for hours. The traffic was heavy despite the poor weather and he had to hurry to get across the streets without getting run down. So, typical day.

Fourth Street wasn't exactly the jewel of the city's crown, but it wasn't Times Square, either. In the narrow alleys between the closed storefronts girls were hiding and waiting for drive-bys.

"Looking for Cassandra," Harry said to a stick-thin dark-haired girl who made a lackluster eye at him. "Know where I can find her?"

"I can do anything you need-"

"Is your name Cassandra?" Harry asked.

"It could be, if you want," the girl said. Her pupils were blown and she sounded fuzzy.

"No, I don't want it to be. I *need* it to already have been before I got here, honey," Harry said.

She digested that and said "Piss off, pig." She turned her back on him and wobbled off on six-inch heels. The snow impeded her flouncing exit.

"Nice talking to you," Harry said. A block later he asked a second girl.

"I'm looking for Cassandra," he said.

"Why?" the girl asked.

"I need her to answer some questions," Harry told her.

"You're a cop?"

"No, I'm not a cop. Used to be, though." Harry pushed his balled-up hands into his pockets. His companion was wearing a short skirt, nylons, and a trench coat wrapped around a halter. She looked faintly blue around the cheeks and nose.

"Used to be? What are you now?" she asked.

"What's your name?" Harry asked.

"I asked you first," she said with a wry smile.

"I'm a private investigator," he said. "I'm Harry."

"My name's Katy," she said.

"Who's your manager, Katy?" Harry asked her, bunching his shoulders against the cold.

"What's it to you?"

"Well, I'm looking for a girl named Cassandra so I can find her pimp. It occurs to me that you might be working for the same guy."

"If you don't know who she is, how's a name I give you gonna help?" she asked.

"Beats me," Harry said with a smile.

She laughed. "You're honest, anyhow."

"Yeah, I got that going for me," Harry said to her.

She said, "You got ten bucks?"

"Yeah," Harry said. "So?"

"So that's what my time's worth. You want an answer, honey, make with the money."

Harry studied her innocent-looking face for a full minute and then sighed. He pulled his wallet out and fished out a bill. She stuffed it in her halter, grinning at him as he looked away. The color in his cheeks might have been from the cold.

"Darius," she said, as though agreeing the day was a bit chilly. "His name's Darius."

"Wonderful. Any idea where I can find him?"

"Beats me. Probably at the pool hall on Tenth. He lives there. Beckett's, it's called," she said.

"Thanks. And do you know where I can find Cassandra?" he asked.

The girl pouted. "You got another ten?"

"Nope," Harry said.

They locked gazes. She stared hard at him while he looked back at her, blandly smiling. She shook her head. "Fine. Redhead, over there."

Harry looked where she pointed and spotted the woman half-hidden in a doorway. "You're sure?"

"Yeah," Katy said, her voice dry as dust. "She's my sister."

"Huh. Family business?" Harry asked.

"It's a living," Katy said. "Now beat it, unless you got more money, or you're looking for something else I got. You're driving off all the trade."

Harry nodded amiably and turned to walk away. He stopped. "One more thing?"

"Jesus, mister," Katy sighed.

"Real quick. Did you know a girl named Bebe?"

She pursed her lips. "Sounds familiar. Why?"

"Just wondering," Harry said. "Black girl. Liked sequins. Know her? Usually worked around here, I'm told."

"I don't… wait. Yeah. I think I seen her once or twice. Why?" Katy asked him.

"You know anyone that hung around with her regular?" Harry asked. "Friends, like?"

"No, and the time your money bought is out, mister," Katy said.

"All right," Harry said. "Have a good one."

"Yeah, you too," Katy said, looking up and down the street.

Harry crossed over and went to the doorway that Katy had pointed out. As he approached, the girl peeked at him and leaned back. "Hey," he said.

"What?"

"You're Cassandra," Harry said. It wasn't a question.

"So what?"

"So, a girl I know told me to come talk to you. You know a girl named Annette? Works for Mr. Jay?"

"Yeah," Cassandra said. She had flat, uninterested eyes and a hard set to her jaw. She seemed unfriendly, and even hostile to Harry. *Hell, I look like a nice guy, so you can never figure people by their look,* he thought. "I know Annette. So what?" she asked.

"I'm looking into something for Annette and her friends. You heard about Bebe?" he asked, hoping to prime her for the conversation by assuming she knew, rather than questioning her.

"Yeah," Cassandra said. "I heard. You're a cop?"

"No, I'm a PI. Can I ask you a couple questions?" Harry fished another bill out of his wallet. He held it up.

"Save it," she said. "Bebe was a friend of mine from way back."

"Oh, yeah?" Harry didn't want to sound incredulous, but he did.

"Sure," Cassandra said with irony dripping. "We went to prep school together. Cotillions and shit like that."

"Sure," Harry mimicked her tone unconsciously. "I could see that."

"Screw you, asshole," Cassandra said. "Get bent."

Harry held up his hands. "Look, I'm sorry. I didn't mean to be an asshole. I'm serious. I'm looking into it for them, and I need a couple answers. Five minutes, ten bucks. What do you say?"

"I said save it," Cassandra said. "I don't want your money. What do you want to know?"

"Your manager's name is Darius, right?"

"Manager. Yeah. Manager. He's a pimp. Darius Cheeseborough," she said with a smirk.

"Cheeseborough," Harry repeated. "Huh. New one."

"Yeah. They call him Cheddar. You can't miss him. He looks like he should play center for the Knicks," Cassandra said.

"Cheddar," Harry said. "Great. Let me ask you something, Cassandra. Do you think Cheddar could have killed Bebe?"

Cassandra blinked, surprised. She'd never considered it. Harry didn't miss it. She shrugged. "If he did, I haven't heard about it. And he would have blabbed that all over the girls. That's exactly the kind of thing he'd like to use to keep us in line."

"You're sure?" Harry asked. He didn't figure it'd be that easy, but he'd hoped. No crime against hope. Just odds.

"I said so, didn't I?"

Harry nodded. "All right, all right. Here. Take the money."

"I told you I didn't want it," Cassandra said.

"Come on, I took your time, take the money," Harry insisted.

"Look, would you leave me alone?" Cassandra turned her back. "Go away."

Harry stuffed the bill back in his pocket and pulled out a card. "Fine. Thanks for your help. If you think of anything, you can reach me here."

"Yeah, whatever," Cassandra said. She stuffed his card into the little space between her stomach and her dress.

"See you," Harry said. He walked away. He plodded steadily through the snow, thinking and shivering in equal measure. He turned right onto Tenth and found Beckett's Pool Hall halfway down. The door was fogged and dirty, and there were at least two cars out front that wouldn't be moving in the near future, even if they hadn't been plowed in. The yellow lock boots showed on the front wheels over the snow. There was a rusty Eldorado half a block away with two black guys in the back, just watching the street. Harry slipped his hand around the grip of his gun and went to the door of the bar. He couldn't see inside. As he put a hand on the door, the Eldorado's doors opened and the two enforcers stepped out. Harry smiled at them and went inside.

The place was packed, even for two in the afternoon, and hotter than a bakery inside. Harry stepped to the left of the door and stood with his back to the wall just looking around and waiting. The door opened and the two guys from the car stepped in and walked past him. Belatedly, one of them looked around and spotted Harry, who waved at them.

The music pounded through the air and covered the conversations and clatter of billiard balls on the tables. Harry waved at the two guys and they stared at him, clearly at a loss. Harry brushed past them and went to the bar.

"Beer," he told the bartender. The bartender had scars on both cheeks and over his eyes. Harry thought they looked like glass wounds, maybe from a car accident. The bartender slammed a longneck on the bar. Harry twisted the top off and looked around the room.

At the far corner table stood a man who could have been seven feet tall, easily. His midnight black skin looked almost blue under the swaying fluorescent lights.

Cheddar. Had to be. His muscular frame was molded by a tight-fitting blue tee shirt with a bright yellow frowning face on the front of it. He held a pool cue and it looked a little ridiculous in his hands-like a toy or a prop. He sipped his beer and watched the game.

Cheddar looked over the table as one of the two guys from the Eldorado approached him. The other stood behind Harry at the bar. He whispered in Cheddar's ear and pointed. Cheddar looked up and Harry waved at him. Cheddar nodded and went back to his game. The other guy joined his friend at the bar.

"So," Harry said loudly. "Think I could get next game?"

The two enforcers just looked at him.

Harry said, "I'm a billiards enthusiast."

They didn't blink.

Harry finished his beer and set it on the bar. "Okay, then."

He made it three steps before the two goons appeared in front of him. "Where you going?"

"Gonna go talk to my friend," Harry said. "What's it to you?"

"You ain't *got* no friends here, man," the left one said.

"You need to get outta here, whiteboy," the other one said. "Before whatever friends you *do* have need to chip in and buy you a coffin."

"Does that ever work?" Harry asked.

"Huh?" goon one said reflexively.

"Do you guys ever actually scare anyone off?" Harry gripped his gun more tightly, trying to appear relaxed.

"Listen-"

"No, *you* listen," Harry said. He stepped closer to the one on the right, and stood nose to nose with him. People around them started to take notice. A few grinned, expecting to see a fight. "You're going to get out of my way. The choices you have are simple- do it voluntarily, and no one here'll think you're a pussy. Do it hard, and everyone here's gonna remember the day you got your ass kicked by an old white boy. Pick one."

"Man, I oughta take you out right here, Homes," the left enforcer said. He seemed a little uncertain, but he was game. Right Side, however, was staring into Harry's eyes. Harry stared right back.

"I'm going to go over and ask Cheddar a couple of questions. You're gonna get out of my way and let me, or you're not going home tonight, man, you're going to Mercy. You wanna go to the hospital and explain to some doctor and nurse why you got a boot stuck up your ass?"

The guy swallowed. Harry looked like a middle-aged accountant, but he talked like the baddest mother in the valley. Right was clearly torn. Harry saw the guy was teetering and gave him a little push. "We're old friends. You just forgot until now. I'm cool. Right?"

Right glanced at Left.

"I just wanna ask him questions. And no, I'm not a cop," Harry supplied.

Right hesitated. "What kind of questions?"

Harry said softly, "The personal kind."

Right looked at Left. Left shrugged.

"Five minutes, maybe less, and I'm out," Harry said. "If it makes you feel better, you can toss me outta here."

Right grinned. "You sure about that?"

"If it helps you, why wouldn't I be? After all, we're friends now, aren't we?" Harry smiled at them both.

They didn't know what to do about him, so while the two guys looked at each other again, Harry stepped around them and went over to the pool table where Cheddar was trying a complicated back-spin trick shot. He stepped up to the table just as Cheddar sank the shot. His crowd whooped and clapped. Cheddar looked at Harry. Then he straightened up and looked *down* at Harry.

"You're Cheddar, aren't you?" Harry asked.

"What's it to you, little man?" Cheddar's voice was deep and clear and Harry had no problem picturing him having his own radio show. His voice was a golden baritone that would put most funk singers to shame.

"I'd like to ask you something. No, I'm not a cop," he said.

Cheddar grinned. He had startlingly white teeth. "Wouldn't matter if you were."

"Why'd you kill Bebe?" Harry asked, watching the taller man's face closely.

Cheddar's eyes went wide in surprise. "What?"

Nuts, Harry thought. He'd been on the far side of plenty of interrogations, and the guy looked startled, but not scared, not guilty. He just looked surprised. Still, he had to press.

Harry said brusquely, "Bebe. You know her. Why'd you kill her? What'd she do to you?"

"Man, I don't know what you're talking about. Who killed Bebe?" Cheddar demanded.

"I thought *you* did," Harry said.

Cheddar put his cue down. "Why would you think that, man? Who the *fuck* told you that?"

"You're fighting with Mr. Jay over on Bleecker, right? Bebe was one of his girls. You did it for retribution, or a first strike, or whatever," Harry said. "Didn't you?"

"No, I *didn't* kill Bebe. And I don't give two shits what you think. I was trying to get Bebe *away* from that fuck. Girl's a… girl *was* a moneymaker," Cheddar groused.

Harry nodded. "What I hear. So this is the first you're hearing about it?"

"Yeah, man," Cheddar said angrily. "Fuck."

Harry studied the man's face, but Cheddar didn't seem to be lying. Harry sighed and said, "All right. Listen, I'm looking into it. Can I leave a card for you?"

"Why? I know who you are, man. Ex-cop. You live over on Elizabeth, right? In the old Chinese place," Cheddar said.

"Yeah." Harry felt a little unsettled by the fact that some pimp he didn't know knew *him*. He looked casually around to cover his unease. "Anything else you think I might need to know?"

69

"Nope. Best you get the fuck out of here now," Cheddar said. "My boys will show you out."

Harry opened his mouth to say something else, but a hand clapped down on his shoulder and spun him around. Right stood there with a cheesy grin on his face.

"Oh yeah," Harry said. "All right. Just go easy on the coat."

Right grabbed one arm. Left grabbed the other. Together they marched him to the door and hurled him at it. Before he slammed into the dirty doors, Harry raised a foot and kicked it open instead. He walked outside without looking back, hoping it played as cool to the patrons as it had to him.

Outside a bitter wind had begun to whip the snow around. Harry shrugged his collar up. He raised a hand in the air and used the other to whistle piercingly. A cab pulled over.

"Yeah?" the cabbie asked genially, for a cabbie.

"43rd and 45th, over in Queens." Harry said. "And take your time."

"Sure thing, pal," the cabbie said.

Chapter Nine

It wasn't a great building, but it wasn't the worst in the neighborhood. The police precinct stood just a block away, so the neighborhood was sullenly decent. Harry told the driver to wait and climbed the steps. He buzzed at the intercom. A man's voice answered. "Yeah?"

"Uh… delivery for Mrs. Angelo?" Harry temporized. He hadn't expected the husband.

"Yeah, come on," the man said, and the door buzzed and clicked. Harry stomped the three flights up. He found the apartment halfway down the hall and knocked.

Mrs. Angelo opened the door and smiled wanly. "Hello, Mr. DeMarko. Come in, please."

Stomach knotted, Harry did so. She closed the door behind him as a man came out of the bedroom. He was shirtless and in decent shape. A sinking feeling began in Harry's gut. He stood between them both and swallowed hard.

"What's this?" Peter demanded.

"Sit down, Peter," Mrs. Angelo said primly. She seemed remote.

"What?"

Harry stared at the floor and considered his options. He could jump. It was only three stories. And there was snow. It probably wouldn't be that bad.

"Sit down, please. I have something I'd like to show you. Mr. DeMarko?" Mrs. Angelo prompted.

Peter dropped into one of the chairs around the scuffed Formica table and waited while Harry pulled the packet of pictures from his pocket. He handed them to the woman. She opened it, rifled through the pictures, and nodded to herself, one quick jerk of her head. She tossed Peter the envelope.

"Go ahead, Peter. He got your good side," she said. The look on her face was pinched and bitter, and matched her voice.

Peter looked puzzled, and pulled out the pictures of himself and his secretary. Harry looked away. They weren't good shots, and neither Peter nor the secretary were flexible. The pictures were pretty blasé, but there were several clear shots of both their faces in the paroxysms of pleasure.

Peter's face turned red, flushing from his chest to his neck to his hair.

"What the *fuck*? You had me *followed*?" he barked as he shot up out of the chair. Harry gripped the .38 in his pocket more tightly. *I thought Cheddar would be the worst part of my day,* Harry thought. *I should know better.*

"Oh, don't play the injured spouse, Peter," Mrs. Angelo said. "You're caught. I suspected for a while, but I wanted proof before I came to you. I didn't want you playing mind games, telling me it was all in my head."

She smiled at him without any trace of warmth. "Now I know. And now you can get your things and get out," she said.

Peter thundered, "Bull*shit*. I'm not just-"

"Leave, Peter," she said, and Harry realized his role in this little drama. He was the enforcer. Shit. No wonder she'd wanted him here after five. She was waiting for Peter to get home. Set up by an angry housewife. Harry's mouth went dry. She wouldn't have done it this way if she had thought Peter would just yell a little.

Peter growled, "I told you, bitch-"

"All right" Harry interjected, as much to his surprise as theirs. "That's enough. Cool it. Just do as she asks. Later, after you're both calmer you can talk this out."

"Fuck you," Peter said. "You don't get to tell me anything in my house-"

"*My* house," his wife corrected. "This apartment's in *my* name, Peter. Leave. Take your shit and your swagger and get the hell out, you lying sack of-"

"You, too, Mrs. Angelo," Harry said. "That's not helping."

"It's Agnes," she said primly. "I'm changing my last name back as soon as I can. You'll hear from my lawyer soon enough, Peter."

Peter didn't bother replying. He just leaned across the table and back-handed his wife. Harry exhaled. He gripped his gun more tightly.

"You shouldn't have done that," he started, but Peter lunged at him and landed a punch squarely in the center of his face. It was an awkward reach across the table, but Peter had the reach for it. Harry felt his nose crunch and a huge bolt of pain lanced across his vision. He howled and stumbled backward. Peter came around the table and pressed the advantage, kicking at Harry a couple of times for good measure. After fending off a kick to the chest, Harry came up off the floor with the gun drawn. He pointed it at Peter, squinting to see him clearly. He felt the blood running down his chin.

"All right, God damn it," Harry snarled. "That's fucking *it*. I have had a shitty day and you're just making it worse. I'm done. I'm *done*. Get your shit, Peter. Whatever you can carry in one trip. I'm sure your wife'll be happy to toss anything else you need out the fucking window at you. But do it now, or I swear to God I'm going to put two in your leg. You understand me?"

Peter backed away with his hands in the air. "Big man with a gun. Put that shit down and let's see what you're made of, asshole."

Harry barked a laugh. "Yeah, because I'm an idiot. Get your shit, Pete. Last chance before I give you a limp."

Baring his teeth at Harry, Peter slipped on a pair of shoes, grabbed a jacket, and his wallet.

"Leave your keys," Harry instructed.

Peter snarled at him and pulled out his key ring. "How am I supposed to drive my car?"

"Whose car is it?" Harry asked them both.

"It's his," Agnes said. "I wouldn't drive that piece of shit anyhow."

"You never bitched about it when you were bouncing in the back," Peter leered.

Agnes retorted, "I was being nice, you limp-dick-"

Harry cocked the gun. The snap of the cylinder revolving sounded very loud in the room. They both shut up immediately.

"Take the goddamned car key off the ring. Put the ring on the table. Walk to the door," Harry said, and moved so the table was between them. "Now."

"This isn't over, bitch," Peter snarled at Agnes as he opened the front door. "Not by a long shot."

"It is for today. Walk," Harry commanded.

Peter left, tromping down the stairs two at a time. Harry looked at Agnes Angelo. "You *better* have my check," he said.

Her eyes brimmed with tears. "You're all heart, aren't you?"

"Lady, do you *see* my nose?" Harry asked. "Any idea how much this kills?"

"I'm sure it hurts more than having your husband fuck around on you with a no-account bitch of a secretary," she retorted.

"Yeah, because there's a comparison," Harry said. "I did the job, please pay me."

Agnes picked up a check from the kitchen counter. "There. Take it," she said with a sneer.

Harry did so. "Thank you. Any time you need help, give me a call."

She froze him with a stare. "Of course. You're the soul of discretion and a humanitarian. I'll tell all my cheated-on friends about you."

"I'd like that," Harry said, countering her broad sarcasm with sincerity. "Also, get a pen."

"What?" Angelo asked, startled.

"Get a pen and a piece of paper. Write this number down," Harry told her.

"I already *have* your number, Mr. DeMarko," she said, but got the pen. He gave her a number to write down.

"And this is what? The number I call to rate your service?" she asked, arching an eyebrow.

"That's the direct desk line of Officer Cathy Michaels. She's at the 6th precinct over in Manhattan, but she'll know what to tell you. You call her if that asshole tries to come back. Cathy can get you a restraining order or send some units this way to help.

Tell her I gave you the number and she'll do it without questions. She'll save you a lot of wasted time."

Agnes Angelo had the grace to look contrite. In a low voice she stammered, "I-I'm sorry, Mr. DeMarko. I didn't-"

"Yeah, you did. But it doesn't matter," Harry said, stuffing his gun back into his pocket after releasing the hammer. "Your husband *looks* like a blowhard, but he's too free with his fists for my taste. Give Cathy a call if you need help dealing with him."

She nodded. She bit her lip and then reached for a kitchen towel. "Here," she said. "Would you like some ice?"

"No," Harry told her. "I'm good. It's already cold out. And get your locks changes as soon as possible. Do it today. *Now.* He'll most likely go out and get hammered. Around three in the morning it's going to seem like a good idea to come back here, and he might have a spare key. I'd just as soon not read about it in the morning papers, you get me?"

"Y-yes," she said. "I will. I'll call right away."

"Good," Harry said. He left, pausing on the stairs until she locked the door and shot the chain behind him. On the street, the car nearest the door was gone and so was Peter. Harry climbed back into his cab, dabbing at his nose with the towel.

"Bleecker and Elizabeth," he told the cabbie.

"Your dime," the cabby told him, and put the car in gear. He looked up at Harry in the mirror.

"Your nose is busted, pal," he said.

"Yeah, thanks for the heads-up," Harry groused. He pressed the towel to his nose and winced. He fished the check out of his pocket. Harry looked at the check. Another hundred bucks. Super.

Such was the glamorous life of the private eye, he thought. *She didn't even offer to sleep with me out of gratitude. Raymond Chandler lied to me.*

Chapter Ten

After giving the cabbie one of his dwindling bills, handing out a cup of coffee to Jasper ("You know your nose is broke, Chief?"), and throwing the check on the desk, Harry went into the bathroom to examine his nose, which he had on good and repeated authority might have been broken in the altercation with Peter Angelo. He swallowed a handful of aspirin and slurped water from the sink, in a way enjoying the sour, grainy feel of the pills disintegrating on his tongue.

He was gingerly prodding the decidedly-right-leaning nose in question when someone began hammering on the door of his office. Swearing without venom, Harry shuffled out. Toni was waiting to be let in. He unlocked the door. As he opened the door for her, her look of annoyance turned to shock.

"Jesus, Harry! What the hell happened to you?" she demanded, dropping her bag.

"Angry husband," Harry muttered.

She cocked her head. "You been putting it where you shouldn't ought to have put it, Harry?"

He snorted a laugh and winced as his nose twinged. "No. It was a snoop job. Pictures of the guy cheating on his wife. I went to deliver them and he was there. She set me up. Used me as defense. He got in a lucky shot."

"What'd you do?" Toni asked, eyes round.

"Threatened to shoot him. He chilled pretty quickly after that," Harry said. They walked back into the apartment. Toni went to the sink and wet a towel.

"Come here. You're covered in blood. Your shirt's ruined. Coat too, I think," Toni told him.

"I don't care about the coat. A little blood won't make it any worse," Harry said. "But that was my last clean shirt.

Toni chuckled as she dabbed at his neck and chin. "You're a mess, Harry."

"Yeah," he said. He closed his eyes and enjoyed the familiarity of her hands and the feel of the warm water. "That feels good."

"Good. Why are you doing this?" Toni asked.

He opened one eye to peer at her. "Doing what?"

"Trying to get yourself killed," she said.

"Come on, how could I have known he'd be there?" Harry asked.

"I don't just mean this, but while we're on the subject, do you plan on heading to the hospital any time soon?" Toni asked him.

"What for? It's just a broken nose. Not my first," Harry added. "Probably won't be my last."

"It's all… crooked," she said, examining his nose critically.

"Why does everyone think I don't know that? I was about to fix it when you interrupted me. Come on. I might need your help, actually," he said. He went back into the bathroom and she followed. He took the towel from her and wiped blood from the bridge of his nose. He gingerly wiped the blood away from the cut. He sucked air through his teeth as the towel stung the raw flesh.

"What do you need me to do?" Toni asked him, wincing in sympathy.

"Just be ready. I'm going to put it back in place. There's gonna be more blood. And… it's gonna hurt.

A lot. I may yell. I may scream. Or I might just pass out. I don't know. Never done it before. Would you make sure I don't clock myself on the way down? Most accidents in the home happen in the bathroom. I wanna try and avoid becoming a statistic."

Toni nodded, eyes solemn. "You're really going to do this? I mean, yourself?"

Harry nodded. "Yeah. It's not a big deal."

He reached up with both hands and gently laid his fingers to his nose. He winced at the flash of pain, and Toni winced with him. He took several deep breaths, psyching himself up for the coming storm of pain.

"Here we go," he whispered, squeezed his nostrils closed between his fingers and pulled downward sharply. He yelped as he wrenched the cartilage. He both felt and heard a crunch, his vision went red, and he dropped bonelessly to his knees.

Toni caught him before he toppled over. She held the towel under his nose as a fresh gout of heavy dark blood poured from his nostrils. Harry rested against her for a moment. She put an arm around him and cradled him tightly. He shook his head gently to clear it, sniffed blood back, and swallowed it. The coppery-slick taste and feel cleared his head even more. He leaned away from her and with her help struggled to his feet. He examined his face in the mirror. It was straight, mostly, but both of his eyes had begun to blacken and the cut across the bridge oozed.

"Well, shit," he said, in an attempt to make light of it. "I'll *never* be a model now."

"You're already handsome enough," Toni said in a quiet voice. "This just… just makes you look more rugged. Less pretty, but more rakish. Like a bad boy."

"I was pretty?" he mumbled. Harry looked at her and smiled. He realized she had tears in her eyes. He reached up with both hands and wiped them away. "It's okay, Toni. It's just a little pain and some blood. No big deal."

She slapped his hands away. "Bullshit, Harry. That's the same bullshit you said when-"

"I know," he cut her off. "I *know* what I said."

She pushed him back a little and he realized she was suddenly, fiercely angry. He was confused. Her elfin features darkened as her face flushed and she screamed at him, "You're going to get yourself killed! Will *that* make you happy?"

"It's not vital, it's just a broken nose. A couple lumps. What's the big deal, Toni?" he asked.

She stalked into the bedroom and stood by the bed with her arms crossed over her chest. He followed, stripping off his shirt. The front of it was dark with blood. He balled it up and tossed it at the trash. It lay half in and half out of the basket. Toni stood with her back to him, arms crossed and head down.

"You gonna talk to me?" he asked, "or just pout?"

She snorted and looked over her shoulder. Heatedly she snapped, "You don't hear *anything* I say. I don't know why I bother at all. Why I bother coming back here. Why I bother with *you*."

Harry's head throbbed, and he didn't think about his words. He said off-handedly, "So don't. There's the door. I didn't ask you to adopt me. I didn't ask you to live here. The couch is killing my back anyhow. You leave, at least I get my bed back."

She whirled to stare at him. Her mouth dropped open. The anger was gone, replaced by what he was alarmed to realize was a deep, deep hurt. He raised his hands in surrender. "I'm sorry. That was bitchy. I'm not in a good mood."

She closed her mouth and set her jaw. She looked away from him again. He sat down on the bed near her.

"Seriously, Toni. I apologize. Forgive me," he said quietly.

After a minute, she put a hand out and took his. "You're an asshole, Harry," she said, but she squeezed. He squeezed back.

"Yeah," he agreed.

"Do you want me to put some ice on that?" she asked in a quieter voice.

"If you don't mind?" he asked.

She smiled at him, a half-smile that seemed sad and happy all at once. "I don't mind."

He lay back on the bed while she broke up some ice and wrapped it in a small dishcloth. She came back and sat beside him, gently holding the cloth to the bridge of his nose, wincing when he did as he hissed in pain.

"I'm sorry," she soothed.

"It's okay. It feels good," he said, and closed his eyes.

They sat in companionable silence for a while, and Harry started to relax. She curled up to make herself more comfortable, and continued to hold the ice to the bridge of his nose. She looked at his serene features, wondering what he was thinking about. He started to snore. Toni blinked in disbelief. Harry didn't snore normally, but he normally could breathe out of his nose. She couldn't believe it, but he was out cold. She sighed, and shook her head with a fond smile. She leaned over and kissed him on the cheek. He woke up, cracked one lid, and peered at her.

"What was that for?" he asked in a sleep-filled voice.

"You. Letting me help you. I'm thankful," Toni said.

"Thankful? That's an odd way to put it," Harry said to her with a frown.

"Most guys would have been all *manly* or whatnot," she said with a smile. "You don't mind looking human."

"Like I have a choice?" Harry asked.

"You always do," she said, "but you *usually* make the right one."

"Oh, good," Harry said told her. "I was *hoping* I made the right choices. Good to know this fabulous life of ease and luxury is what you get when you make the right choices."

"Silly. This is the life you get when you make the choices you want to make. You built this life. God alone knows why, but this is what you made, and this is the life you apparently want," Toni said, brushing his hair out of his eyes. He smiled at her touch.

"All *I* ever wanted was to make detective. Maybe get married some day. Go to ballgames and have a shitty house in Queens or Brooklyn with a postage stamp backyard. Maybe with a grill. I didn't want *this*," Harry said, gesturing at his nose and then around the room. "I bought this place because it was in the middle of my beat. But let's be real, huh? I live in an old restaurant. I always smell like chow mien. I get beat up on a ridiculously consistent basis. I make money breaking people's marriages up and… and finding lost cats. My only friends are cops who are too polite to tell me to get a life and a hooker who keeps trying to sleep with me. I..."

Harry trailed off thoughtfully. Toni smiled down at him. "Just realized you're an idiot?" she asked.

"You know, I *might* be an idiot," he said.

"Yes, but that's okay. You have other redeeming qualities. Trust isn't high on that list, though. Why can't I have a key to the front door?" she asked him. It wasn't the first time.

He looked uncomfortable and didn't answer.

"I get it," she said with a shrug. "You don't want me dragging all my hooker friends home. I might fill the house up with sexy, loose women who fuck for cash, or in a pinch, for a place to keep warm during a shitty blizzard. That's the kind of favor for which they'd be lewdly and accommodatingly grateful."

He blinked up at her.

"You're an idiot," she supplied helpfully.

"Yeah, I'm getting that." He took the ice off his nose and sat up. "How's it look?"

She hemmed and hawed, tilted her head to the left and then to the right, then gave him a big grin. "You look like DeNiro in Taxi Driver. You know, the beaten-up parts, not the scary Mohawk part."

He grinned at her. "I didn't know you liked DeNiro," he said.

"Who doesn't like DeNiro?" she asked. "*That's* idiotic."

He laughed and his stomach growled. "What time is it? I'm starving."

"How can you be hungry? Doesn't that hurt?" she asked.

"Not enough that I'm not hungry," Harry said.

"Hey," she said with sudden inspiration. "Let's go out tonight. What do you say? Feel up to it?"

He didn't say anything.

"You know, dinner, maybe a club?" she asked.

"I'm not much for dancing," he said.

"No, but you do like to drink," she pointed out.

He allowed that he did occasionally like a drop. "What are you in the mood for?"

"Getting hammered and stumbling home to have sloppy drunk sex," she said with what he privately admitted to himself was a cute little leer.

He sighed impatiently. "You know what I mean."

"I know, I know. Grump. How about Italian?" she asked.

He considered it. "Yeah… yeah. I could go for Italian. In fact… I think it's a good idea." He looked around with a smile. He felt a million miles away from himself. Maybe a good sock in the nose was good for him occasionally. "Do I have a clean shirt left?"

"Over on the chair," she said, pointing.

"Thanks," Harry said, and went to get it.

"What should I wear?" she asked.

"I don't know… something nice?" he suggested.

"What, like my day-glo plastic skirt and a mini halter?" she teased.

"How about a nice dress?" he countered. "Do you… do you *have* a nice dress?"

She didn't take umbrage, only considered the question. "I think I have an old dress in my bag." She rummaged in a shopping bag by the couch and came up with a crumpled red dress, not too formal, but nice. Wrinkled as a ball of yarn, though.

"I don't have an iron," Harry said dubiously.

"No problem. I'll hang it in the bathroom while I take a hot shower. That'll help a lot," Toni said. She took the dress into the bathroom and started running the hot water. She closed the door and came back out. "You want to come scrub my back, Harry?" she asked.

He shook his head, hunting for his dress pants that he knew for a fact were around somewhere. "No thanks. You go ahead."

"You're no fun," she told him. She went back into the bathroom. When she closed the door he stared at it thoughtfully while she sang, loudly and more or less on-key. He slipped on his least-rumpled slacks and even went so far as to look for his dress shoes. Not his shiny plastic-feeling cop's shoes; those he'd thrown away. But he still had a pair of funeral shoes. Every cop did. He found a pair of dress socks balled in them and sniffed. Not dirty, for a wonder. *Makes sense*, he thought. Since he left the force he hadn't been to one funeral. So, retirement wasn't all that bad a deal. He put on his slacks, socks, shoes, and his last clean shirt, buttoning it up to the collar and shooting the cuffs. He looked at himself in the mirror. He suddenly realized what he looked like. He sighed and got undressed all the way to his skin.

He banged on the bathroom door. "Toni! Leave me some hot water! I need a shower, too!"

"So come join me! There's plenty!" she yelled.

"Hurry up, girl!" he yelled back. "Or I'll leave without you!"

"You wouldn't dare, you dirty tease!" she bellowed. A moment later the water shut off and she came out in a skimpy towel. "All yours, honey."

"Thanks," he grumped and tried not to stare. She had not-bad legs, he thought. And her ass was-

He froze. Across the middle of her back and stretching to her ribs on both sides were a new set of bruises. "What the hell happened to you?"

She turned to look at him and dropped the towel. "I've been working out," she said, throwing a hand to her hip and modeling her shape for him. "Doesn't it show?"

"Knock off the shit, Toni," Harry said with a glowering frown. "What's with the bruises?"

Toni looked down and spun around, trying to see all the way around her own back. "Oh. Oh, those. Uh, John."

"A *john* did that?" he barked.

"No, Harry. John. Mr. Jay," she clarified. "For, you know, for this morning. He tuned us all up a little as a warning."

Harry's fists were tightly clenched and he could see the red mist floating over his vision as his blood came up. "He. Beat. You."

She nodded, and bit her lower lip, suddenly wary of him. "Yeah. It happens. It's nothing. Worse than it looks. He used a belt this time, instead of fists."

He drove his fist into the wall with a growl, and she flinched at the gunshot sound of it. Naked, he should have been ridiculous. He wasn't. "He's a dead man," Harry swore.

"Harry, no- you *knew* this would happen when you stopped him at Dahli's," she pleaded. "It *had* to happen. He lost face. He had to do *something*. You knew he was going to do something. And more, we did, too."

She touched his shoulder tentatively and surprisingly he let her. She could feel the vibrating passion and anger within him. She ran her fingertips over the splayed scar on his chest and he exhaled.

"We knew the score, Harry, and we talked to you anyhow. You *have* to let it go. It's just… it's just the cost of doing business. You aren't going to change it. Even if you got rid of him, it'll be someone else we *don't* know. At least with John- Mr. Jay- we know what to expect. There's guys out there who like to torture their girls. Stabbing, acid, all kinds of screwed-up shit. Jay at least only hits us, and never in the face. So we take lumps now and then. It's not that bad, all things considered. It could be so much worse."

He stared at her. "You're *okay* with this?"

She snorted. "You *are* an idiot, Harry. Of course not. But what choice do we have?"

"You have a-"

"No," she snarled angrily, suddenly irritated and exhausted. "*You* have a choice. You're all set. You have a job and a home and money. You can do what you want and tell anyone to fuck off if they don't like it. We don't *have* that luxury. You think we're here because we *like* it? Are you retarded? Are you *stupid?* How long have you lived in this city?"

He shook his head. "Come on, you have to realize-"

"Harry," she said gently, "I'm lucky enough to have a place to stay that I don't have to pay for. I'm, like, the *only* girl in the stable that can say that. Half the girls live in shitty hotels, or worse, they have to slum it with whatever john lets them stay. Sometimes they try to get apartments with each other, but no one wants a bunch of hookers as tenants, and even when they do get a place, the girls don't get along forever. Like I said, sometimes they can crash with a john, but if you think it's free you're crazy. Even if we don't pay, we *pay*. You *know* that. You're not some country bumpkin, fresh from Iowa. You know what this city is *like*. You know how bad it is out there. It's getting worse all the time. And it's *winter*. It's not like the girls can huddle in a doorway all night. Its freezing out there, and we have nowhere to go, and we have to come across with the money, and it's the worst situation, but there's worse than this. He could *kill* us, Harry. Remember Bebe? No one knows why she got killed, or who did it, but I guarantee you she was picked on because she was a hooker. We're... we're *things*. We're not people. And when you're not *people*, well... then you're a pet or you're property. But you're not *safe*. And you don't have choices."

She sat down and looked at him. The hopelessness of her face caused him to look away. She seemed both hopeless and resigned and the combination of the two almost broke his heart.

"You've been really nice to me, Harry, for whatever reason. I think you're probably crazy, but I'm not gonna argue about *why*," she said softly. He started to protest but she held up a hand to stop him. "I told you, I don't care *why*. You let me stay here, you're nice to me, and you make me feel... safe. Safer, anyhow. And I'm never going to question that, but it's dangerous out there, and I leave here every day and wonder if I'll come back. And when I do come back, I'm always grateful. You've never been mean to me, not really. You've never made me afraid. I kind of... I kind of *count* on that, Harry. But if you do anything about this, I'll have to face even worse than a beating, and I'll have to do it without you watching my back. So please, *please*, let it go. And not just for me. For the other girls. God only knows what he would do. And there's something else, Harry. What if you went after him and you get *killed*? What happens to me then?"

He didn't say anything. There wasn't anything to say.

"I'll *tell* you what happens then. We get killed too. Or worse than dead. But John wouldn't just let that go either. He'd make a huge example of us. We might still be able to work, but we'd be hurt bad, probably permanently. And then I'd be without *you*, too. So what's it gonna be? What are you going to do?"

Harry hung his head. He hated what she had said, but it was... it was all true. How could he argue with the truth? He said, "I don't... nothing. Nothing I guess. Nothing I *can* do."

She smiled at him and stood up. "There is, though. You can go take a shower and take me out. You never know. Maybe you'll get lucky." She put her arms around him and kissed him softly, her lips touching his briefly. "You take care of me, Harry, and I'm grateful. I give you a lot of shit, and I'm a pain in the ass, but I really am grateful."

He became immediately aware that she was warm, damp, and naked as he was. He patted her awkwardly on the arm and backed away. "I know, Toni. I know. And I don't... I don't know *why-*"

"I know," she said in a soothing voice, "I know you don't know. It's plain you don't. When you do figure it out, I'll still be here."

He nodded. "All right. All right. Good enough. Let me get this done."

With a last glance at her, he went into the bathroom and closed the door. He got into the already lukewarm shower and gingerly washed his face.

Toni sat down on the bed and wrapped her arms around her body. Tears streamed from her face but she didn't made a sound. She was quick and efficient and she let the grief and pain pour out of her. When she was finished, she was finished. She ran a cloth under the cold water tap and wiped her eyes. She examined herself in the mirror. Not bad. She fluffed her hair with the towel and took out eyeliner and lipstick. She primped quickly and efficiently, smiling at the result. She sprayed deodorant under each arm, and followed it up with a spritz of perfume on one wrist. She rubbed her wrists together, and then pressed them to her breasts. She heard the shower shut off and quickly arranged herself on the edge of the bed, leaning back and crossing her legs. She gazed at the door of the bathroom until he came out.

He stepped out of a cloud of steam, and froze as he caught sight of her. Swallowing thickly, he quickly busied himself, drying off and putting down the towel. He was careful to keep his back to her, but she could see his honest interest in the mirror.

"Harry," she asked.

He looked at her over his shoulder. "What?"

"Why don't you want me?" she asked with a purr.

He cleared his throat. "Come on, Toni. Don't do this."

"I'm being serious. Especially since I know you *do*," she said with a cat-like wicked smile.

"Toni, come on. Knock it off, okay?" He struggled into his slacks and zipped them, covering the evidence of his interest. He slipped on his shirt and busied himself with the buttons. "I told you, just let it go."

She sighed and uncrossed her legs. She caught him watching in the mirror and smiled. "It's okay to want to. It's okay to watch. It's *okay*, Harry. I'm giving you permission."

"It's not okay," he said. "I told you, I'm not looking for payment for... for the things I do."

"You're just a nice guy?" she asked.

"Am I not?" he countered, piqued.

"You are. You're certainly the nicest guy who ever turned me down. Idiot," she added with a smile. She went to the bathroom and swung on the door, leaning toward him. "Are you sure?"

He nodded and sighed. "I'm sure. Get dressed, brat."

"Yes, daddy," she said. She closed the door. He looked at himself in the mirror. His nose was messed up, but at least the bleeding had stopped and the swelling had started to recede somewhat. He'd found a tiny bandage in the bathroom and taped it across the bridge of his nose. He dried his hair quickly and combed it with his fingers. It wasn't terrible. He turned to the opening door as Toni finished up and stepped out.

Holy... shit. She wears the hell *out of that dress,* he thought. It clung to her like a second skin, and it complimented every slender curve she had. The dress matched her lipstick, and somehow, even her eyes.

"Stop drooling, Harry," Toni said in her least serious, playful voice, but color appeared high on her cheeks and she looked away with a nervous smile on her lips.

"You look *really* good," he said, and meant it. "Very elegant."

"Huh," she said. She eyed him for a second. "You mean for a street chick? Who would have thought?"

"No," Harry said sincerely. "I mean for *anyone*. You're gorgeous, Toni."

She blushed again. "Thank you," she whispered.

"You make me feel underdressed," he said.

She grinned at him. "I could strip down again, if it'll help."

He sighed. "Never give up, do you?"

"Nope."

"Good. I like that about you," he told her truthfully. She blushed again. He cleared his throat and looked away again. "So, uh, you ready?"

She fished out a pair of heels from her bag. He frowned thoughtfully at them.

"What?" she asked nervously. "You don't like them?"

"No, no," he assured her. "They're fine. I like them. I just… do you think I should buy a dresser?"

She guffawed. "Really? *That's* what you wanna ask me?"

He shrugged uncomfortably. "Well, yeah. I have nowhere to put my clothes aside from the floor unless I hang 'em. And you don't have- I mean-"

"Careful, Harry," she said as she slipped on the heels. They brought her up to nearly his height. "Your self-interest is showing."

"Hey, that's not-"

"Where you taking me, stud?" she asked.

Thrown by the change of conversation, Harry groped around for a second. He gave his audacious thought voice. "Uh, I uh, I thought maybe we'd try Bellini's uptown."

She stared at him in awe. He'd actually intended to take her to Gino's Bar & Grill, but realized she looked way too good for that. They kind of both did. Bellini's was far more elegant, in the same way a high-heeled shoe was more elegant than a ratty old sneaker.

"Wow," she said. "You're *really* trying to impress me."

He shrugged uncomfortably, trapped in his decision now that he'd said it. "No... I just... it's been a hell of a day, and I thought it'd be nice to, you know..."

"To what? Celebrate a broken nose with a dinner that would probably cost a hundred bucks?" she asked him.

She was right, and he wasn't sure his checking account would handle the hit, or even if Bellini's would *take* a check, but he put on a confident face and nodded. "Sure. Why not?" he asked with a bravado he did not feel.

"Harry... you don't have to do this to make me feel better," Toni assured him solemnly.

"Who said anything about how *you* feel? This is for *me*. My nose hurts like hell, and I have the distinct feeling that it won't feel better unless I find a nice restaurant full of classy people so I can stick it in the air." He did so, looking down the sides of his bruised nose at her. He put on a posh voice. "Now then, young lady, I do believe it's nearly time to arrive fashionably late."

She giggled. "You're a loon."

"Indubitably," he said in the same voice. "But I'm one of the happy kinds."

He grabbed his coat, and she picked up hers. As they left she poured a cup of coffee for Jasper. She sniffed it and made a face. "Ew. This is just that side of burned to a crisp."

"Doesn't matter. I'm not sure he drinks them. I think he just likes the warmth," Harry told her.

"It's cold out and getting worse all the time," she said.

They donned coats and scarves, she unlocked the door, and he put his hands in his pockets. He looked at her. "I uh, I forgot my wallet. Be right back."

Back in the apartment, he grabbed his wallet and his check book. He looked at the side table by the bed, where his gun sat. After a moment of debate, he grabbed it and stuck it in the coat pocket, a familiar comfortable weight. Joining her outside, he locked the door, nodded at Jasper's thanks, and they walked to Bleecker, where he whistled down a cab.

They got in and he told the driver, "Bellini's, uptown."

The driver whistled. "Fancy," he commented, and threw the meter. Toni hugged Harry's arm the whole way, a childlike grin on her, he admitted to himself, beautiful lips. Reality began to intrude and snapped him back to himself. He looked out the window at the city going by and heaved a sigh. He liked Toni. Always had, more or less. She wasn't stupid, no matter what she said. She was… she was *complicated*. And so was their… whatever they had. Friendship. Arrangement. Deal? He didn't know what it was or how he really felt about her, or why. *Complicated* didn't even begin to describe how he felt about her.

"Don't we need a reservation?" she asked suddenly, intruding into his dark thoughts. He didn't mind. It was easier to play the part than it was to think about all the things he didn't want to think about.

"We have one," Harry told her, smiling at the skeptical look. "Don't worry about it."

"Well, okay…" she said dubiously.

He grinned at her and looked out the window.

Chapter Eleven

The door of Bellini's was flanked on both sides by huge side-of-beef bouncers in tuxedos. It didn't seem possible for them to move in the tightly-fitted suits, but they did, and with surprising grace. One opened the cab door and handed out a speechless Toni, and one opened the door of the restaurant for them both.

At nearly ten o'clock the lobby was packed with people standing, waiting, and leaving. Inside gentle music seemed to hang in the aromatic air, buoyed on waves of delicious aroma and cigar smoke. The maître d' glared at them as they walked into the lobby. Harry looked around, looked at the crowd of people who probably had more money than he'd ever seen, and felt lost. What the hell was he doing here? He didn't belong here. He was out of his depth. Maybe he should just admit it, take his lumps, and go for a burger. He-

"Can I 'elp you, sair?" he asked in possibly the most dismissive way Harry could imagine. The tone, more than anything, got his hair up, and suddenly it all crystallized. He'd gotten the short end of a bunch of sticks lately, and he was fed right up. Besides, Harry was, when you got down to it, a New Yorker. Not just a New Yorker, but from the Bowery. Harry wasn't impressed by *this* guy. He'd lived in the city his whole life. He'd be damned if some fake French accent would throw him off his game. Ditto twice for a real one.

"DeMarko," he said off-handedly. "Two for dinner."

After a cursory glance at the list, the man looked up at them, a gleam in his eye. "I'm sorry, sair," he said in his prissy accent. "But I don't see you on the leest."

Harry leaned over and looked. "I do."

"Sir?" the maître d' said uncertainly. "I'm sorry, but you *aren't* on my leest."

Harry set one hand on the list and made a fist. The knuckles popped menacingly. "You absolutely sure about that, pal?" Harry said, purposely thickening his speech with an accent. "One hunnerd percent sure?"

The man swallowed with difficulty. "Sair, I assure you-"

"Don't 'sir' me, pal," Harry said. He lowered his voice. "You sure you want the Boss to hear about this?"

The maître d' swallowed again, looked at his list, and shook his head. "Sair, I'm terribly, 'orribly sorry, I seem to 'ave made a mistake. Of *course* I see your name! I apologize, sair, wiz all my 'eart."

Harry patted his cheek. "No sweat, pal. Don't even worry about it."

The man picked up his pencil and made a note on the seating chart. "Please," he said, "if sair and madam would care to accompany me?"

Harry stuck out his elbow and Toni slipped her hand into it. They followed the man through the restaurant. Eyes followed them, some wondering who they were, some just admiring the sight of Toni. Harry pulled out her chair and she sat. He took his place across from her. The maître d' signaled a waiter and turned to leave. Harry grabbed his arm.

"Sair?" the maître d' asked, trembling slightly.

"Bottle of champagne. You pick. And two scotches right now. *Good* ones. Mine's on the rocks, the lady drinks hers neat."

The man smiled painfully. "O-of course, sair, right away."

The poor man scuttled off and Harry watched him go. He turned to look at Toni, who was gazing at him with a very amused grin.

"What?" Harry asked.

"*What* boss?" Toni asked.

Harry shrugged. "I don't know. Everyone has a boss. Or knows a boss, or is afraid of some boss or another. Who needs a name when you know a boss?"

"Do you know a boss?" she asked.

"No, but he didn't know that. Seems like it worked out," he said.

"No wonder you don't worry about reservations," she said. "You rogue, you."

"Yeah, well, between you and me, I didn't know it was gonna work. But once you start the con, you have to go with it, you know?" Harry nodded as a waiter set down their drinks, and then the maître d' came back with their champagne. The waiter seemed nonplussed the maître d' was serving them himself. He assumed, quite wrongly, that Harry and Toni were someone to know about and watch for.

The beleaguered maître d' asked, "Would sair care to-"

"Naah. I know how to find you if it sucks. Put it down and vanish, pal," Harry said without looking at the man. The waiter didn't smirk, quite.

"Y-yes, sair," the terrified man readily agreed. He set the bucket of iced champagne and two glasses on the table and retreated. The waiter watched his maître d' scuttle away, bemused in spite of himself.

"Wow, you're kind of a jerk to the help," Toni said with a smile.

Harry stuck his nose in the air again and waved a hand gaily. "I'm sure I have no idea what you mean, my lady."

She laughed, a chiming, bell-like laugh. People around them turned at the sound, and several men smiled at Toni. One or two of the women smiled at Harry.

"You're fearless, aren't you?" she asked him.

He shook his head and poured them each a glass of champagne. "Oh, no. I fear plenty. But what's the sense in being afraid of things that *aren't* scary? What's the worst that would have happened? He would have had his bullies throw us out. Worst thing about that's being embarrassed in front of a lady. That wouldn't have been the worst of my day."

She cocked her head, admiring him. "You're awful sure of yourself, Harry."

"I just know how the world is. I've seen worse and I've seen better. It's just a lark," Harry said. "Just a meal."

"You sound like you're having fun," Toni said.

Harry raised his glass and she did the same. The crystal chimed as they touched the rims together and then sipped. "You're not?" he asked as the waiter came back with their menus.

They looked over the menu, and Toni glanced at Harry with worry on her face. "This is… uh… this is kind of expensive, Harry."

He nodded. "Yeah. But get what you want. It's okay."

They ordered their food and sipped their drinks while waiting, alternating champagne and scotch. To the harried maître d's credit, the scotch was very, very good. The ambiance of the restaurant was a little cloying after a while, with the studiously casual jazz playing in the background and all of the well-dressed people surrounding them obviously trying very hard to be seen by everyone else. Harry found it all overwhelming, but he found he was enjoying himself.

Harry smiled more than Toni was used to, laughed more than he ever had. She found that she was also having a very good time. They talked about nothing in particular as they ate. Later on, Harry wouldn't able to remember what they talked about, just that they'd laughed and enjoyed each other's company greatly. Eventually, plates cleared away, the waiter asked if they wanted dessert, but neither had room.

"Just the bill," Harry told the waiter.

Toni grimaced and Harry shook a finger at her. "Don't worry about it. I don't care. I needed a blow-off, and I'm having a good time. It's worth it. Good food, excellent company, and pretentious atmosphere. What's not to like?"

She giggled as the waiter came back. His hands were empty.

He said to Harry, almost apologetically, "Pierre- our maître 'd- wanted me to let you know that your meal comes with compliments from Bellini's, sir."

Harry blinked. "I, uh, okay… tell Pierre I said thanks."

The waiter nodded. "You're welcome. Have a wonderful evening, sir, ma'am." He spun on his heel and left. Harry and Toni stared at one another.

"Uh, so…" Toni said. "Are you *sure* you don't know who the Boss is?"

Harry shrugged. He pulled some money from his wallet and dropped it on the table for the waiter. "Beats me, like I said. But I think we should probably go. *Now*. Before anything else happens."

"I think that's an excellent idea, Harry," she said.

He stood to help her out of her chair. They walked casually to the front door, got their coats from the check girl, and headed for the door. Harry snapped his fingers and looked over at the podium. Pierre was talking on two telephones while snottily informing a trio of blondes that Bellini's wouldn't be serving them. Harry held up a finger to Toni and went to Pierre's side. He tapped the man on the shoulder. Pierre turned, irritated at the interruption, and comically his face fell, he dropped one of the hand sets, and slammed the other one down onto the cradle.

He sounded as if he were near tears. He said, "Sair, if zere's anysing else I can do-"

Harry handed Pierre a pair of bills. Pierre blinked at them, and slowly reached out a hand and took them.

"Sair, if I-"

Harry clapped the man on the shoulder. "Just wanted to say thank you, personally. I get a chance, I'll put in a good word for you, Pierre."

The man's chest puffed out and he looked almost pathetically grateful. "Sair, sair, of course, sank you so much! If you evair need anysing, please don't 'esitate to ask! J' suis votre homme! I'm your man, sair!"

Harry nodded. "I appreciate that, Pierre. Thanks again. Have a good night."

The man smiled painfully and nodded, and Harry walked away. Toni was watching with her mouth open. Once they were safely on the street and away from prying ears, Toni said, "You're a dastardly fiend, you know that?"

Harry snorted. "'Dastardly'? Who talks like that? And what do you mean?"

"You told me you didn't know who the Boss was."

"I don't."

"But-"

Harry darted a sidelong glance at her. "Come on. I was just following through on my bluff. And besides, the tip was way less than the bill would have been. And next time, I won't have to even *ask*. He'll bend over backwards to accommodate me. No one gets hurt."

"What about the bill? Someone's gonna have to pay for that," she said.

"Naah," he replied. "You really think they pay for the food? The liquor? Come on. You're not that naïve. Are you? Look where we are. Odds are, Bellini's is owned by the Gambinos."

Toni stared at him. He shrugged.

"You lying little shit," she said. "You *did* know what you were saying."

Harry didn't bother to reply.

"Didn't you?" she asked.

"I know what the rumors are," he said. "Sometimes that's enough to get a free meal."

She grinned at him. "Well aren't you just the clever one," she said, impressed.

"I have my moments," he replied. They walked for a while, and she reached out and took his hand. The champagne, the scotches, and the night were working on him, and he let her. They strolled hand in hand for a while, and he had to admit it felt okay. Finally, he noticed she was shivering.

He whistled for a cab. It took a while but finally he got one, and they huddled in the warmth. "Bleecker and Elizabeth," Harry told the driver.

They arrived in short order, Harry paid, and they walked down the street to Harry's office. She slipped her arm through Harry's and scooted closer to him. He put his hand on her and they walked in companionable silence. They reached the door and Harry reluctantly disengaged himself from Toni's arm and pulled out his key. He unlocked the door and went to the apartment door.

"Take Jasper-"

"A cup, yeah, I am," Toni said. She poured a cup of coffee for the bum and handed it to him. The old man winked at her and pulled his several coats more tightly around himself. She winked right back and went inside. After locking the door and pouring a second cup for herself, she went into the small apartment.

Harry was already in the bathroom, and the shower was running again. She sat on the bed sipping the bitter coffee. It warmed her, and she drank it only for that reason. She kicked off her heels and set the cup down on the table. Relaxing backward, she closed her eyes just for a second.

The next thing she knew, Harry was gently rolling her over and unzipping her dress. She whispered sleepily, "It's about damned time, Harry."

"Zip it, twit," he said with a smile. "I'm undressing you for bed. Don't want to ruin a beautiful dress, do you?"

She hummed to herself and let him work the dress off her body. He turned to put it on the chair and she reached up and grabbed his waistband. "My turn."

"Knock it off, Toni," he said without heat. "It's time to get some sleep. I've got a headache."

She rolled up on one elbow and stared at him, awake now. "You're serious? You're going to sleep?"

"Yeah," he said, slipping off his shoes. "Already brushed my teeth and everything. Why?"

"Harry, what the hell's wrong with you?" she asked him. "Are you insane?"

"I don't think so," he said, unbuttoning his shirt. "Just tired. Why?"

"You wined me, and you dined me, and you *know* what comes next. Don't leave a girl hanging," Toni said. "Finish the job, honey."

Harry shook his head. "You know the answer to that."

"You're a fucking idiot," she snarled, but she was smiling. "At least no one can accuse you of running a con to get into my panties."

Harry nodded. "At least I have that going for me."

He rolled her over suddenly. She yelped. He yanked the covers out from under her and rolled her back. She giggled as he tucked her in.

"Good night, Toni," he said. He kissed her on the cheek. She slung an arm around his neck and kissed him back.

"Thank you for tonight," she whispered in his ear. "I really had a good time."

"Me, too," he said.

He climbed onto the couch and pulled the covers up. "Good night," he said again.

"Good night, my idiot," she told him. He chuckled and she turned out the light next to the bed.

In the darkness he listened to her squirm around and get comfortable. He frowned to himself. *I think maybe she's right,* he thought to himself. *I kind of am an idiot.*

Chapter Twelve

The next morning was the same as usual. He woke up, rolled over, and she was gone. He padded to the bathroom. On the bathroom mirror she'd written in red lipstick, 'I had an amazing time, Harry. Tonight, I'm taking *you* out. I'll be back around six. Be ready and be pretty- you're *my* arm candy tonight. XOXOX Toni.'

She'd dotted the I in her name with a heart, for God's sake. Shaking his head and smiling in spite of himself, he got in the shower.

Afterward, looking at himself through her note, he gingerly pinched the bridge of his nose. The swelling had gotten worse in the night, and his eyes were thoroughly blackened now. He looked like a boxer who'd gotten the worst of it. He puttered around in the office for a while, purposely not doing much thinking. He finished up his notes for the Angelo case and filed them in his broken cabinet. He gave Jasper a cup of coffee and finally listened to his messages.

"Hi, is this Ming's-"

Delete.

"Do you or someone you love-"

Delete.

"Mr. DeMarko, this is Agnes Angelo. I wanted to thank you again for what you did today. In fact, Peter did come back, as you predicted, drunk and angry and with a key. I called your friend, and she sent two patrolmen who were forced to hurt Peter badly to remove him. Thank you so much, and if I can ever repay you, please let me know how. Thank you."

Harry smiled. *Couldn't have happened to a nicer guy*, he thought. Delete.

"Mr. DeMarko, my name is Catherine Blankenship. I got your name from a mutual friend. I wonder if you have a moment to give me a call? My daughter is missing, and I need your help. Officer Montrose gave me your number. My number is-"

Harry grabbed a pen and jotted the number on the back of his electric bill.

"Please call me as soon as you can. Thank you."

Harry picked up the phone and dialed the number. After four rings, someone picked up.

"Hello?"

"Mrs. Blankenship? Harry DeMarko. You left a message," he said.

"Yes, Mr. DeMarko," she said. "My daughter Catherine-"

"If it's all the same, I'd like to meet face to face. Where are you?"

The woman paused. When she spoke again she seemed a bit miffed that Harry had interrupted her. "I'm in Midtown, Mr. DeMarko. Would it be convenient to meet now?"

"I can do that. Where?"

"I don't suppose you're close to the Four Seasons?" she asked.

"I can get there. Noon?"

"That would be fine, Mr. DeMarko," Blankenship told him.

"All right. I'll see you there, ma'am." Harry hung up. He looked around the office. She wouldn't be back until later anyhow, and he didn't want to sit around waiting for her. Might as well get something done.

He grabbed his keys and a cup of coffee from the fresh pot she had made and headed out the door.

Chapter Thirteen

The doorman didn't want to let Harry in without a tie. Harry walked past him and told him to fuck off. The doorman called the hotel detective, who took one look at Harry's ID and let it go.

Smiling to himself, Harry went into the bar.

At noon, the hotel bustled, and people were shuttling from the bar to the restaurant in waves. At the bar, in the exact center seat, sat a very beautiful woman in a flawless red pantsuit and white pearls. Her blonde hair was freshly-coifed and her makeup looked like a painting. Harry took the seat next to her.

"Mrs. Blankenship?" he asked.

Her eyes fell on him like a blessing and she nodded. "Yes. Hello, Mr. DeMarko."

"Hi." The barman came over, and Harry said, "Whiskey, neat."

The woman took several photos out of her purse. "Mr. DeMarko, I'm in something of a hurry. This is my daughter, Cecilia. She's a sophomore at NYU. She hasn't called in two weeks and no one seems to know where she might be. It was suggested to me that you might have better luck than the detectives who don't seem to be devoting nearly enough time to the case. Officer Montrose intimated that you may have better luck digging. Why do you think that might be?"

Harry shrugged. "Morgan's a good cop. Maybe they're busy. I hate to say it, but sometimes missing persons takes a back seat to murder. It's possible they're working something big and have to put your case on the back burner. I couldn't say. Luckily, NYU's only six blocks from my office. I can do a lot of digging. If Morgan gave you my number, he thinks I can help. Maybe I can."

"You make no guarantees?" she asked.

"No, ma'am. But I can tell you this- I don't stop until the job is done," he said.

She didn't look satisfied with that answer but she couldn't do much about it. She nodded. "What do you charge?"

"Fifty for a retainer. Thirty a day. I'll call you once a day to report, or more if I have something new. I'll keep at it until you pull me or I find her," Harry thanked the barman for his whiskey and sipped. It wasn't bad. "I'll need the usual information. Address, dorm number, or whatever, phone numbers, acquaintances, boyfriends, anything you have. Do you suspect foul play?"

It sounded so hokey when he said it, but it was nicer than saying 'Do you think she was grabbed and killed because you're rich?' Mrs. Blankenship shook her head.

"No. It doesn't seem to be… to be malicious. But one never knows, I suppose. She stopped going to class, and no one in her sorority has seen her. She stopped calling home, and more importantly, she hasn't cashed her latest living expense check. Here, I've written everything down." The woman slid a photo over to him, and on the back were details. Harry studied the face. She seemed like a happy kid.

"All right. I'll get on it. As it happens I have nothing else pressing, so I'll probably give you a call tonight with an update. I'll have to retrace everything the cops did. It can take some time."

"I'm not worried about the time, Mr. DeMarko, nor am I concerned about the expense. I want my daughter found," the woman signaled the barman for her bill. "Put his drink on my tab," she told the man. Harry nodded.

"Thank you. About my retainer-"

Mrs. Blankenship took out a hundred dollar bill. "Here. I'm not going to argue your prices. You're significantly cheaper than many of the... the-"

Harry took the bill. "You can say it. The more professional detectives. The big guys. Yeah, I'm on the cheap. But if Morgan gave you my number, he also told you I have a good track record."

"Officer Montrose spoke rather highly of you, in fact. He said you were a police officer before you went into business for yourself. Why did you leave? If you don't mind my asking," she added.

"Not at all. I was shot in the line of duty. Had to give it up. Luckily, I can still be of some use," Harry said.

"I'm sorry that happened," she said.

"I'm not," he told her, surprised that it was more or less the truth. "I think I've done almost as much good in the years since then as I did in uniform. It balances."

She finished the drink and set the glass back on the napkin. "All right. I have to make a meeting. Please do keep me up to date. You can reach me at my home number after six, or my office number during the day. You can leave a message with my girl."

"I'll head over to the school right now," he said.

"Then this is goodbye," Blankenship said to him. She stood up and shook his hand. "Good luck, Mr. DeMarko."

"Have a good afternoon." He watched her walk away. She went to a table across the bar where three businessmen sat drinking. They stood when she approached, and he watched curiously as she embraced all three, laughing at one of their comments. As they headed into the restaurant area, she looked back. He looked at her face, which wasn't concerned at all. She nodded to him and turned her attention away.

Harry finished his drink. He dropped a single on the bar, nodding to the barman. He left, clapping the doorman on the shoulder as he went.

"Have a good one, pal," he said.

Through a clenched jaw, the doorman mumbled, "And you, sir."

Harry whistled for a cab and got in. "Washington Square, NYU," he said.

Chapter Fourteen

After paying off the cab, Harry walked around a bit, getting a feel for the campus. He'd gone into the academy right out of high school, but he'd always liked NYU. They showed cheap movies and the libraries always had some kind of interesting art exhibit to go see. He walked along University Place to Weinstein Hall, the last place anyone had seen Cecilia Blankenship. He crowded into an elevator with a bunch of what looked to him to be nine year old kids and rode up to the seventh floor, where her room was located.

"Visiting your kid?" one of the tiny, seemingly-grammar-school-aged students asked him. Someone told him once that the older you got, the younger everyone else seemed to be.

"Something like that," he said. "Looking for someone. You know a girl named Cecilia?"

The students all looked at each other. "You mean Blankenship?" the young man asked.

"That's the one," Harry said. "I'm looking for her. You seen her?"

"No," the boy said, and the crowd echoed the sentiment. "She didn't show up for physics today."

"When's the last time you saw her?"

"I don't know, a week ago, maybe?" the boy said. His hair was hanging in his eyes, and he brushed it out of the way. "She missed the last mixer, too."

"Mixer?" Harry asked.

"Yeah. She's a Zeta."

Harry shrugged.

"Zeta Tau Alpha?"

"I'm not familiar," Harry said.

"They're pretty big. Anyhow, the Zetas and the Alphas have a mixer every weekend. Mandatory attendance. She hasn't been there," the boy said.

"How do you know?" Harry asked.

The boy laughed. "I'm an Alpha, man."

"Were you going out with Cecilia?" Harry asked. The boy laughed again.

"No, we just went to the parties. I think she was with Brad at some point, but they might had broken up."

"Brad?" Harry asked.

"Anderson. Hey, why are you looking for her?"

"Her mother hired me to find her. She's been missing for almost a week," Harry told him. The students around him made impressed noises.

"So you're like a private eye? Like Marlow? Or Spade?"

Harry shrugged. "Yeah, I guess. Except I'm real."

"What happened to your nose?" one of the girls asked.

"I got into a fight with an angry husband. He got in a good swing."

They made more impressed noises. The elevator stopped at seven and most of them got out. Harry looked up and down the hall. The boy pointed. "Ceci's room's down that way. She's in 711. Her roommate is probably there."

"Thanks. So what's your name?" Harry asked.

"I'm Tom. Tom Morrison. I'm in 701, that way," the boy said.

Harry shook his hand. "Thanks for the background, Tom. I appreciate it."

"No sweat. I hope she's okay."

"Me, too," Harry said and walked down the hall. The smell of pot was redolent and the music was loud. He knocked on 711.

After a moment, the door opened. A tiny redhead looked up at him. She had huge green eyes and fading freckles.

"How much?" she asked.

"I'm sorry?" Harry asked.

"You're the pizza guy?" she asked him.

Harry held up both hands. "Do you see a pizza? My name's DeMarko. I'm looking for your roommate."

The redhead shook her curls so they bounced. "Sorry. Ceci's not here. Excuse me." She tried to close the door. Harry stopped it with his foot.

"Wait a minute. I'm not looking for her to chat, or anything. I'm a private investigator." Harry showed her his ID. "Her mother hired me to find her."

He checked the back of the photo of Cecilia.

"You're... Constance?" he asked.

She nodded. "Constance Smithe. You're what now?"

"Private investigator. Looking for her. May I come in for a moment?" The redhead nodded and opened the door all the way. The room wasn't big by any stretch of the imagination, and it strangely mirrored itself, although one reflection was obviously the real world, and one was Wonderland.

Two beds, two dressers, and two desks. The left side of the room was almost painfully neat. The bed was made to within an inch of its life, the dresser was closed and had three pictures of family on it, all arranged at precise angles, and the desk held two open books, a typewriter, and an unopened can of Coke.

The right side of the room was an explosion. The bed was covered in clothes, the dresser's drawers were all hanging out with clothing cascading from them like waterfalls, and the desk was covered with record albums and pizza boxes. Harry looked at the neat dresser. The pictures were of Constance and her parents.

"Not exactly a neat-freak, is she?" he said.

Constance laughed. "God no. Ceci is pretty messy sometimes. She usually cleans up, especially if she's going to have a boy over, but she didn't clean up after last weekend, and she hasn't been back since then. You know, the cops were here a couple days ago, and they already asked me all kinds of questions."

Harry nodded. "I know. But I'm following in their footsteps and I'll probably ask you the same questions. Do you mind?"

"Oh, no," Constance said. "I miss her. She's a good roommate. I mean, aside from the disaster area. But she can iron faster than anyone you've ever seen."

"Well, let's start at the top. When did you last see her?"

"Um, last Monday when I got up for class. I have an eight. Ugh. I took a shower, grabbed my books, and went. She was still asleep. Ceci doesn't like early classes. When I came back at two she was gone."

Harry stared at her desk. "Did she go to class that day? I mean, I don't see any books."

"They're under the bed. Ceci doesn't study."

"How does she do in her classes?" Harry asked. He got down on his knees and looked. There were eleven texts under her bed, covered in a fine layer of dust. They didn't look like they'd been opened since she bought them. He fished them out and went through them all. Not so much as a receipt.

"See? She doesn't open them. But she's always getting Bs or better. I wish I could," Constance said. "I have to study, like, all night every night just to hold onto my scholarship."

Harry nodded. "Doesn't seem fair, does it? I knew some cops like that. Aced exams I couldn't pass in a Porsche."

Constance laughed.

"All right, on to the other stuff. Was Cecilia seeing anyone regularly? I heard she was involved with a boy named Brad for a while."

"Brad? Oh, God no. That was, like, a one-time thing. Brad's a wolf. He never goes out with anyone. At least, not for more than two nights," she said, and colored.

"Okay. So no boyfriend?"

"Well," Constance hedged, "not steady-steady. But she hung around with a guy named Mike more than a little. Mike Zeist, that is."

"Zeist. He's a student too?"

"No, he works off-campus at the Rice Bowl, over on Uni. He's a nice guy, I guess. Sometimes he'll give me my food for free, if I give him a kiss. But he's not a student. He's, like, older? I think he's twenty-five."

Harry snorted. "Older. Sure. The Rice Bowl. All right. Anything else you can tell me?"

"No..." she trailed off. "But... I hope you find her. You said her mom hired you?"

"Yep," Harry said.

"Weird," Constance said.

"Why's that?"

"Ceci and her mom never get along. They're always fighting, you know? Ceci hates that bi… uh… her mom." Constance finished lamely. "Ceci's always bitching about her mother."

"Interesting," Harry said. He looked around the room. "All right, I'm not going to keep you. Thanks for the information."

"No sweat. I'm here all the time at night studying if you have any more questions. You want the phone number?"

"No, I've got it. All right, have a good night, Constance. Thanks a lot." Harry went to the door.

"I hope she's okay," Constance said. "I kinda miss her."

"I hope she's okay, too," Harry said. He opened the door. The pizza delivery guy was standing there, ready to knock. "Pizza's here."

"Oh, yeah! I'm starving!" Constance grabbed her purse as Harry pushed past the teen holding a box of what smelled suspiciously like heaven.

He found the floor RA and grilled the girl, but she didn't know anything new. He asked up and down the hall, but no one really seemed to know much about Cecilia. She got good grades, partied a lot, and wasn't reckless. No one had seen her sloppy drunk or passed out anywhere.

Harry headed back down to the street and stopped the first student he saw. The girl gave him directions and he walked over to the Rice Bowl. He worked his way through the crowds of students on the sidewalks until he came upon the little Chinese restaurant. Of *course* it was Chinese; he could smell it two blocks away and it made his skin crawl. Once inside he went up to the counter.

"What do you need?" the kid behind the counter asked him. He was a handsome enough kid, about six feet tall, with dusky mocha skin and kinky black hair cut short.

"Hi. I don't want food. I was wondering if Mike Zeist's working. I want to ask him a couple questions."

The kid's face went blank. He looked down at his own chest and Harry's eyes followed. The boy's nametag said 'Mike Z'. Harry smiled.

"Everything's going my way today," he said.

"Who're you?" Zeist asked.

"Harry DeMarko. I'm a private investigator." He flashed the ID card again. "I'm looking for someone. You know Cecilia Blankenship?"

Zeist's face went completely bland. Harry watched with interest. "Yeah, I know Ceci. Why?"

"I'm looking for her," Harry said. "When's the last time you saw her?"

Zeist shrugged. "I don't know. Week? Two? It was at a party."

"Did you leave with her?"

"Nope."

"You're sure about that?"

Zeist chuckled. "It's the kind of thing I'd know, man," he said.

Harry nodded. "You know she's been missing for almost a week now."

"Yeah, there was a cop in here a couple days ago. You with them?"

"Occasionally. This time it's her mother," Harry said. "She hired me."

Zeist laughed. "You're kidding."

Harry cocked his head. "No. Why would I kid about that?"

"They didn't get along, man," Zeist said. "She was always complaining about her mom."

"You're the second person today to tell me that. But there's a difference between having problems getting along with your parents, and them getting upset when you vanish off the face of the Earth. Whatever personal problems they had, it's still unsettling. Her mom's pretty upset about this."

"She told you that?" Zeist laughed. "I'd have liked to see that."

"You know Mrs. Blankenship?" Harry asked him.

"Me and Cecilia went to a party her mom threw. She took one look at me and threw us out," Zeist said.

"Why'd she do that?"

Zeist just stared at Harry.

"Why'd she do that?" Harry asked again.

"I clashed with the linen," Mike said. "Come on, man. *You've* met her."

"I have. I didn't get to know her or anything," Harry said. "So she has a problem with you dating her daughter?"

"Yeah, you could say that. She told me to clear out before she called the cops." Zeist's lips twisted. "She's a bitch."

"Sounds like it," Harry said.

"Hey man, you gonna order, or what?" a voice behind Harry said. Harry turned around and looked at the student standing behind him.

"Hurry up, man. I only have half an hour before class," the kid said. Harry nodded. He pulled out a card and handed it to Mike.

"This is me. If you hear from her, give me a call, huh?"

Mike nodded. "Sure thing, man."

"All right. Can you think of anything I might need to know?" Harry asked him.

"Naah... wait. Ceci said something about wanting to go to school in Florida. Maybe she skipped town?" Mike said.

Harry studied the boy thoughtfully. "Florida?"

"Yeah. She hates it up here. She wanted to get as far away as she could from her mom," Mike said. "She wanted to just move to Florida. Orlando is what she mentioned."

"Orlando. Huh." Harry nodded. "All right. Thanks for the info, Mike."

"No problem."

Harry moved out of the line so that Mike could take the next order. He turned and left the restaurant, pulling up his collar against the chill. He decided it was nice enough to walk back to the apartment. He shuffled along, not really thinking about anything in particular. He let the facts of the case jumble around in his head. He crossed over to Bleecker and headed down Elizabeth to his place. Jasper was gone, which was odd. There was a piece of paper stuck to the door. Also odd. Why hadn't they just pushed it through the mail slot?

He reached the door and saw that it wasn't stuck, it was glued. Someone had smeared glue all over the door and plastered a piece of paper to it. In a heavy hand in red marker someone had written 'asshole.'

He sighed. He tried to unlock the door and realized they'd also glued his lock. The mail flap was glued shut, too. He laughed.

Figured.

He went down the block to the payphone and leafed through the yellow pages. He called a locksmith, gave his address, and walked around the corner to the market to pick up a couple things. One hour and twenty bucks later the door and the mail slot were open again. Harry hadn't been able to get the paper off the door, but he found a marker in his desk and colored it all black. Inside, he checked his messages and wrote some notes about Blankenship's case. He picked up the phone and dialed.

"Motor Vehicle Department."

"Shelley Mendoza, please," Harry said.

"One moment." The hold music was terrible as usual. After a couple of minutes, the line clicked on.

"This is Shelley."

"Shelley, it's Harry DeMarko."

"Harry! Haven't heard from you in a while! How's the arm?" she said. Shelley was an old friend from way back, and she'd been one of the only people to visit him in the hospital.

"Hurts when it's cold," he said. "How's Manuel?"

"He's fine, same as always. Got a big contract with Bank of America, doing their renovations over in Jersey. Busy busy busy," Shelley said.

"Glad to hear it. Hey, I need a favor."

"Of course. You never call just to shoot the shit, Harry," Shelley said.

"Well, no," Harry admitted. "I guess I don't. Can you run down a name for me?"

He heard the click of her pen. "Go ahead."

"Last name's Zeist, First is Mike. Unknown middle. About 25, black, lives somewhere near NYU, I think. I need an address if you can find one."

"All right, Harry, but you owe me one," Shelley said.

"One? I owe you like a thousand, Shelley. This one's for a missing person. I think he knows where his girlfriend is, but I need to see his digs," Harry told her.

"Can do, but only for you, big guy," she said. "Still got that same place off Bleecker?"

"You know it."

"All right. I'll dig in and give you a call when I have something," she said.

"Okay," he said. "And thanks, Shelley."

"Thank me if I get you a lead," she said. "With a bottle of red wine. *Good* red wine, Harry, you cheapskate."

"Cheapskate? For you, Shelley, I'll spend ten, maybe even twelve dollars. Possibly fifteen."

"Ooh, business must be good," she said.

"Eh," he said. "It's keeping me in the lifestyle to which I've become accustomed."

"So, takeout pizza and cheap beer, huh?"

He laughed. "The beer's not cheap."

"Says you. All right. Let me get back to work. Take it easy, Harry. We're still waiting for you to come around to dinner some weekend."

"Soon, I promise," he said.

"Yeah, yeah," Shelley said, and hung up on him. Harry smiled and put the phone down. Shelley had been his contact at the DMV for the best part of five years before his accident, and had run down many a name for him. Her voodoo with the labyrinthine files of the motor vehicle department were legendary. If it existed, she'd find it. He looked at the clock. Almost five. He peeked out of the door, but Jasper was still gone. He took a cup of coffee for himself and went into his apartment.

He showered and went through his wardrobe. All his white shirts were dirty. He chose a black one. With the dress pants and shoes, he looked like an undertaker or a priest, but he combed his hair neatly, at least, neatly for him, and sat fiddling with the aerial on the TV, watching Dan Rather report the day's events.

At six o'clock someone beeped their horn out front several times. Harry went out to see what was going on, and Toni was in the back of a cab waiting for him. He opened the door and started to climb in and stopped short.

She was beautiful.

She wore a blue sequined sleeveless dress that hugged her diminutive curves. She held in her hands a tiny purse made of the same material. Her hair was swept upward and piled on the top of her head in a curling crown. Her makeup was stunningly subtle and bold as well. Her lips were perfectly sculpted with a dark red color, and the eyes were lined with a similar shade. Her legs were frosted with dark stockings, and her heels were barely there, both elegant and understated.

She was beautiful.

He stammered and slid onto the seat next to her. The cab driver appeared to know the destination and drove off as soon as Harry closed the door.

"Hello, lover," Toni said in a sultry voice. She smiled at him with half-closed eyes. It took him a moment to find his tongue.

"Uh, h-hi," he said. He blinked. "You look amazing, Toni."

She blushed and looked down. "Thank you, Harry. You look very handsome."

He grinned. "You said I was arm candy. I tried to look the part."

She smiled at him. "I appreciate that."

"Where we headed?"

"Don't spoil the surprise," she said.

"Okay," he said.

They drove for forty minutes, most of the way downtown. They drove into the financial district. Harry looked around in confusion. They rounded the corner on William Street, and stopped at No. 2 South William. A line of people waited outside a restaurant. The cab pulled up at the steps.

"Holy shit. When did Delmonico's reopen?" Harry asked.

Toni grinned. "Tonight."

Harry stared at her as the driver went around and opened her door. He handed her out. They waited while Harry's brain caught up with him and he slid out of the cab. He fished in his pocket for a bill and handed a five to the cabbie.

Harry looked at the line, but Toni took his hand and led him up the stairs to the doorman.

"I have a reservation," she told the doorman. "Bonanno. Party of two."

The doorman checked a list and gestured them inside. Toni and Harry went into the restaurant. The wood panels on the walls interspersed with huge murals and extravagant paintings gave the huge room an intimate feel. The band in the corner played Mozart. Each table was full of pretty, handsome, and rich-looking people laughing and talking and eating. The doorman led them to the table in the middle of the wall under a mural of people at the very tables through which they had walked which had hung in Delmonico's in the Forties and Fifties. The owner had the furnishings removed in 1977 when the restaurant closed and stored against the day he could reopen. Harry was awake enough to hold her chair out for her and help her sit. He took his own seat.

"Champagne," she told the waiter, who smiled and nodded. He set down two hand-written menus and retreated. Toni picked up Harry's menu and her own and set them aside.

"We're not eating?" Harry asked.

She smiled and shook her head. "We're eating, but we don't need the menu. Did you know that Delmonico's invented lobster Newburg?"

Harry shook his head.

"Yup. No reason for anything else, from what I understand," she said. She had a smile a mile wide, and he admired her coolness.

"So, there's a question I want to ask," Harry said.

"Give me three guesses?" Toni asked.

"Bonanno?" Harry asked.

She dipped her head. "Yep. That's what the B stands for, Harry."

"Toni Bonanno? Your name's Toni Bonanno?" Harry asked. "Any relation to…"

She laughed. "Harry, do you really think I'd be a hooker if I was related to the Bonanno Family?"

Harry shrugged. "I don't have a clue. You're pretty stubborn. I wouldn't want to be the man to try and make you do something you don't want to."

She grinned. "Thank you, Harry, I think. Sounds like you just called me a bitch."

He shrugged. "You hear what you want. But I figure a bitch is more interesting than a pushover."

She laughed. He smiled at her. The champagne arrived. They drank. "You look great, Harry," she said.

"I appreciate the lie. I know what I look like. But thank you. *You*, on the other hand, look like a million bucks. How in the world did you pull this off, Toni?" Harry asked. He regretted it immediately, because the smile slipped from her face as she took the meaning he hadn't intended.

"Meaning how does a hooker clean up so well, or score prime reservations at a popular restaurant?" she asked.

"I didn't mean that," he said.

"What *did* you mean, Harry?"

He didn't get to explain because the waiter chose that moment to arrive for their dinner orders. He looked expectantly at Harry, who pointed to Toni.

"She'll have the Lobster Newburg," he said.

"Excellent choice, ma'am," the waiter said to Toni. "And for you, sir?"

"Do you have crow?" Harry asked. Toni snorted and looked away.

"Sir?"

"I've accidentally insulted the lady," Harry said. "And I'm not sure she'll accept my apology. Maybe the chef's got a bowl of crow I could eat instead."

"You're a silly ass," Toni said, but she smiled when she said it. Harry nodded. "I am."

The waiter looked from one to the other. Harry let him off the hook. "Two orders of the Lobster. And don't spare the Newburg."

The waiter looked uncertainly from one to the other. Toni shook her head and laughed. "Ignore my companion," she said. "He's a little drunk."

The waiter nodded, picked up the menus, and left gratefully.

"I'm sorry for what I said," Harry told her. "I didn't mean to sound like that."

"I know, Harry," she said. "It's all right."

"You gotta admit, this is a little… strange."

She shrugged elegantly. "Of course. After last night, I wanted to do something big. Actually, the entire thing is a little boring, I'm afraid. As luck would have it, I happened to know someone who told me about the opening tonight. He had a reservation that he wasn't going to use. I asked if I could have it. He agreed."

Harry waited.

"As for this," Toni said, gesturing at her dress, "I splurged. I've got a little money squirreled away so I treated myself. It's not as expensive as it looks if you know where to go. And I wanted to treat you, the way you did for me last night."

Harry just watched her talk, fascinated with the way her mouth moved.

"So," she said, a trifle uncomfortable with his stare, "that's all there is to it. Not a mystery, really."

He didn't say anything.

"Harry, you're kind of scaring me," she said. "What's wrong?"

"Just seems a little coincidental," he said.

"What's that?"

"Knowing someone who had a reservation here with the same last name as you," he said.

She colored.

"So," he said. "Name's not really Bonanno, is it?"

She shook her head. "No."

"And of course, the guy you got the reservation from, his name *is*?"

"Yes."

Harry nodded. "And... you just happened to know a guy?"

She didn't say anything. He nodded again. "He's a john, then."

"So?"

Harry opened his mouth and couldn't think of a thing to say. He shut his mouth.

"I didn't think so. Can we just enjoy our meal?" she asked.

"Are we done lying to each other?" Harry asked.

She grimaced, but said, "Sure, Harry. Why won't you sleep with me?"

His mouth dropped open. She smiled sweetly.

"Until you're done lying, don't you judge me," she said.

He raised his hands in surrender. "You're right. I'm sorry. Thank you for this surprise. It's lovely. And so are you."

She ducked her head. "Thank you."

The waiter brought over the dishes and they spent a few minutes discovering why Delmonico's reputation had always been deserved. Afterward they had dessert and more champagne. Harry enjoyed himself. They laughed. She touched his hand several

130

times, and he tried not to flinch. He waited for the bill to arrive. Instead, the waiter came by with a slip of paper and handed it to Toni. She frowned.

"I have a phone call," she said. "I'll be right back."

Harry stood up and held out her chair. She went with the waiter. He finished his champagne. She came back to the table and poured herself another glass, and downed it all in one go.

"What was that all about?" Harry asked.

"Nothing," she said. "Want to get out of here?"

"Uh, sure," Harry said, frowning. "But… we haven't paid."

"It's handled," she said. "Come on. I want to go home."

Harry stood up. "Everything okay, Toni?"

"Everything's fine, Harry. I just want to go home. Would you take me home, please?" she asked. "I'm fine. I promise. I'm just tired."

Harry nodded. "All right. Come on. Let's get lost."

He took her hand and led her out of the restaurant. On the street he whistled up a cab and they got in. He gave the address and they sat back. Toni was humming and looking out the window.

"Why didn't they charge us?" Harry asked her.

She smiled. "They did."

He frowned. "Wait… the phone call?"

"I had them pull me away for that so I could pay without you getting all weird," she said.

"Weird?"

She patted his cheek. "Weird."

He shrugged. "Fair enough. What did dinner there run you, anyhow?"

"Harry," she chided, "if I were going to tell you, I wouldn't have bothered setting it up like that."

He grinned. "Can't blame me for trying."

"I don't," she said.

They arrived. Harry paid the driver and they went inside. Toni hummed to herself and spun around. She bent and took a new bottle of Harry's favorite whiskey out of a paper bag by the bed. She held it up.

"Nightcap?" she asked.

"Sounds great," he said, unbuttoning his shirt collar. She poured two shots into some glasses she scrounged and handed him one. He took a healthy swig. She downed hers.

"Turn on the radio," she said. "I'm in the mood to dance. Dance with me, Harry."

He put his glass down. "I'm not much of a dancer," he said.

"I don't care. No one cares. There's no one here but us anyhow. Dance with me. Please?"

He nodded and switched on the radio. He spun the dial until he found a station playing soft jazz. He turned to find Toni close to him. She stepped into his arms, and in reflex he put an arm around her. She put her head on his chest and they swayed slowly to the beat.

They drank and danced for an hour, and finally she looked up at him. "I'm tired, Harry."

"Let's go to bed," he said. She shook her head.

"No, Harry. I'm *tired*," she said again. Her tone froze him.

"What can I do?" he asked.

"Go to bed with me," she said. He started to protest. "I didn't say fuck me, Harry. I said go to bed with me."

He looked at her for the longest time. Finally, he nodded. "Okay."

They brushed their teeth together, which struck Harry as an oddly intimate thing to do, but he couldn't figure out why. After, she crawled on the bed still wearing her dress. Harry lay down next to her. She took his arm and snaked it over her, pressing it to her belly. She rolled on her side and pulled him against her. He stretched his left arm out and she pillowed her head on it. He held her closely and shifted his cheek to move her hair out of his face. He felt dampness on his arm and realized she was crying. He panicked. But he couldn't think of anything to say. He lay there, mind racing.

Eventually, she stopped crying. She never made a sound. Not a sniffle. Finally, she whispered, "Thank you, Harry."

"For what?"

"For just being there. Not trying to help. Not trying to fix me, or change things, or stop me. Placate me. You just held me. You're smarter than you play it up."

"I think you're giving me too much credit, but okay. I expect if you need something, you'll tell me, won't you? You did this time." Harry shifted a little and pulled her tighter. She hummed and snuggled closer.

"I try. You don't always come through. But," she said quickly, cutting him off before he could protest, "it's never on purpose. I know that. You always come through when you can. You're wonderful to me in every way you can be. But when I need something from you, I tell you. And almost always, you're there for me."

"Almost?" Harry couldn't stop himself from asking.

She craned up to look at him and chided, "Harry, sometimes a girl wants to get laid. You think guys have a lock on horny?"

He cleared his throat and looked away.

"The reason I put up with you is because I *know* you want me. I *know* I turn you on. I've felt it." She wiggled. "I can feel it now."

He pulled back a little, and she laughed.

"Whatever your deal is, I know it's not because you're not interested. You are. But you're also fighting something inside. I think if you knew what it was, you'd tell me. Since you don't, I figure you don't understand either. So, I'm content to wait. You'll either figure it out, or you'll kick me out into the street, right?"

Harry thought about it. "I think that's probably true."

"So, just keep me in the loop, Harry. I'm not going anywhere until you tell me to."

He stared into space for a while, trying to understand what she was telling him. He shook his head. He didn't like to think about it.

"Tell me about your day," she said in a sleepy voice. "What's the great detective got on his plate now?"

He told her about Blankenship and what he found out.

"Sounds like she ran away on her own," Toni said.

"That's what I figure. If Shelley can run down an address, I'll go check it out. It's the likeliest outcome. If not, I guess I'll have to find out when the kid gets off work and follow him home."

"You need any help?" Toni asked.

134

"I don't think so…" Harry trailed off. "Well, I don't know, really. What can you do?"

"What do you mean?" she asked.

"What are you offering? You gonna tail the kid home, or do you have some kind of contact that can get me more info?"

Toni shrugged. "I don't know. But I'd like to help if I can."

"I appreciate it. If I think of something, I'll ask," he said.

"Okay," she said, and she sounded happier.

"Let me ask you something," Harry said.

"Okay."

"What's your last name?" he asked.

She was silent for long enough that he didn't think she would answer. Finally she said in a small voice, "Why?"

"What do you mean 'why'?" he asked. "I don't know anything about you, Toni. I don't know what your last name is. I don't know where you're from. I don't know if your parents are alive or not. I don't even know if Toni's your real first name." He rolled his neck and she winced at the pops.

"Jesus," she said. "Are you okay?"

"Been a little stiff. I'm fine."

"Want a massage?" she asked.

"I… actually, yeah. That'd be good, thanks." He disentangled himself and sat up. She scooted around behind him and started to rub his neck. He made the right noises and slumped his head forward. Toni smiled to herself. She played her hands over the muscles in his neck. He had cable-strength tension in the tendons along the sides, and she worked them as hard as she could. He groaned with pleasure.

"God, that feels good," he sighed.

"You should see what I can do with the rest of you," she said.

He chuckled. "I'm tempted, believe me."

She stopped short and smiled to herself. Resuming the massage, she said. "Bennett."

"What?"

"My name's Bennett."

He digested that. "Bullshit," he decided.

"What?" she asked.

"Your name is *not* Toni Bennett. I refuse to believe that anyone would be that cruel to a young woman."

She laughed. "You know my first name's not Toni, Harry. It's a nickname."

"Yeah, but still," he said. "Nickname for what?"

She hesitated. Toni never told anyone anything. It was an old policy that had stood her in good stead for many years. But... she *trusted* Harry. He wouldn't abuse it. He wouldn't hurt her. She *wanted* to believe he wouldn't hurt her.

"M-my name," she said for the first time in seven years, "is Antonia Marie Bennett."

He was stunned as he realized what she had done. What she had given him. He turned to look at her. "Antonia?"

"Watch it, DeMarko," she warned.

"No, no... I like it. I like it a lot," Harry told her.

She smiled, a beautiful sunny grin. "I'm glad."

He nodded. She continued rubbing his back. "You know, you could do this any time," Harry said. "You're really good at it."

"All you have to do is ask, Harry," she said shyly.

He nodded. "All right. I will."

"Good." She finished up and patted him on the shoulder. "Can we go to bed now?"

"Sure. Let me change out of this-"

She took his hand and pulled him slowly back down on the bed. She curled up again with his arm around her, pressed against her tight belly. He disengaged himself long enough to turn out the light. In the darkness, the soft jazz played from his tiny radio, and they curled up together. He dragged the blanket over both of them.

"Thank you," she whispered.

"You're welcome," he said, and realized he meant it. He didn't feel like she was manipulating him, or trying to get something from him he wasn't willing to give. He liked being next to her. The clothing kept him relaxed. She wasn't haranguing him about sex, she just wanted to be held. He relaxed against her, realizing he was enjoying it at least as much as she seemed to be. He tried to recall the last time he'd held a woman in the night. With a guilty start, he realized it had been more than five- no, six. Six years. Six years he'd denied himself this simple pleasure.

What is wrong with me? he wondered.

They fell asleep listening to the radio and to each other's breathing. She fell asleep before he did, and he enjoyed the steady rhythm of her body swelling and deflating with each relaxed breath.

"Thank you for today," he whispered into her hair. "Thank you."

As he fell into a dreamless, restful sleep, he thought he heard her reply, "You're welcome."

Chapter Fifteen

He woke in the morning confused. He was on the bed, and he was still dressed. What-

He suddenly remembered the night before, and he smiled. He looked around, knowing by instinct that she was already gone again. He had no idea when she left. She worked the early mornings, and she was gone until five or six every night. He wondered how she got enough sleep. Or where she-

He cut off that line of thought. He needed to try and not think of her out there, working. It just pissed him off. He undressed and got into the shower. She had cleaned off the bathroom mirror at some point. Everything but the tiny heart she'd dotted the I in her name with. He reached out and touched it. He shook his head and busied himself brushing his teeth. She was a little crazy, he thought, and a little wonderful. But that didn't change what she did, and he couldn't let himself get involved.

Why? he thought. *Why not?*

He decided he needed a shave and he slid a new razor blade into his old safety razor. He lathered up and managed to get through the entire job without slicing himself apart. Wiping his face with a towel, he meandered around the apartment. The place was kind of grungy, now that he looked at it. Or maybe it was that there wasn't any natural light besides the cheap lamps he had bought when he moved in.

He looked around and wondered to himself if he would bring a girl back here. If he met a girl on the street, would he bring her here? The dingy, cobbled-together efficiency apartment he'd built for himself was all his, sure, and it was cheap enough, but there was a stainless steel slop sink on the one wall next to the walk-in freezer and refrigerator. The floor was grimy red tile with blackened grout between, where he hadn't thrown cheap rugs down. Even the rugs were matted and a little sticky.

The bed was unmade. The sheets hadn't been changed in God alone knew when. The television was broken down and dusty, the radio was a cheap silver box he'd scrounged from a dump pile.

He had a pressboard wardrobe in the corner and a Formica table and two cheap chairs in the middle of the floor. Looking around, Harry suddenly felt shame. He was living in a slum.

In a fit of anger he stripped the bed and gathered up all of his clothes. Time to do some laundry. He went back to where the emergency door was padlocked shut (private residence didn't require it to be accessible) and where a fifth-hand washer and dryer sat. He stuffed everything in the washer and topped it off with a pile of soap powder. While the machine churned and walked all over the back of the apartment, he peeled the rugs off the floor, wincing at the sticky sounds they made. He dragged them into his office. He lifted the bed up and leaned it against the wall. He swept everything and considered his next move.

He'd covered the walls with cheap wooden panels, but underneath they were clean painted sheetrock. Maybe he could pull the panels off and paint. And get the whole place carpeted. Maybe he wouldn't do it himself. Maybe have a professional come in and give him an estimate.

He padded out to the office. The machine wasn't blinking. Odd. He usually had at least one call, even if it was a wrong number. He dragged the rugs outside and draped them in the stunted oak tree that against all odds had survived the last few years.

He went inside and grabbed the broom and went back outside. He spent the next hour beating the rugs within an inch of their ratty lives. When he finished to his satisfaction, the snow around the tree was dark with dirt and dust. Jasper watched with some amusement, sipping fresh coffee. Harry dragged the rugs back in and rearranged them a little more carefully, trying to make it appear neater. He put the bed back down and moved the table to the far wall. He realized he had no decorations. No pictures on the walls. No photographs on the mantle. No mantle.

He swapped the laundry to the dryer. His mind whirled and he didn't notice he hadn't switched the dryer on. He sat down on the bare bed, thinking. What the hell was wrong with him? Why did he give a shit what the apartment looked like? He rolled it over in his mind. Why *didn't* he give a shit? What changed when he got shot? Did he think he wouldn't go on living? Had he forgotten *pride*?

He needed a couple more lamps, he figured, and the place would be bright enough for humans. Looking around, he likened it to cave dwelling. A knock on the office door brought him out of his reverie. He went to the door and tried to peer through the film of soap. He used his thumbnail to scrape a clear spot to see out.

Porter. He didn't look happy.

Harry opened the door. "Hey, Porter. Come on in."

Porter came into the office, looking around in disinterest. "Harry, how's it going?"

"Eh. Quiet day. Doing laundry. What's going on?"

"Harry, let's take a ride," Porter said.

"What's going on?"

"I've got another one," Porter said. For just a second, Harry didn't understand what was going on. And then he got it. The bottom dropped out of his stomach.

"Let me get my coat," he said.

Chapter Sixteen

Eight blocks away, hidden in the snow behind a dumpster, was the corpse of a girl who was too young to drink legally. A girl who didn't belong crammed between a dumpster and a dirty barroom wall. A girl Harry realized he recognized.

"Shit," Harry said. "Her name's… uh… Katy. At least, that's the name she gave me."

Porter watched Harry looking at the girl. "When was this?"

"Day ago. I was running down a lead. That girl Bebe, she worked for a pimp called-"

"Mr. Jay. I know. So?" Porter said.

"So, Mr. Jay's main competition for the streets hereabouts is a big black guy named Cheddar. Uh, Cheeseborough. Darius Cheeseborough. I found him in Beckett's Pool Hall, over on…" Harry trailed off as he looked around. He thumbed over his shoulder. "There."

"Yeah," Porter said. "We picked up on that. What'd you get out of Cheddar?"

"Nix," Harry said. "He wanted to recruit Bebe, but he didn't kill her. I believe him. He was broken up about it. Or, you know, as broken up as you'd expect him to be. He liked her, I guess."

"So, you got dick," Porter said. Harry eyed him.

"I got some answers," Harry said. "Just like you asked me to get. That's as far as I've gotten."

They looked down at the girl. She'd been stabbed in the chest, just below her left breast. The blood stain wasn't much. Her heart had been stopped almost instantly.

"I got Cheddar out of our girl, here," Harry said. "And another name. Uh… what the hell was- Cassandra. Redhead. She was working the other side of the street."

Porter cocked his head a little.

Harry said, "Two dead hookers. Both stabbed."

Porter nodded.

"Someone's targeting street walkers," Harry said.

"Looks like," Porter said.

"With a second body, they gonna throw more manpower into this, do you think?" Harry asked him. Porter snorted.

"Yeah. Because hookers are a priority. I don't know, Harry. This feels wrong," Porter said.

"Yeah," Harry said. "I know what you mean."

Eugene came trudging down the alley with his helpers in tow. "Harry, Porter. Long time, no see."

"Gene," Harry said.

"Been meaning to ask you, Eugene," Porter said, "you get anything outta Bebe? Something I can use?"

Eugene shook his head. "Autopsy's gonna be a while. Got a backlog. I'll call you when I get it done. What have we here?"

"Instant replay," Porter said. "Only white. Bebe looks like the first in a series."

Eugene shook his head disapprovingly. "Someone ought to be shot. This's a crime."

Harry guffawed. Porter smiled. Eugene looked up, startled. He realized what he said and colored. "You know what I mean. No reason these girls should be getting whumped and dumped."

"We thought maybe it was a territorial beef, but now we have two dead hookers, each one run by one of the two guys in the territory."

"And you don't think that's a beef?" Eugene asked.

"Too neat," Harry said. "Like someone was trying to start some shit. If it were a turf war, there'd be all kinds of signs. This is just…"

"Wasteful," Porter said.

"Exactly. No statement. No advertising. A war means two camps sniping at one another, and they always make damned sure the other party knows who did what. This is… this is *Yojimbo*."

"What?" Porter asked.

"The movie. *Yojimbo*? Akira Kurosawa?" Harry sighed. "You've seen *A Fistful of Dollars*, right?"

Porter nodded. "Sure. Loved it."

"That's what this feels like. Stranger comes to town, starts working both sides against a middle. This feels like that kind of a setup," Harry said.

Porter nodded slowly. "Maybe. Could be. Stranger, or someone close to both of the sleaze bags."

"Maybe a third player looking to clear a path for himself. Wants Jay and Cheddar to take each other out, maybe?" Harry said, wondering what the truth would turn out to be.

Porter said. "All we know now is what we knew twenty minutes ago. Two dead whores and no more answers than we had. All right, Gene. Do your thing. Send me the reports."

Eugene nodded and signaled his lackeys, who began taking photos and jotting notes. Porter walked toward the street. Harry followed, lost in thought.

They stood watching the traffic and the passers-by. News vultures snapped photos of them. Porter walked toward his car, still not speaking. Harry followed along, thinking about Antonia.

Antonia, he thought. He didn't realize he was thinking of her using the name only he knew, but he was.

Porter got into the cruiser on the passenger side. Harry slid into the back. The uniform started back to Harry's place.

"Harry," Porter said.

"Yeah?"

"You holding out on me?" Porter asked.

Harry blinked. "Fuck you."

Porter turned around in his seat to look at Harry. Harry didn't especially like the way Porter eyed him.

"Excuse me?" Porter said.

"You heard me. I said 'fuck you'."

The uniform looked out the window and wished he was anywhere else. He knew Porter, and he knew of Harry. They were supposed to be friends.

"Harry, come on. You're holding something back."

"I'll say it again, Porter. Fuck you. You asked me to help. I didn't ask you if I could jump into it. You think I don't have shit to do? I have *paying* clients. I know full well you aren't gonna send in my voucher. And I said yes anyhow. And you accuse me of fucking around? Go to hell." Harry stared out the window.

Porter nodded. "All right. All right. I had to ask."

"Bullshit," Harry snarled. "You didn't have to ask. You should fucking well *know* better."

"Harry," Porter chided. "You know how this works. I have to ask all the questions. It's nothing personal."

"Sure as hell *feels* personal, Porter," Harry said. "When have I ever given you any cause to doubt me?"

"Why'd you get in a fight with the pimp, Harry?" Porter asked, instead of answering the question.

"What?"

"Matisse and Bender mentioned having to break up a fight. You clocked Jay's bodyguard a good one the other day. What's that about?"

"That happened *after* you found Bebe's body," Harry reminded him.

"Yeah," Porter said, and seemed to think he had made his point.

They pulled up in front of Harry's. Harry got out. Porter rolled the window down. "Harry, if you find out anything more-"

"Are you fucking kidding me, Porter? After that, you want me to keep helping you?"

Porter smiled. "Come on, Harry. You're you. I could tell you to walk away and we both know you won't. Just keep me in the loop as to what you find."

Harry grinned despite himself. "Yeah, all right. See you tonight?"

"I'll be there," Porter said.

The cruiser took off, and Harry watched them go, rounding the corner and heading back toward the crime scene. He thought about it while he fixed a pair of coffees. He handed one to Jasper.

"Thanks, Chief," the bum said.

"Jasper, how do you know when you're into something you shouldn't be?"

Jasper grinned, a gap-toothed smile filled with yellow teeth and humor. "Come on, Chief. If you gotta ask, *that's* how you know."

Harry laughed in spite of himself. "I guess that's true. Thanks, Jasper."

Harry went inside and found things to do. He had cleaning to do, and he had decided to pull down the ridiculous wood paneling and paint. He sat at the desk to make a list. As he jotted notes, he noticed the light on his answering machine blinking.

"Mr. DeMarko, my name is Lucille Martin. I'm a nurse at New York Downtown. I have this number as a contact for a Miss Bennett. Miss Bennett was admitted to the ER at one this afternoon. Please give us a call at-"

Harry was already moving. He grabbed a cab at Houston and made it to the hospital in fifteen minutes. At the desk they gave him a room number. He pelted down the hall, suddenly having a momentary flashback. This was where they'd brought him after the shooting. He skidded to a halt in front of the room and opened the door. She didn't have a private room. There were three other beds, two of which had the sheets drawn around them.

She looked like hell. One eye was swollen closed. She had stitches on her right cheek, one arm was in a sling, and one foot was in a soft cast. He rushed to the side of the bed and her eye opened. She smiled and winced. He gritted his teeth in sympathy. He took her non-injured hand.

"I hear you been looking for me," he said softly. She smiled.

"All my life, lover," she said. The woman across from them cleared her throat.

"Toni, what the hell happened?"

"What's it look like?" she asked.

"It *looks* like you got hit by a car," he said.

She nodded. "Yep."

"You're serious?"

She nodded. "I was down by Houston. A car swerved, jumped the curb, and plowed into me. If it'd been going any faster, I'd be dead."

"Jesus, Toni."

"Yeah. I'm screwed."

"What do you mean?" Harry asked.

"Come on. As soon as Jay finds out I'm in here? And not on the street? He's going to flip his lid. A couple of the girls were with me. He's bound to know by now I'm not working," Toni said.

"You're kidding. You're all messed up. He's not gonna put you back out there," he said.

"You don't know him, Harry. I do."

Harry's jaw clenched. He said, "Fine. I'll make sure he understands-"

"Harry, *no.*"

"Why not?" Harry said. "It's not like you can get any worse off."

"Harry- we've been over this!- he'll just make it that much worse on me. Please. Swear you'll stay out of it," she pleaded.

He ground his teeth. But... she had a point. "All right. All right. I won't say anything."

"Thank you, Harry." He sat with her for a couple of minutes, not speaking. She reached up and touched the stitches, wincing.

"You've looked better," he offered.

"I know. Best part? The guy drove off. Left me lying in the snow, or so they tell me. I was out cold. So I'm stuck with the bill." She shifted her shoulders and gasped. "The drugs aren't touching the pain."

"Let me get someone," he said.

She nodded. "Please."

"Be right back." Harry went out to the hall and looked around. He spotted the nurse's station and walked down. It took him a second to find a nurse.

"Hey," he said. "Room 214, Bennett? She needs something for the pain. She said it's pretty bad."

"All right, let me find the doctor and see if we can up the dose. Wait here." She left.

Harry leaned against the counter, waiting. He looked down the hall toward Toni's room in time to see Mr. Jay walk in. Harry went down to the door, but didn't peek around, he just listened.

"Fuck's wrong with you," Jay said. "Don't you have sense to get the hell out of the way?"

"Excuse me, you can't talk to her that way," the woman across from Toni said imperiously.

"Bitch, I ain't talking to you," Jay snarled. "Shut your mouth or I'll break it."

The woman gasped.

"You need to climb your ass off that bed, Toni," Jay said. "Get back on the street. You ain't getting a vacation."

"Jay, come on," she pleaded. "I broke my foot, for God's sake."

"Ain't nobody wants to fuck your *foot*," Jay said. "And ain't nothing wrong with what they *do* want, is there?"

"Jay, come on-" she started, and yelped in pain as Jay did something to her. "Ah, okay-okay-okay! Stop it! Please!"

"That's better. You hobble your skinny ass out of here, Toni, and get back to fucking work. I bet it's not as bad as they say it is, is it?"

Harry could hear the tears in her voice. He closed his eyes. His fists clenched. "No, Jay."

"What'd you say, bitch?"

"Mr. Jay! Mr. Jay! I'm sorry!" Toni fairly yelled.

"Damned *right* you're sorry. You get your shit together, bitch. Get your ass back on the street and bring me some cash. Don't you and I *ever* speak you don't give me some green. You get me?"

Another sound like flesh on flesh and another gasp from Toni's roommate. Toni sobbed, "I understand! I'm sorry! I'm sorry, Mr. Jay!"

Harry thumped his head on the doorframe. He drew his fists so tightly that his nails cut into his palms. He held his breath so he didn't start panting. Starburst spots behind his eyelids flared in time to his heartbeat. *I'm in a hospital,* he thought to himself desperately, *I'm in a hospital, I'm in a hospital. She doesn't want me to do anything. I'm in a hospital. I'm in a hospital.* He was thankful that he hadn't thought to bring his gun.

"Better be," Jay muttered. He turned on his heel and started for the door. Harry ducked into the room next door and stayed out of sight until he heard Jay's steps fade. He peered out of the doorway. Jay stepped into the elevator and the doors closed. Harry counted to two hundred to give her time to put herself together. He went back into the room. He sat next to her and took her good hand. She clasped his fingers in hers.

"I need to g-get out of here, Harry," she whispered. "Can you t-tell them I need to leave?"

He didn't say anything. He just looked at her. She looked away. "You heard?"

He considered and rejected half a dozen retorts. "I heard," he told her softly.

Tears welled in her eyes, and she said quickly, "Look, Harry, I don't need your bullshit right now. I'm-"

"What do you need from me, Toni? How can I help?" Harry asked quietly. "We can fight later. Right now, I'm here. Just let me help you. Trust me." Toni closed her eyes.

"Just get me out of here. Take me… take me home. Please?" she asked. He didn't trust himself to speak. He just nodded.

"I'll go get-"

A doctor came into the room followed by the nurse Harry had spoken with.

The doctor started to speak. "I understand-"

"We're leaving," Harry said. "What do you need from us?"

The doctor blinked. "No, you can't leave. She's still-"

"This conversation ends with me wheeling the lady out of here. What do you need for that to happen?" Harry said.

"I can't allow that," the doctor said.

Harry grinned and stood up. He went up to the doctor. The doctor shifted eyes uneasily from Harry to Toni and back.

"I did not ask you to allow it. I did not ask you to condone it. I did not *ask* you a goddamned thing, pal," Harry said. "I *said* we're leaving. You can either tell us what we need to do to make that happen, or I can go find another doctor who isn't a moron. And I should warn you, I've had a shit day, I have a headache, my girl's been screwed up by a hit-and-run,

151

and I'm in the mood to break someone's hands. So what do you think I'm going to do to you if the next words out of your mouth aren't 'I'll get your paperwork and a wheelchair'?"

The doctor blinked.

"I'll…" Harry said, rolling his hand in the air.

"Uh… I'll get your paperwork and a wheelchair." The doctor said. The nurse looked at the floor and very obviously didn't grin.

"Thank you, doctor."

"Uh, My name's-"

"Don't care," Harry said, turning away. "Write me some prescriptions for her meds, and we'll be on our way. Have someone call a cab."

"Nurse, do as he-"

Harry looked back at him. In a deadly quiet voice, he said, "I told *you* to do it."

The doctor swallowed thickly. He turned to leave and stopped. "Uh, may I-"

"Yes. Get gone," Harry said. He looked at Toni. Her eyes were wide and startled until he winked at her. She smiled.

The doctor rushed out of the room. The nurse watched him go. After he was out of earshot, she said quietly, "If there's anything I can do, please let me know. That was… fun."

Harry grinned. "Yeah, maybe a little."

The nurse left whistling. Toni said. "You're kind of a jerk."

"Yeah, I get that way. Especially about you."

She didn't say anything. Her eyes were downcast and she swallowed hard.

"Toni, this isn't over. But let me get you home first, okay?" Harry said.

Toni nodded faintly. He leaned over and put a hand under her chin and gently lifted her face. "Listen to me, okay? You can trust me. You can depend on me. You know that."

Toni nodded again, but she looked away as soon as he let go of her chin. The doctor came in with a wheelchair and a clipboard.

"Here, here, here, and here," he said, pointing. Harry scribbled random letters, figuring that if it worked for the doctors, it would work for the patients. The doctor handed him a sheaf of papers.

"Antibiotics, painkillers, and a topical ointment. Follow up on the foot in a week. Stitches can come out in three or four days. The sprain should be all right in a couple of days. Just come back here, we'll take care of it." He looked at Harry uncertainly. "If… if that's okay?"

"Her foot's not broken?" Harry asked.

"No, just sprained," The doctor said. "Same with her wrist. Is there anything else?"

"That'll do it," Harry said. "Thanks. I'll take her down."

"Uh, sure," the doctor said. He stepped aside, hovered for a second, and then realized his presence was superfluous. He left abruptly. Harry chuckled. He waited as the nurse unhooked the IV and put a bandage over the puncture. They helped Toni into the wheelchair. Harry wheeled her down the hall and into the elevator.

It took patience and care to get her into the cab without hurting her, and Harry discovered he had a certain touch for cradling her so she didn't feel any more pain than necessary. He stuffed the wheelchair into the trunk, not caring that it belonged to the hospital. In the cab, she leaned against him, and he put an arm carefully around her. He had the cabbie stop at the pharmacy and they filled Toni's prescriptions. At the apartment, it took even more care, but he finally finessed the wheelchair through the front door and into the apartment.

"You cleaned up," Toni said.

"Yeah," Harry said. "It was about time. Been a year already." She laughed.

He looked at the bare bed, swore, and went to the dryer. He puzzled over the damp sheets for a moment, realized he never switched the machine on, and did so.

"Sorry," he said. "No sheets yet. Are you hungry?"

Toni sat in the chair and didn't say a word.

"Toni?"

She looked up at him. "What?"

"Hungry?"

She shook her head. "No. I'm tired. I'm really, really tired."

He nodded. "I don't want to put you on the bed without sheets, but if you're really tired…"

"No," she said. "I guess I can wait."

He nodded.

They sat quietly for a moment. Finally, Harry said, "I can't do this anymore, Toni."

She didn't say anything.

"I'm sick of putting you back together. I'm sick of trying to ignore your bruises and your tears. I'm sick of wondering if you're going to come walking back through that door every night. I'm sick of watching you simper and bow to that fucker. I'm *done* with it," Harry said harshly. He could feel everything coming up like vomit and couldn't stop it. He needed to suck it up. All the rage and hurt and frustration and impotence and lack of understanding about her, her place in his life, how he felt, and what she was came up in a heaving, bile-sour mass of foul words and feelings and he couldn't seem to stop.

She didn't say anything.

"You *look* at me, Toni! I'm fucking talking to you!" he barked. His hands became fists and his knuckles crackled tightly in the quiet of the room. Instead of looking at him, she reacted in a way he'd never seen from her. Not tough Toni B. Not the sassy, flippant street chick. Not *his* Toni.

She flinched in the chair, drawing away from him as though his words had physical form. Tears flowed down her cheeks. His eyes widened, and the skin on his arms and neck tightened as the hairs there stood. He was shocked by his own reactions, swore softly and hung his head.

"Stupid, stupid, *stupid*," he said to himself disgustedly. She flinched every time. He realized what his words were doing. All the heat fled from him. The anger was gone, and in its place was only an empty hole. He went to her then, kneeling in front of her, but she cried out and leaned away. His mouth dropped open. She was afraid of him? Of *him*? He did the only thing he could think to do. He backed away as far as he could. He grabbed the chair from the table and put it against the fire door and slumped into it. He hung his head and rubbed his hands together. *What the fuck is wrong with me?* he berated himself silently. He squeezed his eyes shut. He took a calming breath.

When he opened his eyes, she was looking into them. She struggled upright out of the chair and limped toward him. He started to get up, to go to her, but she stopped. He frowned, thought about it, and sat. She limped toward him. She came to him and cupped his chin in the same way he had done to her. He looked up at her hopefully.

She slapped him as hard as she could.

She slapped him again. And again. He didn't flinch away, he didn't say anything, and he made no attempt to stop her. She slapped him five times as hard as she could. Tears streamed from her eyes and sobs began to shake her. She slid to the floor in a boneless heap. He dared not reach out for her.

She looked up at him with blazing eyes, anger and hatred- no. He realized she wasn't angry. She didn't hate him she... she *loathed* him. it was loathing he saw in those familiar, stranger's eyes. She snarled, "Y-you... you *bastard*. You... how *dare* you? You son of a *bitch*."

She climbed painfully to her feet and limped back to the chair. She shot him another dirty look. "Son of a bitch."

They sat there, not speaking, until the dryer buzzed. Almost instinctively, he got up and pulled the sheets out. He carried them to the bed and made it up. He pulled the blankets off the couch and flapped and straightened them across the bed. He went back to the couch and sat down. She got up and crawled into the bed, pulling the covers around herself. He stared at her forlornly, and wished he were born mute. Or that he could take it all back. But once you said some things, you couldn't unsay them. He wouldn't be surprised if she-

She sighed. "You coming, or what?" she asked in a whisper.

He shot to his feet and went to the bed. Kicking off his shoes he lay down beside her. She said, "Okay. Tell me what it is you need to tell me."

He thought about his words carefully. He struggled for a handle on it. He sighed. "I don't know how to say what I want to say."

She nodded. "Figures."

"I… I need-"

"I think I'm hungry, Harry," she said. She sounded remote. Dazed, almost. And exhausted. He felt it, too. They were both empty of whatever had filled them both only moments before, and he was afraid that things would never be the same. But he could go through the motions if she were willing to.

"Oh. Okay. What can I get you?"

"Pastrami on rye," she said.

"Okay. I'll run over to Katz's," he said.

"I want to come," she said.

"Hey, no," he said. "You just got out of the hospital, Toni. You're all messed up."

She craned her head back and glared at him. "You don't get to tell me what I can and can't do, Harry."

He nodded, but said, "It's going to hurt. I'll get us a cab-"

"I want to walk. I want to be outside. I'm tired of being indoors. I need fresh air," she said. "I need a change of scenery. Shut up and help me?"

He shut up. He grabbed his shoes and his overcoat. While she struggled into her own coat, Harry looked around for his wallet. It and his gun sat on the night stand. He shoved both into his pocket.

They dressed warmly and left, handing off a cup of coffee to Jasper. It took an hour for them to walk the eight blocks down Houston to the deli. They took their tickets and shuffled along the counter picking out what they wanted. The register girl bagged their food and Harry paid, tipping a little extravagantly.

Toni was pale and sweating as they rounded the corner of Elizabeth. "Thank God," she whispered, "I'm ready to drop."

"Well, you're the idiot walking around on that screwed-up drumstick," Harry said. "I'm not surprised you're beat."

"Shut up, smart ass. I haven't forgiven you yet for being a jerk," she said angrily, but he heard the smile on her lips as she said it. He looked at her out of the corner of his eye, and yes, she was smiling wanly. His hear lightened.

"Shutting up, ma'am," Harry said. She looked angry, but she slid an arm through his, and he smiled. His heart lightened. Harry pulled his key as they got to the apartment. Before he could open the door, a voice stopped them.

"Figures I'd find you here, you bitch," came a familiar growl.

They both turned. Mr. Jay and his bodyguard Marvin came out of the darkness. Salano had a gun in his hand. He had stitches across his nose and cheek, and two black eyes. Harry realized that he and Marvin looked at lot alike, at least where the damage to their faces was concerned. Harry dropped the food bag and went still. He didn't feel worried, he realized. He didn't feel upset, scared, angry, or even surprised. His vision went ultra-clear, and he recognized this immediately. It was adrenaline and the instant call to action he remembered from his few scrapes in uniform. He watched

"Mr. Jay," Toni stammered, "w-what-?"

"The fuck you doing with him, bitch? You're supposed to be working," Jay snarled.

She put up her hands. "N-no, I mean, I am. I am working. He's my- he's the *client*, Jay."

Harry watched them, his eyes flitting back and forth between their faces. His breathing went low and even. The pimp looked murderous, and Toni looked terrified. Harry interjected, his voice dangerously calm.

"That's right," he said, "and it's none of your business."

"Bitch *is* my business, you fuck," Jay snarled. "Shut the fuck up."

Harry shrugged and said as soothingly as he could, "Okay."

"Date night's over, honey, Get back to fucking work." Jay grabbed Toni by the arm and yanked her out of the circle of the yellow streetlight. She stumbled and went to her knees in the snow and slush. She gasped in pain.

Jay kicked her in the ass and she went down on her stomach with a cry. Although that cry cut through Harry like a razor, Harry stolidly looked over at the grinning Salano. He didn't want to take his eyes off the gun. That was important. Suddenly, with a silent whir like gears meshing and advancing, Harry's heart made a tiny, minute adjustment as a prelude to his coming actions. He knew he'd made the decision. No debate, not questions, no illusions. He'd made his decision and now he knew he would follow through. Jay and Marvin were real people, right in front of him, and suddenly they seemed to change. They were paper targets, outlines of people, just paper and ink. Harry measured the distance.

Jay turned to Harry. Harry's eyes went to Jay's. Jay sneered and said, "Stay the fuck away from my girls. I came here to tune you up, asshole. Drop a beating on your ass. Took me a little while to find you. I was *gonna* warn you never to get fucking involved with me and mine. And now I find you renting out *my* pussy like you're Joe Blow. I don't fucking think so, you piece of shit. But I'm gonna let it all ride, man, just to show you how generous I can be, and to remind you to keep off my streets. But if I see you looking at my meat again, talking to them, renting them out, *anything*, I'll have my boy here blow your fucking dick off. You get me?"

Harry nodded amiably. His lips bowed in a gentle smile. He said softly, "I get you. I'm sorry. Won't happen again."

"Better not, asshole. Now, I'm-a have a word with my girl here. You better pull whatever cash you got. You don't talk to *me* without paying." Jay turned to Toni, who had begun picking herself up off the sidewalk. He kicked her again in the ribs, hard enough that she lost her air in an explosive choking burst and slumped back down. Harry looked away from Jay and back to Salano. The bodyguard laughed. Harry counted backward from one hundred in his head. Marvin smirked at him and said, "What's the matter, hero? Worried he'll damage the pussy? Don't worry. He won't hurt the moneymaker, not that it'll do *you* any good. It's the yap wrapped around it needs the lesson."

Jay laughed. "That's funny, what you said. And he's right, you know, Toni. You *do* need a lesson. You've been getting uppity, bitch. Ornery. Been meaning to reeducate you. So, I'll tell you what. I'm gonna give you that lesson right here and right now. Pay attention, boyfriend."

Toni turned look at Harry. Harry's eyes found hers. She started to speak, but before she could say anything, Jay went to his haunches and slapped Toni across the face. Her stitches broke open, blood spattered the snow, and she wobbled. He slammed his fist into her ribs. The force of the punch knocked her over on her side, and she lost all her air again. She wheezed, struggling to draw breath, curling into a terrified ball, knees coming to her belly. Harry had to look away. He had to reign it in. He wouldn't help anyone if he let himself get mad. Maybe he could-

Marvin the bodyguard chose that moment to do exactly the wrong thing. When Toni went over on her side in the slush, he laughed aloud. His high, mocking bark of laughter echoed in the street for just a second. Harry looked up at Marvin. The bodyguard was watching Jay and Toni, not Harry. Harry rolled his head on his neck, the bones of his spine making little popping sounds, his shoulders relaxed, and his hands moved in his pockets.

"Hey, Marvin?" he called softly.

Salano looked over at Harry with an irritated look on his bruised face. He said, "What the fuck do you want, man?"

Harry's right pocket exploded as he fired his .38. The bullet caught Marvin low in the belly on the right-hand side, and the man gasped and spun, falling into the snow with a sodden thump. He groaned and whimpered, scrabbling at his belly. Jay and Toni both gaped at Harry and he noted remotely, in a far-off part of himself, that they looked too alike. Wide eyes, open mouths, unbelieving stares.

"All right, asshole," Harry said in a conversational tone, "Step away from the lady and go see if your fuckboy's still alive."

Jay didn't move. Harry took the gun out of his pocket. He pointed it at Jay and his hand didn't waver.

"You heard me," Harry said.

Jay's face didn't change as he suddenly, convulsively moved. He went to Marvin and knelt next to him, rolling the man onto his back. Salano cried out as the pain rippled across his belly. The blood had spread across his shirt in a wide bloom of wet crimson.

Jay looked up at Harry. "He's hurt bad, man."

"I hope it's worse than it looks," Harry said. "The question is, what about you?"

"Me?" Jay asked.

"Yeah. How you feeling?" Harry's face had gone curiously blank. Toni stared at Harry, realizing she'd seen that look on his face before. Once.

"What?" Jay whispered. Fear rippled across his face. He didn't want to believe what was happening. Beside him in the snow, Salano made a choking, gasping, ghastly rattling noise. The exhaled plume of steamy breath that issued from his lips was not followed by an inhale. Jay didn't notice his man die, but Harry did, filing that tidbit of information away somewhere else. His primary attention was focused on the pimp.

"How's that bullet feel?" Harry asked him. Toni's eyes darted from Harry's face to Jay's and back. "Harry?" she whispered.

"Shut up," Harry said distantly. He didn't sound like himself. He sounded faint to his ear and hers, as

162

though speaking from the other end of a long-distance phone call. She shuddered. He didn't look like himself. In fact, he hadn't looked like that since the day they'd met. Her eyes went to Jay, and she felt a cold shiver that had nothing to do with the weather or the slush covering her.

"I asked you a question," Harry said. "Do you want me to repeat the question?"

Jay stared daggers at Harry. "Man, are you crazy, or what?"

"No, I'm not crazy." Harry looked at Toni. "I don't like the way you treat women."

"Why do you care, asshole?" Jay demanded, his face flushing dark red.

Harry's eyes settled on Jay again. They were faded blue, and empty. He smiled hollowly and shook his head. "I don't know," Harry told the pimp truthfully. "But I do."

He shot Jay in the chest. The pimp made a croaking noise that couldn't be heard over the shot, and tilted backward in the snow, one leg bent awkwardly under his body. Toni screamed involuntarily. The barrel of Harry's .38 didn't waver. He sighted over the barrel at Jay, but Jay didn't move and didn't breathe. Harry put the gun back in his pocket and went to Toni. He gently, carefully helped her to her feet.

"Are you okay?" he asked in a soft voice.

She stared at him. Her wide eyes were glued to his face. He didn't look away or flinch. He looked at her and looked at her, and was relieved to see that, unlike Jay and Salano, she was still real, still a person, and not made of paper and ink. She wasn't a target. She was alive. He felt something struggling inside of him to break free, but he couldn't let it. Not yet.

"Are you okay?" he asked her again.

"Why do you care?" she asked him. It was Jay's question, but her voice, and he felt differently about her asking him.

He didn't look away. "I said I don't know. It was true. But... does it matter?"

"You killed him, Harry," Toni said, and her voice trembled. "You *killed* them."

"Yes," he replied calmly.

"Why?" she asked.

He looked over at Jay's body. The street was quiet and no lights appeared anywhere. No sound anywhere. He looked back at her. It was as though they were the only people in the whole world. "You really have to ask me that?" he asked her. She followed his gaze, looked at Jay, and back to him. She touched the reopened cuts on her face, rubbing the blood between shaking fingers.

"Because of this?" she asked in a tremulous voice.

He nodded.

"B-because of *me*?"

Another nod.

"Not because he killed Bebe?" she asked.

Harry shook his head. "Toni, he didn't kill Bebe."

Toni stared. He looked again at the men lying in the snow. The blood that mixed with the snow steamed in the pale light. "You... you killed him because of *me*?"

Harry shook his head. "Not because of. *For* you. For the shit he's *done* to you. For the shit he's *made* you do. For the bruises. For the fear. For *all* of the things he did. *That's* why I killed him. Never *because* of

164

you. You aren't responsible for this. *I* did this. I wanted to."

She backed away from him. He nodded to himself.

"Yeah. I know. I sound like a bugnuts lunatic. I'm *not*. I'm just…" he shrugged, and the adrenaline suddenly ebbed away. The weight of everything settled on his shoulders. He was tired. So tired. But not of her, he realized. Not of the complications of her. He was tired of himself. He struggled for words, and finally managed to say, "I'm just *tired* of it. I'm tired of the bodies. I'm tired of the fighting. I'm tired of-of *all* of it. I'm tired of you."

She looked up at him quickly, hurt on her battered face. She looked at him closely, but he didn't look angry. He didn't look upset. He looked exhausted.

"I'm tired of you leaving. I'm tired of you working the streets. I'm tired of wishing and wanting and hoping and waiting. I'm tired of waiting for the idea of *you*," he finished, almost whispering. He felt something threaten to break inside him, and wondered what that meant.

"The… the idea of me?" Toni asked. "What does that mean?"

"Or whatever. But… I'm tired of waiting for you to…" he almost stopped, but forced himself to continue. He didn't know what he was going to say, but like Toni, he really wanted to find out. He said, "waiting for you to…to stop being what you are."

"What… a hooker?"

"Yes," he said, and realized it was the truth.

They stared at one another. Toni made an angry noise.

"What?" Harry asked.

"Fuck you, Harry!" she blurted.

He didn't say anything.

She turned away and hugged herself. "Fuck you," she said again.

He didn't say anything. She didn't walk away. They just stood in the snow beside the bodies of Jay and Marvin and didn't talk for a while. Finally, she turned around, eyeing him suspiciously. "*That's* your fucking problem?" she asked. "That's the reason you won't fucking touch me? Because I'm a *hooker*?"

He shrugged. "I-I guess so."

"So you look down on me? Because I'm a whore," she said. "You *asshole*."

"No! I don't care what you *do*. It's not what you *are*, but just what you do. I think you made choices that made sense at the time. I- I don't care about that, and I don't judge you, I swear I don't. But... you're who you are. And I'm who I am. And I... I can't be with someone who's a whore. Not because there's something wrong with being a *hooker*. Everyone's paid to do *something*. Yours is sex. At least it's honest. But *I* can't live with it. And I don't want to live *without* you. I don't want you for a *night*. I want-" Harry rubbed a hand over his face. I-"

"What?" she asked. Her eyes were round and her face had gone solemn and still. She stared at him and couldn't believe the words coming from his, Harry's, mouth. *Him.* Saying these things. Her heart began to gallop.

"I don't know. There's no point to this conversation. *You* know how I feel. I'm pretty sure you feel the same. But... but I wasn't going to *make* you quit. I didn't want to *force* you to choose, or whatever. I wanted *you* to quit. To *want* to quit. I was... I was waiting for you to choose *me*," he said, forcing the words out. He gestured at the bodies. "Kind of immaterial now."

"You wanted me to choose you over hooking?" she asked.

"I want you to *want* to choose me," he said sheepishly.

She guffawed.

"Yeah," he said, blushing. "Dumb, huh?"

She shook her head. "Harry, you're an idiot. You should have *said*."

He shrugged. "I don't think I knew. I didn't know. I knew something was- I could-"

He kicked at the snow at his feet. Her heart melted at the sight of him. Big, bad, Harry. Always in control. Always calm. Always knowing what to do. Tough as anybody, looking like a lost little boy. She could see the trouble he was having, could see him trying to understand the words even as he spoke them.

"I *couldn't*. I didn't want you to have to make a choice because I *asked* you to. I wanted *you* to choose me over the life," Harry said. He looked up at her, nakedly open and honest. "So I'd *know*."

"So you'd know what?" Toni asked.

He took a deep breath. "Whether it was me or security. Whether it was me or a place to live. Whether it was me, or money. Whether it was me or *not*," he said.

She slapped him. She caught him off-guard, and his head rocked with the blow and one hand went to the reddish mark on his cheek.

"Again? Jesus, what was *that* one for?" he demanded.

"Because you're a dumbass, Harry. You've been an idiot since we met, but you're really *dumb*," she said.

"Well, yeah," Harry said unhappily. "Obviously."

"You really think I would choose *you* over hooking? That I'd choose you over the life? That I'd rather be with *you* than walking the streets at two in the morning, wondering what I'm going to have to do for twenty bucks this time? That I would choose to be with *you* rather than work with..." she waved at hand at Jay's body, "...*for* a pimp who liked to beat me when he wasn't fucking me just because he *could*? Like I was property. You really *believe* that?"

Harry looked away, wincing. "I'd *hoped*."

"Do you ever *listen* to yourself talk, Harry?" Toni asked. She went to him, grabbed his chin with one hand, and made him look at her. "Do you have any idea how moronic you sound? How idealistic and starry-eyed and *fucking* stupid?"

He pulled his face away from her. He wouldn't even look at her. "Fine, fine. You don't want me, I get it. Quit being-"

"Being what?" she demanded. "Quit being a dick? Quit being unreasonable? Quit being a fucking *imbecile*? Look at me, Harry. *Look* at me!"

He raised his eyes to her face. She was smiling.

"Harry, you should have *said*. You *idiot*. You should have *told* me you cared," she told him gently.

"You know I-"

"That you cared about the *hooker* part, not the *me* part! You should have fucking *told* me. Harry, I don't give a shit that you have a place to live. I don't give a shit if you give me money. I don't care if you can get me off the street. I don't need to be *rescued*. I didn't need to be here. If I wanted, I could have left any time. You think I couldn't figure out how to make my way in the world? Come on, if it came to that, I know five johns that would have been happy to set me up as a part-time mistress. Apartment, car, money, the whole nine yards. I could have been gone any time. Harry, one of the guys I know... his name's *Bonanno*. Think I couldn't deal with Jay if I really *wanted* to?" Toni laughed then, really laughed. Harry looked at her with suspicion. She shook her head so that her hair bounced and flopped and she laughed long and loudly. "Oh my *God*, Harry, why do you think I keep coming back here? It sure isn't for the smell."

He eyed her uncertainly. "You need a place to stay. You need a safe place."

"Safe places are all over, Harry. I make- made- a hundred bucks a day, if I want. You think I can't afford a hotel room? You think I couldn't afford *food*? Or a *bed*? Or a safe place to hide when I needed it? Think, idiot. *Think* about it," she told him.

He looked down. Finally he looked up at her, and the hopeful, cautiously daring look in his eyes almost broke her heart. *I'll be damned. He was so afraid of getting hurt*, she thought. Well, at least *that* she could understand, because God knew nothing else about him made a lick of sense to her.

"Me?" he asked in a small voice. "You came back for me?"

"It's not a question, Harry," she said. "Say it like you mean it. Say it like you *know* it, because I'll be goddamned if you *shouldn't* know it by now, you idiot."

He cleared his throat. "Me," he said, with more confidence. "You came back- you kept coming back- for... for me."

She smiled at him. "Of course I kept coming back for you, Harry. Why the hell else would I come back?"

She saw him trying to deal with it, and it melted her heart again. He swallowed a couple of times, and looked lost and scared and... and human. Different. He looked different. She saw him reel away from that. It was too much, too soon. She saw him retreat again, and trying to shield himself. This time, she let him.

He cast his eyes around, and they settled on the bodies in the snow. He seized the distraction. He at least knew how to deal with this. She let him have his distraction, because she knew him. And she knew he wouldn't forget or hide or retreat from her. He just needed time.

"I need to call this in," he said. His voice was back to normal. All business. "There's gonna be questions."

"Always are," she said. "Make the call."

"Hold on. Here's the scenario. They jumped us. Pulled the gun. He was going to kill us. Beat on you, I protected you. Get it?" Harry asked.

"I get it."

"Repeat it, Toni."

"What's the big deal, Harry? They're jerks. Dead ones. What-"

"Because earlier today, my friend Porter questioned me about them and now they're dead. Not seven hours after telling me to my face he thought I was holding out information about these guys, I *shot* them. So you need to get this right, because otherwise I'm not coming home tonight. Or for maybe six to ten," Harry told her.

Toni blinked. "Jesus, Harry."

"Remember, I was looking into Bebe's murder. There was another killing last night, Toni. One of Cheddar's girls. Name of Katy. Did you know her?"

Toni shook her head. "No. We don't really socialize, you know?"

"Yeah. Anyhow, Porter read me the riot act because I'd been in the fight with Jay, and then I was seen harassing Cheddar about Bebe. That happened right before I came to get you at the hospital. So you see the thing," Harry said.

"Yeah." She looked miserable. "So… they jumped us?"

"Yep."

"A mugging?" Toni asked. She sounded dubious.

"Sure. What else-"

She said, "How about the truth, Harry? I'm a hooker, he's my pimp, he was slapping the shit out of me. You interfered, Marvin pulled a gun, you did what you had to do."

"That explains Marvin. Why'd I shoot Jay, Toni?" Harry asked.

She looked at the bodies. She bit her lip. Looking up at him, she said in a small voice, "He went for Marvin's gun?"

Harry considered it. In reality, despite letting Jay crouch next to his fallen enforcer, within arm's length of Marvin's gun, Harry had never considered for a moment that Jay would try and use it. It hadn't mattered. He realized that he'd made Jay and Marvin dead in his mind well before he made them that way in life. They weren't going to have walked away from this encounter no matter what had happened.

It was the first time in his life he'd ever actually murdered someone in cold, calculated blood, and he

171

didn't feel the slightest remorse. He nodded slowly. "Yeah. He went for the gun, I warned him, but he didn't listen. But we don't have to-"

"Your friend Porter… is he gonna buy that they stumbled across us randomly? In front of your place?" she asked.

Harry didn't speak. She was quick, he realized. She wasn't stupid, but he hadn't realized how quick she could be.

"You know the only way it works is if you were picking up a girl for the night, and *this* happens," she said.

Harry stared thoughtfully at the bodies.

"You think they'll look down on you because you're hiring a girl? Does that bother you?" she asked.

He shook his head. "No. I don't care. But… it might be more helpful if I tell Porter you came to me with some information. That's why Jay wanted to… *shit.*"

She cocked her head. "What?"

"Won't work. You don't actually know anything. That'll be the first question. Falls apart right there."

"Harry, tell him the truth," she said. "I don't care. Maybe *you* do. You're living with a hooker. Your friend is gonna find that out. Am I a secret? Are you ashamed? Embarrassed?"

Harry stared at her. "I… maybe. Maybe I am. I'm sorry for that."

She shrugged. "You and I know the truth, Harry. Does it matter what anyone else thinks? Really?"

Harry looked at her as though seeing her, really seeing *her*, for the first time. Finally, he smiled. "You know what? Fuck 'em if they can't get over it. You're right. You're right. I'm wrong. What else is new?"

She laughed. "Now you're talking."

"All right. Truth. We'll try that." He picked up bag of the sandwiches and brushed it off. "Come on, it's cold out here."

He unlocked the door. He turned suddenly and looked at her strangely.

"What?" she asked.

He smiled sweetly and shyly, and tossed her the key. She almost dropped it in surprise. She stared at it, and looked up to see him watching at her intently. She grinned and tucked the key down her shirt, between her breasts. She laughed aloud when he blushed and turned to go inside. She stood there on the street for just a second, hugging herself to keep warm. She stared down at the bodies of Mr. Jay and Marvin.

Hell of a way to tell someone you love them, she thought. She followed him into the apartment.

Into *their* apartment. She felt like someone punched her in the stomach. *Their.* She smiled and went inside, delighted with new thoughts, and with no consideration for the bodies behind her.

Chapter Seventeen

The station was exactly as Harry remembered. He hadn't been back for more than a year, but he knew how the next hour, and the evening, would go. He'd done it a million times from the other side of the desk, hadn't he? So he started off on the right foot. He broke away from Porter, went to the coffee pot and poured himself a cup of the thick, hours-old concoction, using a mug someone had left next to the pot. He creamed and sugared it within an inch of its life, although normally he didn't take much of either. He couldn't handle the station coffee without that buffer and never could. He sipped it on the way to Porter's desk.

The coffee was still lukewarm and bitter, the chairs still squeaked badly, and the air of sullen relentlessness was the exactly the same. Harry walked to Porter's desk and sat in the chair in front of it. More than a few glances from the officers in the room, a lot of whom Harry knew by sight, fewer by name. He nodded to one or two acquaintances.

They had spent four hours at the scene, walking through the details. Three times. Both he and Toni had been questioned by Porter, who clearly believed none of it. Finally, they had taken Harry down to the station. Toni was at the apartment. After a call to the hospital to verify the accident story, Porter agreed that Toni could stay and get some rest. He couldn't resist telling her to stay by the phone. Harry pointed out to her that she'd have to turn the ringer on.

Porter sat down and took out his notebook. Harry didn't smile. He'd done this a thousand times. He sipped the cup of coffee again, staring politely but disinterestedly at Porter, who opened the notebook, read a few lines, and closed it again.

He put the folder on the desk and folded his hands across his stomach. "So, what's with the hooker, Harry?"

He'd been waiting for that. "What hooker's that, Porter?"

Porter's eyebrows knitted as he frowned. "The girl. Uh… Toni? She's a hooker."

"She's my roommate," Harry said.

Porter blinked. "You're living with a hooker?"

"I'm living with a woman," Harry said. "Millions of people do it."

Porter frowned. "You seem… angry, Harry."

"Do I?"

"Why you angry?" Porter asked.

"I'm not. Why would you think I'd be angry, Porter?" Harry asked.

"You tell me, pal."

"Nothing to tell, Porter. Can't imagine why I'd be angry if an asshole suddenly snuck up on me and beat my friend in front of me. And now you've dragged me down to the station at one in the morning to ask me questions you already know the answer to instead of me being home taking care of my friend." Harry sipped again. "Can't imagine why I'd be angry."

They stared at one another for a while. Porter sighed. "Couple days ago you got into an altercation with one John Leslie and his associate, Marvin Salano. Then you were spotted in a bar questioning one Darius 'Cheddar' Cheeseborough. These two pimps

175

control the female workforce for fifteen blocks around your apartment. Marvin Salano got a broken nose during your little chat. Cheeseborough claims you threatened him. And John Leslie claimed you bragged about having 'reduced his workforce'. Now, given that Mr. Leslie's a pimp, and one of the girls working for him was found dead, that looks a little suspicious. The fact that you're the connection between two pimps looks a little suspicious. The fact that you're… uh… consorting with one of Leslie's girls is a little suspicious. You don't live with a hooker, Harry. You either fuck a hooker or you run them."

There it was, Harry thought.

"So I'm going to ask you politely and informally, what the hell's going on?" Porter leaned forward and lowered his voice. "I asked you to ask around about the first girl. I thought I was talking to an ex-cop. A private investigator who's done some work for the force on occasion. I didn't think I was asking a fucking pimp-in-the-making who wanted to carve out an empire to scout the territory. Dead hooker? Beating on an enforcer? Threatening a second pimp? That's got all the earmarks of a territorial *move*, Harry. What the shit?"

Harry didn't say anything.

Porter threw up his hands. "You're forcing my hand, Harry."

"No one's forcing you to do anything, Porter. You're in control of yourself. So you need to be a man and fucking do what you know is right, asshole," Harry snarled.

"There's no call for that," Porter said.

"There's *every* call for that. We've known each other for ten years, Porter, and you're talking to me like I'm a fucking scumball you pulled out of a lineup to sweat," Harry snarled. He sipped more coffee.

"Harry, come on. You do the math," Porter said.

"I can add, Porter. I also know when shit *doesn't* add up. If someone told me *you* were putting together a string of girls, I'd punch them in the mouth before laughing in their face. Dick." Harry stared evenly at Porter, who had the grace to look away.

"Okay, I take your point," he said. "But come on. You get kicked off the force for something that ain't your fault. You're living in an abandoned restaurant. You can't make shit for a living being a half-assed private eye. You're basically on the bottom rung, and you *never* talk to us. Is it so hard to believe? You're ex-cop. You know the routine. You know the streets. You know the codes, you know the drill. Who's better at getting around the rules than someone who *knows* all of them?"

Harry said, "It's a fair point. Unless you know me."

"I know. You think I didn't think about this shit before I came to you?" Porter asked.

"It's a fair point if the ex-cop in question *isn't* a friend of yours. We play poker every week, Porter. I've been to your *house*. I know your wife. We worked together. Played softball. Worked out in the gym. Got drunk together. You asshole."

Porter just stared evenly at Harry. Harry cocked his head. It was almost like Porter was trying to tell him something. Something he couldn't say out loud. Harry sighed. Aha.

"Well *fuck*," he said bitterly. "Fucking Captain Wells?"

Porter's half-smile said it all.

"You're covering your goddamned ass. He's leaning on you," Harry guessed. Porter said nothing, but his body language changed. Harry chuckled. "All right, all right. Let's get it over with. Permission to treat the witness as hostile, counselor."

"About damned time," Porter said.

It was Harry who looked away sheepishly. "Hit me, Porter."

"All right. Run it down for me again, Harry. But start at the part where you've been living with a woman for *two years* and didn't think to mention it to your friends?" Porter grinned. "You're a tight-lipped son of a bitch, man. And a hooker? You dog, you."

Harry shook his head impatiently. "It's not like that."

"Come on, it's exactly like that," Porter grinned. "You think I disapprove? Hell no, man. I'm glad you finally found a girl. I mean, it's been, what... ten years? Unless... you've always had women on the side and you never told anyone?"

Harry grinned. "Naah. But Toni, she's different. She's not just a girl."

"No, she's a hooker. I mean... does she... does she *know* stuff? Like, kinky stuff that your average woman doesn't know? Or won't do? Is that what it takes to get you-"

Harry's hand slammed down on the desk. Heads turned. Harry glared at Porter. "Watch your mouth, Porter. You're *not* talking about some bit of fluff I picked up for the night. First, it's not *like* that. And second, she's my *friend*. You have no fucking *idea* what you're talking about. Trust me on this. But Porter, if you talk about her disrespectfully again, I'm going to have to kick your ass all over the station."

Porter was silent for a long moment, and then said, "Again?"

He and Porter stared at one another for a long moment, and then both of them burst out laughing. Porter scrubbed his hands through his hair.

"All right, all right. Jesus, it's late. I'm sorry. You know? For what it's worth, I apologize. I'm sorry." Porter glanced at his notebook. "So, you met him for the first time in Dahli's. What was that about?"

"I told you, I walked in on him threatening Toni and two other of his girls. Even if it hadn't been Toni I would have had to get into it. He was pissed off about Bebe and thought the girls were talking to the cops."

"Which they weren't," Porter said.

"No. But Toni talked the other two into throwing me a tip," Harry said.

"Cheddar?"

"The name of one of his girls, actually. Katy. From her and the other girl on the corner I got Cheddar's name and hangout. So I went to chat with him. You said he told you I threatened him?" Harry asked.

"Yes and no. He was a little vague as to the threat. Said you harassed him in public. You know, a bunch of random noise. But… it got back to Wells. After that and the thing with Jay in Dahli's, the word came down from on high. Wells never liked you much anyhow, and you *know* how he feels about bent cops. Even one who retired a hero."

"Hero's a little strong," Harry said. "I got shot by a punk in an alley."

"You saved the hostage at the cost of your career. Almost your *life*. You're a grade-A, gen-you-wine heeero, boy!" Porter thickened his speech and did a passable imitation of Captain Wells. Harry chortled.

"He ever hears you doing that, you're going to end up on pooper-scooper duty in the mounted stables," Harry said.

Porter nodded. "Probably."

"We done?" Harry asked.

"Not even close. So the first time you met Jay was the store, and the second time was at the hospital?"

"No," Harry said. "He didn't know I was there. Toni asked me not to interfere. She was... she was worried if I leaned on him, he'd come down harder on her, or maybe the other girls. So I wasn't in the room when he threatened her. But... there were three other women in the room. You question them, all three'll probably tell you about it."

"Okay, I'll follow up on it. Now, the second time is outside your place?" Porter checked his notebook.

"Yeah. He came to the hospital to scare Toni, get her back on the street. That's why we checked out," Harry told him.

"She was gonna go back to work?" Porter asked.

Harry shrugged. "She kept asking me to stay out of it, but I don't know what she was going to do. I got her home, we talked for a bit, and decided to go get some food. We went to Katz's-"

"Good choice," Porter said.

"-thanks. We went to Katz's, and when we got back Jay and his little buddy were waiting. He said he was looking for me, but since Toni was there, he went for the convenient target."

"He roughs up the girl, you get pissed and try to stop him. Jay's flunky pulls the gun, you shoot him. He goes down. Jay goes for the gun, you shoot him, *he* goes down. That about right?" Porter asked.

"That's what happened," Harry said.

"You warn Marvin before you shot him?" Porter asked.

Harry's eyes went hard. "Nope."

"Good," Porter said.

"Yep," Harry said.

"Your girl going to be okay?" Porter asked.

"Well, she's gonna need a new job," Harry said. "I killed her boss. But she was looking to change careers anyhow."

Porter snickered. He sobered. "Okay, so, let me ask you this-"

"No," Harry said. "I don't believe Jay was the killer."

"You sure? I like him for it. A lot. It *fits*."

"It wasn't Jay, Porter."

"Come on, man," Porter said. "It ties up in a neat bow, Jay being the doer. My paperwork is clean, you're off the hook, everyone wins."

"Except that it wasn't Jay. Or Marvin. What happens when another body drops? I don't think it was Cheddar, but I haven't spoken to him since this morning. I know you had to interview him. What'd he say about his girl turning up in the alley?"

Porter hesitated. "Uh, Harry…"

"What?"

"I can't really talk about it anymore. After you putting away his competition, you're involved in this mess. You're not on the outside anymore. You know what Captain Wells'll say if I feed you information."

Harry raised an eyebrow.

"Don't give me that shit, Harry. Subject change."

"Yeah, because we have so much else to talk about," Harry said.

"We do, actually. You're coming to the game tomorrow night, right?"

Harry blinked. "Uh…"

"You should. We can kick back and shoot the shit, just like usual," Porter said.

Harry nodded. "Gotcha. I'll definitely be there."

"Good. Grab a top-shelf bottle this time. And we're done here. Get the hell out, don't leave town, blah blah blah…"

"Yeah, I know the drill. Get a uni to drive me home, would you?" Harry asked.

"Private citizen DeMarko, you can get a cab," Porter said.

Harry put his feet up on Porter's desk. He sipped his coffee.

Porter snorted. He yelled, "Hey, Carnaheim, run my suspect back to his shithole apartment, would you?"

The uniformed man by the door looked up and smiled. "Sure thing, Porter. You want me to lump him up a bit, as a warning?"

Harry laughed. "Joe, you better bring two or three more guys. And it doesn't matter. I'll tell your wife you were mean to me. How *is* Mary, anyhow?"

"Oh, she's good, Carnaheim said, getting his keys. "Pregnant again."

"Jesus, man," Harry said. "Again? What is this, four?"

"Five," Carnaheim said with a grin. "You been gone a while. How's the arm?"

Harry raised his left arm and flipped off Carnaheim. They both laughed. "At least you got the critical functions," Joe said.

"True. Come on," Harry said. "I'm beat."

"All right. Let's go."

Harry got up and finished his coffee. "Porter... I think something crawled into the coffee pot and died."

Porter nodded. "Yeah. We keep meaning to empty it out and check, but... Harry? What if it's not dead?"

Harry laughed. He dropped the empty cup in the wastebasket, clapped Porter on the shoulder, and headed out.

Chapter Eighteen

Toni was waiting in his office when he finally stepped through the door. She came off the couch and hugged him. He almost pushed her away before the day caught back up to him. He smiled against her neck.

"Hey," Toni said. "I ate your sandwich."

He laughed. "Serves me right for being late."

"How'd it go?"

Harry shrugged. "It was an interrogation. Nothing major. I told 'em the truth. It worked. So, thank you for that."

"You should start listening to me," Toni said. "You'd be right a lot more than you are."

He nodded. "That's probably true."

"See? You're smarter already," she said.

He grinned wanly. "Jury's out. How are you?"

She gave him a goofy grin. "I'm on all those drugs they gave me. Right now nothing hurts, which is a wonderful thing."

"I bet."

"I'm pretty tired," Toni said. "You want to go to bed with me?"

Harry eyed her. "Uh-"

"Just to sleep. There's plenty of time to talk about it later," Toni said.

Harry regarded her thoughtfully.

"What?" she asked.

"You've been trying to get me to have sex with you for years, and I've been fighting you. And now that all that is worked out, you're telling me it's okay to wait?" Harry asked.

Toni smiled shyly at him. "Honey, are you under the impression that all our problems are magically solved? But I do feel better about it than I did. So… yeah. I guess that's what I'm saying. Plus… a girl likes a little romance, you know?"

Harry laughed. "You are *so* with the wrong guy, Toni."

She put her hands on her hips and frowned at him. "Okay, rule one: you don't get to be like that. You've treated me like a queen since the first day I showed up here. You've never pushed, you've always been a gentleman, and you have really noble intentions. Don't tell *me* you aren't romantic. You're a friggin' knight in shining armor."

Harry opened his mouth to say something, but she stopped him with a held-up finger on his lips. "Not to mention the fact that you just shot and killed a guy who was beating me up," Toni said. "Come on. You literally came to my rescue."

"Huh," Harry said. "I didn't even think about that."

"I know. You're not the kind of guy who does. But I'll tell you a secret," Toni said, putting her arms around him, "it scored you major points."

He kissed her. She was so startled she almost forgot to kiss back. She closed her eyes and leaned into him. He did a very thorough and good job. They parted and stared at one another.

"…wow," Toni said.

"Yeah," Harry said. He seemed as stunned as she.

They just grinned at each other for a minute. She said, "I didn't take Jasper any coffee."

"Oh," Harry said. "I didn't see him out there. Sometimes he goes to the shelter when it's really cold."

"Okay. Uh, you got a call from someone named Shelley."

Harry nodded. "I've been waiting for her call. What's she say?"

"She gave me an address to write down. It's on the desk."

Harry blinked. "You answered the phone?"

Toni looked up at him curiously. "Should I not?"

"No… just… why would you- oh. From what Porter said."

"Yeah. I turned on the ringer and it rang. I figured it was him, but it wasn't."

"Okay, good," Harry said. "I'll check it out tomorrow."

He started to go into the apartment, but Toni stopped him. "Uh, Harry?" Toni's said in a quiet voice.

"What?"

"He knows who I am," she said.

"Who?" Harry asked.

"That cop. Porter. Your friend."

Harry stared at her uncomprehendingly. "How does he know… he didn't- he never- I've never said-"

He broke off. She stared at the floor. "He's… you and he-"

"Yeah. Didn't know he was your friend. Didn't even know he was a *cop*," she said softly. "I'm sorry, Harry."

Harry stared at her stolidly for a second. She looked genuinely sorry, and he tried to figure out what that meant. Nothing bad, from what he could

186

see. So, don't get mad, he thought to himself. *Don't be a dick. Don't fucking blow this, asshole. You* know *what she does. Did,* he corrected. *And that's going to have consequences for a long time. But hey… you're not exactly a shining beacon of honor and character.* He took a deep breath.

"It's okay, Toni," he said.

She looked up, afraid to believe him. "Really?"

"Yeah. You didn't know. Couldn't know. And it's not a big deal," he lied. His gut rolled and he felt sick, but he tried hard not to show it. "It's over, right? New beginning."

She smiled at him gratefully. "Thank you, Harry."

"Nothing to thank me for," he said. He went to her and pushed her hair out of her eyes. "It's just a thing. I mean, it's not a little thing, but it's just one thing. Don't sweat it. I know this isn't going to be all cake and roses, but today's not as bad as yesterday. I'm okay. We're okay. Promise."

She smiled up at him, and he grinned.

"That's better. I like your smile, kiddo."

She smiled more widely. She took his hand. "Come on."

They went into the apartment. The round Formica table was covered with a sheet and had a pair of guttering candles on it. Their sandwiches sat on clean plates. He looked at Toni.

"You lied to me," he said with a smile.

She said, "Oh, I prefer to think of it as a… okay, yeah. I lied. But come on. Anyone who would eat someone else's Katz's Reuben deserves a fate worse than death."

Harry nodded. "I'd actually been planning on covering you in shaving cream tonight while you slept."

Toni laughed. "Sit down, devious man. You want a drink? I stumped over to Brandt's and got a bottle of Glenfiddich."

Harry's eyebrows climbed. "I'll grab it."

"Sit," she ordered. She pulled open the walk-in door. The bottle turned frosty as it came into the warmer air of the apartment. She pulled the cork.

He smiled at the familiar label. "Twelve-year-old? Damn, Toni."

"It felt like a celebration type of night," she said. She poured two fingers into each glass and sat across from him.

He raised the glass and she did the same. "So... us?"

"Sure," she said. "To us."

They touched glasses and drank. Toni made a face. "Gluh. The ones that taste like dirt. Why are they your favorite?"

"I told you: that's peat, and it's delicious," Harry said.

"It's like licking a campfire," she said.

"You never turn any of it down," Harry said.

"Because after two swallows, I don't care if I'm licking a campfire," she said. He laughed.

They tucked into the sandwiches. Cold, hours old, and still amazing. They ate in companionable silence. After the sandwiches were done and they had both used the bathroom he helped Toni get into bed. He turned out the lights and went to his couch.

"What in the name of all that's holy are you *doing*, you idiot?" Toni said.

Harry stopped in his tracks. "Uh…"

"Get *over* here," she said, "right fucking *now*."

He went to the bed. "I-I didn't want to… to assume…"

"Get in the bed, idiot," Toni said. Harry sighed.

"Are you just going to keep calling me an idiot all the time?" he asked.

"Only when you're an idiot, idiot," she said.

He couldn't help laughing. "All right. Fair enough."

He slipped into the bed beside her. She snuggled back against him and he held her close. They lay in the darkness together for a time. Harry said, "Toni?"

"Yes, Harry?"

"Are you… uh…"

"Yes, Harry?" she asked.

"Will you be here when I wake up?" he asked. "I mean, you always-"

"I know what you mean," she said softly. "Harry, I'm not going anywhere."

He nodded against her neck, not trusting himself to speak. He squeezed her tightly, and she patted his arm. They lay together in the darkness and realized they were together.

Chapter Nineteen

Harry woke slowly, his head a little thick. He looked over at the clock. Eleven. Damn. He hadn't slept that late in a long time. He should get up and-

God damn it. She was gone *again*. He made a fist-

And chuckled to himself, calming down. If he were an idiot, he'd assume she was gone, but she'd really be in the-

Toni stepped out of the bathroom, toothbrush in her mouth. She stopped dead in the doorway, and even stopped brushing. They stared at one another for a moment, and both of them burst into laughter.

"You thought-" she said.

"Yeah, I did," he said.

"Idiot," they both said at the same time, and laughed a little more. She came back to the bed, sitting next to him. She took his hand.

"I told you I wouldn't leave," she said.

"I know, I know."

"Thought I lied?" she asked.

"No!" he said. He paused. "Yes."

She nodded. "I know."

"Yeah," he said. "I know you do. I just... you need to give me time. I just need time. You know?"

She nodded. "I know. I'm patient. I've put up with you all this time, Harry. Think I'm going to run off now? If I were going to give up on you, I'd have done it a long time ago."

He studied her face. "Why didn't you?"

"Because I'm not tired of your bullshit yet, I guess." She smiled sweetly and bent to kiss him. "It's still cute bullshit."

He grinned. "Yeah, yeah."

"So what's on your plate today?" she asked.

"I don't know… I guess I have to go track down that kid's apartment. And… do you know how to get in touch with Jay's other girls?" Harry asked.

Toni looked blank. "Oh, right. I forgot he's dead."

"Forgot? It happened last night."

"Well, kind of a lot has happened," she said. "Yeah, I know how to find them."

"I want to talk to them all," Harry said. "See if any of them know anything about Bebe or Katy, Cheddar's girl that got killed."

She nodded. "I'll find 'em."

"All right." Harry looked her up and down. Her face was bruised and battered, the new stitches EMS had put in were bloody-looking and raw. Her lip was swollen. She still had a haunted, pained look. She was achingly pretty, he thought. "You want to come with me?"

"What?" she looked startled.

"Come with me. Snoop on the boyfriend. Help chase down a murderer," Harry said.

"Why?" she asked. "I'm not-"

"You know the streets. You're smart. I could use someone watching my back anyhow," Harry said with a smile. "I tend to get beat up a lot if someone isn't looking out for me."

"That's true. You want a hooker watching your back?" she asked him.

"No," Harry said. "But… maybe a… partner?"

Her mouth dropped open.

"Come on," he said. "I'll buy you a cup of coffee and we'll talk about it."

He got up and got dressed. She watched with interest. He grabbed a dark shirt and a pair of jeans he scrounged out of the bottom of the wardrobe.

"I've never seen you wear a pair of jeans. I didn't even know you owned a pair," she said.

"Yeah… I never wore 'em," he said. He put them on and tucked in his shirt. "What do you think?"

"Pretty good," she said, and she meant it. He grabbed his clip-on holster and put it on his belt. He shoved the .38 in the clamshell and slid it behind his left hip. He put on his overcoat and held out a hand. He helped her up.

"You're gonna want to wear something warm. We're going to be outside all day."

She thought it over. "You're gonna have to help me. That bag over there."

He picked up her shopping bag and dumped it out on the bed.

"Hey!" she said. "What the hell?"

"You don't need a bag anymore," he said. He stirred the clothes. "Pick."

"Those jeans, and that shirt," she said. He separated her pick and carried the rest of the clothing over to the wardrobe and started to hang her stuff. She sat on the bed with her mouth hanging open. When he finished, he turned to her and her look stopped him.

"What?"

She shook her head. "Harry, Harry, Harry. You don't do anything by half-measures, do you? How long have you been thinking about all of this? All the

192

things you wanted to do with me? Or for me? You made room in your… closet… for me?"

Harry shrugged uncomfortably.

She smiled, eyes shining. "Come here, Harry. Give me a kiss."

He did. They took a goodly time, enjoying the taste of each other. When they broke, she whispered, "Help me take my clothes off."

Harry blinked several times. He looked like a fish trying to breathe air. She laughed merrily.

"Harry," she said, "My arm hurts like hell. And I can't get the thingy off my foot without your help. You want me to come with you, you have to help me change."

He hung his head and grinned ruefully. He didn't bother saying anything, he just knelt and started to remove the soft cast. She leaned back and crossed her legs, watching him. He carefully peeled the boot off her foot. It had swelled a little, and the marks from the straps were red and ridged. He rubbed her foot gently, and she sighed. He looked up in surprise. He didn't stop massaging her foot.

"You can do that any time you want," she whispered. She leaned all the way back on the bed. He rubbed the insoles of her feet while she closed her eyes and grinned.

He moved to the other foot, massaging more roughly and taking his time. He worked his way up her calf, pushing the sweat pants she had worn for pajamas up. She spread her legs a little for him and he almost tripped, despite not moving at all. He rubbed her calf slowly and firmly, and she scrubbed her hands over her face. He finished what he was doing and sat back on his heels. Without getting up, she raised her ass off the bed and pushed her sweatpants down. He slowly worked them off her legs, careful of her sprain. He picked up the jeans and worked them slowly onto her legs and pulled them as far up as he could. She took over as he reached her hips, arching her back off the bed and tugging the jeans all the way up. He slipped a pair of socks over her feet.

"Leave the cast off," she said. "My ankle's feeling pretty good."

He tossed it aside and stood up, helping her into an upright position using her good arm. He unbuttoned her shirt and took it off, and held out the clean blouse. She kept her eyes on his as she slowly worked her way into the shirt. She didn't wear a bra- almost never did. She wasn't large enough to warrant one, most of the time. He buttoned each button slowly until she was dressed again. She caught his hand and raised it to her lips.

"Just so you know," she said softly, "I'm all in favor if you taking your time. I could get used to this kind of attention."

He stood up. "Good. I kinda like doing things for you."

He got her sneakers and helped her put them on. Once she was ready, he helped her to her feet. She hobbled around the apartment experimentally, testing her ankle.

"Sore, but it's okay," she said.

"Good. We might be doing a lot of walking today. Do you need the sling?" he asked.

"No," she said, gingerly moving her arm. "It feels okay."

"You got *so* lucky, Toni," he said.

She beamed at him. "I know."

He frowned. "I meant the car."

"I know," she said again with that beaming smile still turned all the way on.

He sighed and shook his head. They went into the office and he set about making a fresh pot of coffee. He looked at the address scribbled on his electric bill. He knew the place. It wasn't three blocks from the Rice Bowl restaurant.

"We can take a cab over to his restaurant, see if he's there. I don't want to have to break into an apartment today unless I really have to," he said, pocketing the envelope.

"You're not ruling it out, though, right?" she asked.

"I never rule anything out," he said. "Sometimes I don't even intend to get in trouble."

She snorted. "I don't believe that. You were born to be in trouble, Harry. Look at you. Your whole life is about being in the middle of shit."

He rubbed the bridge of his nose and looked thoughtful. "You might be right."

"I keep telling you, I'm *always* right."

He chuckled but didn't say anything. He poured a fresh cup of coffee for each of them and a third for Jasper.

"Come on, Toni. Let's go see what we can see."

They handed the cup to Jasper on the way up to Bleecker where Harry flagged a cab. They rode over to the university district and got out. They went into the restaurant. Harry took a seat while Toni went to the register.

"Hey," she said to the bored-looking kid. "Is Mike here?"

The kid shook his head. "Mike's off today."

"Oh, okay," she said. "Thanks."

She went back to Harry, who nodded when she told him.

"All right, step two. We check out the guy's apartment."

"I feel all clandestine," Toni said. "Like… uh…"

"Sam Spade," Harry suggested. "Mike Hammer? Phillip Marlow?"

"Mannix," she said. "Or Jim Rockford."

Harry shook his head. "Come on, seriously?"

"What? I like Jim Rockford. He has sexy eyes," she said.

Harry sighed. "You want to eat here before we go?"

"God no," Toni said. "I hate Chinese."

"I didn't know that," Harry said, pulling himself to his feet. "You keep coming back to my place."

"Yeah. What does that tell you?"

"You're a glutton for punishment. Come on, Mannix, let's get going." Harry held the door for her, and she eyed him for a second. "What? No one ever held a door for you?"

She said quietly, "No, Harry. Just you."

He smiled. "Good."

They walked hand-in-hand for a while, until they were a block away from Zeist's apartment. Harry said, "Wait here."

"Why?"

"Because I'm armed and you're not. Because I'm the professional and you're not. Because I said so."

"Doesn't he know what you look like?" she asked.

"Yeah," Harry said.

"So… what if I go? He doesn't know me," she pointed out.

Harry thought about it. It made sense, actually. "All right. Zeist, third floor. Three oh eight."

"Three oh eight," she echoed.

"Maybe… you're looking for a friend. You ring the doorbell. Guy answers. Look confused. Ask him where… I don't know, pick a name. Ask him where she is. Any name except Cecilia, okay?"

"Harry, I'm not an idiot," she said.

"Sorry, you're right. See if you spot the girl. If not, look for anything that says 'girl'. Purse on the counter. Coat on a chair. Anything that isn't a man's signature. When he tells you you've got the wrong place, just nod. Walk away. Don't be suspicious. Got it?"

"Got it."

"I'll be on the landing, about twenty feet away. Anything happens, yell. I'll be there," he said.

"I'm not worried. Not anymore."

Harry looked at her. "Anymore?"

She smiled. "Since last night."

He licked his lips. "Uh, Toni…"

"Yes, Harry?"

"I can't just shoot *everyone* that tries to hurt you," he said. "It's not gonna work twice."

She laughed. "I know. But you could beat him up, right?"

"That I can do."

"My hero," she said, and kissed his cheek. "Ready?"

"Yeah." They walked up to the apartment door. Next to the door was a buzz-box, a list of apartment numbers and the intercom buttons. Toni reached for 308 and almost pressed it before Harry caught her wrist.

"You won't make it inside if you're looking for your friend who doesn't live there," he said.

"Right," she said, wincing. "What do we do?"

Harry didn't reply. Instead, he ran his hand down the rows of buttons, pressing them all except for 308.

They waited for a second, and three or four voices burst from the box at once, asking questions. The garbled voices didn't matter, though. Someone on the list was waiting for someone, and buzzed the door open. Harry smiled at Toni. She rolled her eyes.

"Tricks of the trade?" she asked.

"Always," he said with a self-satisfied grin. "Pay attention, kiddo, you'll learn something."

She rolled her eyes and went into the apartment building. Harry followed her in. They trudged slowly up the stairs to the third floor. By the time they got to the top, Toni was gray-faced and sweating.

"My foot..." she said.

He nodded. "Take a minute."

"I'm okay. It just... it hurts."

"Stairs are different than walking on the street. You're using your ankle a lot more." He led her to the stairs up and made her sit. He knelt at her feet and rubbed her ankle gently.

"You're really good to me, Harry," she said, caressing his cheek. He looked up at her, surprised.

"You deserve it," he said. "And anyone who ever made you think otherwise deserves-"

"To be gunned down in the snow by my guardian angel?" she said impishly.

"Look, Toni..." Harry said. "I... I don't regret killing Jay. I don't think I'll lose any sleep over it. But be very clear about this, honey- I wouldn't have done it if there had been any other choice. If he hadn't punched and kicked you, I wouldn't have killed him. I'd have thrashed him within an inch of his life, but he would have lived. But Marvin had a gun and Jay was beating you. But I'm not a guardian angel, Toni. I just have a short fuse."

"You're my hero," she said. "I don't really care about Jay. Harry… you've… you've been my hero for a long time. Since the alley."

He looked up at her.

"Yeah, Harry. I said it. Come on. You're not stupid. You *have* to know I've been hung up on you. You're stuck on me. That's why you let me live in your house. Sleep in your bed. Trample all over your life. It's why you put up with me even though I was a pain in the ass, a horrible houseguest… a hooker. I knew how you felt about me hooking for a living. You were pretty straightforward about it. But you never kicked me out. Instead, you were nice to me. You think I don't know why?" Toni said. Her face was serious and her eyes were bigger than he could ever recall them looking. "I *know* why. I do. You may think I'm stupid-"

"I don't-"

"Stop. This isn't your time to talk. I'm speaking," she said. "You may think I'm stupid, but I'm smart enough to put simple clues together. No one came to see you in the hospital. No one was there to drive you home. No one was there when the cab dropped you off. You were alone, Harry. Where were your friends? Where was your wife? Girlfriend? Fucking casual acquaintances? Nothing. I was there. I was watching when the cab dropped you off. I was watching when you dropped your key and almost passed out trying to pick it up."

Toni reached out put her hands on his cheeks.

"I was there. And I helped you. And you've been helping *me* ever since. I don't believe it's random. You don't talk about it. You don't like to think about it. But you also wouldn't get rid of me, even though you had no reason to let me stay. And it all started in that stupid alley. So you've always been my hero, Harry, but you don't have to make grand gestures. You didn't have to shoot my pimp. You don't have to save me from everything. All you have to do is what you've always done. Just be yourself. That's what I want. Okay?" she said with a smile. "That's all I want."

Harry didn't say anything. He couldn't think of anything *to* say.

"So let's do this, okay?" she said.

He nodded and helped her up. She tested her foot with her weight. "It's better."

"Good. Look, Toni-"

"Harry, don't bother. Think about it. If it's still important later, tell me. When we're home and warm and sleepy and curled up in bed. If it's important, tell me then. Okay?" Toni said.

Harry sighed, but a smile crossed his features. "Okay. Let's go."

She took a deep breath. "Toni Bennett, undercover detective. I-"

She stopped and looked at him with wide eyes.

"What?" he asked.

"Holy shit, Harry. I'm James Bond."

Harry snorted. "You're too short to be Bond. You're Moneypenny. I'm Bond, if anyone here's Bond."

She looked outraged. "Moneypenny!? You're not… you can't-"

"Letsh go, Moneypenny," Harry said in a passable Scottish accent. "The villain awaitsh."

She burst out laughing. "Oh, God. What am I going to do with you?"

"I have a list," Harry said absently. "Now let's go."

She grabbed his arm and tugged on it. "No, let's talk about your list. I'm interested in your list."

"No, brat. Later. Now get with it. The fate of the world depends on you," Harry said.

Toni cocked an eyebrow.

"Okay, so just my paycheck. Still, though."

Toni nodded. "All right. But this list conversation isn't over."

She squared her shoulders and opened the stairwell door. Harry kept it open with his foot while she went down the hall to 308. She flashed Harry a look, and then knocked.

It took twice before Mike Zeist opened his door. The big smile on Toni's face faltered as he said. "Yeah?"

"Uh, is Jessica home?" Toni asked in a bubbly voice.

"Who?"

"Jessica. She lives here," Toni said. She reached up and toyed with her hair. Mike looked her up and down.

"No Jessica here," he said brusquely.

"No, she's here," Toni said with a bright smile. "I wrote the address down right and everything. Don't play."

Mike smiled in spite of himself. "I'm telling you, ain't no Jessica here. Sorry."

"Come on," Toni said in that bubbly voice. "Don't joke with me. It's mean!"

"I'm not being mean. Whoever you're looking for isn't here," Mike said.

"Oh… when will she be back? I could… uh… I could wait. If you want some company, that is," Toni said in a musical tone of voice. Harry blinked. The girl was a genius.

"Uh," Mike stammered.

"What's your name?" Toni asked.

"Uh, Mike, but-"

"Mike… are you and Jessica an… item? Hmm?" Toni stepped a little closer and smiled shyly up at the young man. She bit her lower lip.

"Uh… no. Like I said-"

"Mmm. That's good to know. Are you *sure* you don't want me to come in and wait for Jessica? We could… get to know each other a little better," she said, and put a hand on his bicep, making an appreciative sound. Harry grinned. He was twenty years older than Mike and far more experienced, but if it had been him, he would have gone all tongue-tied as well. Toni was a woman, and she was very good at it.

"Uh, jeez, I wish I could, but… I kind of have a girlfriend."

"Kind of, Mike? That doesn't sound very solid to *me*," Toni purred. "And honestly, I don't care all *that* much."

Harry could practically hear Mike begin to drool. Toni had begin slowly dragging her fingernails up and down the bare expanse of skin on Mike's arm, idly toying with the fluffed hair from his gooseflesh. Mike cleared his throat a couple of times.

"Uh, look…" Mike spread his hands in the air.

"Oh. I'm Toni," she said in a sultry purr.

"Okay, look, Toni," Mike began.

"I like the way you say my name," she whispered.

Mike cleared his throat again. He spoke so softly Harry could barely hear him. "Uh… okay… look, I'm not- I can't… my girl? She's *here*. She's in the back room. Like, right now. So…"

He trailed off and Toni winked at him. "I gotcha, stud. Do you have a pen?"

Mike went inside for a second, and came back out with a pen. She took his hand and wrote some digits on his palm. "Well, if you ever get a free night, call me, okay?"

She handed the pen back and stretched up to give him a kiss on the cheek. "*Use* it, Mike. Bye-bye."

She walked away with an extra swing to her hips, knowing he'd be watching. Mike did watch her sashay away. She pushed open the door of the stairwell and let it swing shut after a lingering glance backward at Mike. Harry was out of sight around the doorframe. She smirked at him.

"She's there," Toni said. "And *he's* a dog."

"He's a dog because a beautiful woman turns his head?" Harry asked.

"Okay," she said, "you get a pass for that one, Mr. Smooth."

Harry ducked his head in acknowledgement. "She's there?"

"Someone's there. His girlfriend. Unless he found a new one while his old one was being kidnapped…"

"…he's in on it," Harry said.

"Do we call the police?" Toni asked.

Harry snorted. "What, and have the client weasel out of the fee?"

Her face went blank. "Oh, right."

"Rule one, Toni," Harry said. "The clients hate to pay."

"Can't you make them pay you up front? That's what *I* did."

Harry chuckled. "Sure, but yours was a high-demand product with a proven outcome. The snoop business is less sure, and takes a lot longer to show results."

Toni pursed her lips. "Hooking is easier," she said judiciously.

"For you, maybe," Harry said. "No one's gonna be paying me."

Toni looked him up and down. "I've got twenty dollars, Mister," she said.

Harry grinned at her. "I'm glad you value me so highly."

"Oh, I do. I might even go as high as thirty-two fifty," she said. "But I'd have to draw the line there, at least until I find out what you're actually worth through direct experience."

He laughed. "That's fair," he said.

"Okay, so… no cops," she said. "What do we do?"

"Well, I go knock on the door and demand to see her," Harry said.

"Can I come?"

"No," Harry said. "If I can't get a look at her, we might need you and your way in to help out later. Let's not blow your cover just yet."

"Okay."

Harry took a breath. "Okay, lemme go do this."

He walked down to the door and knocked. A second later, Mike answered. "I told you, I don't-"

"Hi, Mike," Harry said. "Do you remember me?"

Mike just stared.

"I'm here to see Cecilia."

Mike rubbed the back of his hands over his lips. "Uh, I, uh told you, man, I ain't seen her-"

"Here's how this goes, Mike," Harry said. "You let me in and I look around. If she's here, I ask her one question. If she answers yes, I'm not going to shoot you. If she says no, I'll shoot you. If you *don't* let me in, I call the police and tell them I know where her kidnapper lives. They come in here with guns ready and maybe they shoot you. So, you gonna step aside?"

Mike stared open-mouthed.

"Thought so." Harry tried to brush past him. Mike stopped him.

"What question are you going to ask her?" he asked Harry.

Harry stared levelly up at the kid. "I'm going to ask her if she's here of her own free will. She answers yes, you don't get shot. She answers no, I'm gonna put two through you."

Harry reached back and pulled his gun out of the holster.

Mike stared at him open-mouthed.

"Move," Harry said brusquely. Mike jerked back as if on a string.

Harry walked into the apartment slowly. It wasn't very big, just one living room slash dining room. A kitchen lay off to the right. "Where?"

Mike, all fight and attitude drained, pointed toward the bedroom. Harry motioned with the gun. "You first."

Mike led him to the bedroom. He opened the door. Cecilia looked up in confusion that turned to anger.

"What the hell are you doing, Mike?" she demanded. Harry pushed the boy into the room with the barrel of his gun. When she saw the weapon, Cecilia froze.

"Miss Blankenship, I presume," Harry said.

"Uh-"

"Tell me your story," Harry said.

"What-"

"Your mother hired me," Harry said, "to find you. Claimed you'd been missing, possibly kidnapped."

"That *bitch*," Cecilia said.

Harry eyed Mike. "I told Mike here I was going to ask you a question, and the answer would determine whether or not I would shoot him."

Cecilia Blankenship's eyes popped.

"Are you here because you ran away, or did he grab you?" Harry asked.

"I'm never going back to that bitch! I hate her!" Cecilia snapped. Harry put his gun away. He clapped Mike on the shoulder.

"If it makes you feel any better, Mike, I knew the answer. I wouldn't have shot you. Not anywhere vital, anyhow."

Mike looked sick. "Uh, great."

"Yeah. By the way, the girl works for me," Harry said.

Mike closed his eyes. "Figures. I don't get that lucky."

Cecilia eyed Mike. "What girl?"

"Just a red herring I threw at your boy here to see if you were home. Don't sweat it. He was a perfect gentleman," Harry said. Mike's grateful eyes almost made Harry laugh out loud.

"Look, your mom's paying me to find you. Okay, I found you. So, you going to go back peacefully, or what?" Harry asked.

"I just told you, I'm not going back! I can't stand my mother anymore! She's not interested in me, she just wants someone to show off at her friggin' parties! She doesn't care about me! She doesn't think Mike's good enough because he's black. She doesn't like my classes because I don't want to *be* a lawyer! She doesn't want me to do anything *I* want to do unless it fits into her image!" Cecilia shouted. "I can't stand her anymore! I won't!"

Harry nodded. "Okay… none of that is my problem. But you need to face up to your shit, young lady."

"You're not my father!" she yelled.

"Nope, I'm not, so you know I don't give a crap about your good opinion, or whether you love me, or making peace with you. I'm just going to tell you how it is. And how it is, is it's a bitch to vanish successfully. You can't just go out and pick up a new ID and social security number at the corner drug store. Have you ever been arrested?"

Cecilia looked guilty. "Uh-"

"If you have, they have your fingerprints on file. You're in the system. That makes it worse. I'm not saying you can't make a go of it, but it's going to be hard. You'll have to work jobs under the table. I'm talking cheap, cash-as-you-go jobs. Waitressing, maybe dancing in a topless joint. You never know. But no good jobs are going to take you without the minimum of identification for taxes. You can't get an apartment without ID. A car. A library card. Utilities. I get that you're sick of someone else trying to run your life. Doing it this way, though… you think your mother won't have every cop in the city looking for your boyfriend here? Only they won't be friendly, like me. She'll tell them some bullshit story about how you were kidnapped, or taken, or drugged, or coerced. And what happens to Mike?"

"Uh," Mike began.

"You get caught, Mike goes to jail, and no one listens to you because your mother is who she is. Sound familiar?"

Cecilia looked down.

"However, it doesn't have to be that way. Your schooling, your pocket money… mommy pays for everything, doesn't she?"

"What do you care, cop?" Cecilia sneered.

"Not a cop," Harry said. "And I don't care, not really. But if you want to *really* piss your mother off… why not let her pay for all this shit that she hates? It's going to irk her more that you're living off her dollar doing shit she doesn't want you to… or doing *people* she doesn't want you to."

Harry patted Mike on the back.

"So, keep it up. Let her pay for college. Let her pay for your car. Take her shit and smile, and keep cashing the checks. And when you graduate, get a good job, and you can live the way you want without her cash, tell her to go piss up a rope and slide down the dry side."

Mike and Cecilia laughed together.

"It won't be easy, but if you have the fortitude to bolt and live like a homeless runaway, you surely have the guts to take her shit and smile, right?"

Cecilia nodded reluctantly.

"If she's going to stake you at life, let her," Harry suggested. "And fuck her over later, if it still matters. But you're never going to have a better opportunity to get your life paid for."

Cecilia looked thoughtful. "I guess you're right."

"Yeah, probably," Harry said. "It's a myth that I'm always wrong."

"So… do I just go home, or what?" Cecilia said. "Or… just got back to school?"

Harry said, "I don't know. Why don't you let me take you back to your mother's house?"

Cecilia frowned. "Why are you being so helpful?"

"I'm being paid to be helpful," Harry said.

A knock at the door startled them all. Mike went to answer the door. Harry and Cecilia looked at each other.

"Okay," Cecilia said. "Fine. I'll go deal with my mother. Be a good little girl."

She crossed her arms and stuck out her lower lip. Harry silently wondered what he'd done to deserve this life.

"Hello," said a familiar voice from the next room. "Did you kill my partner? Or did *he* kill someone? I'm just curious."

Harry covered his eyes. "Oh hell."

He and Cecilia went into the other room and both were amused to see Toni standing in the doorway, staring grimly at Mike. When Harry came into view, Toni smiled.

"Oh, yay. You're not dead. Thank you for the heads-up. And you found the girl. Good for you." Toni leaned against the doorframe. "I was bored in the stairwell."

"Well, we're done here. Come on, Cecilia. Let's grab a cab and head over to your mom's place."

Cecilia grabbed her coat. "Come on, Mike."

Harry stopped him. "Look… you want to be taken seriously? Running away to shack up with your boyfriend isn't the way. Tell her you were… uh…"

Toni broke in. "Tell her you went to Atlantic City for a couple of days, just *you*, to see what kind of trouble you could get into."

Harry looked at Toni, impressed. "That's not bad."

"What do I say when she wants to know why?" Cecilia asked.

"She'll probably buy you ditching classes to go gamble for a week or so. We'll tell her I found you at the train station as you got back. Lucky coincidence," Harry said. "And we don't have to mention Mike here at all."

"It's… it's not bad." Cecilia said, a little ungratefully. "Okay."

"All right. Better late than never. Let's go right now. Mike, you stay here. I have no doubt Cecilia will be back soon, right?" Harry asked.

Cecilia nodded. "He's right, Mike. She'd screw you in a heartbeat. This way, at least I get money. I can finish my degree. Then we're gone!"

"Let me use your phone," Harry said. He called Blankenship. "Mrs. Blankenship, it's Harry DeMarko."

"Yes, Mr. DeMarko?"

"I wanted to let you know that I found your daughter," Harry said. He had a smile on his face and sounded happy.

"Oh?"

Harry stared at the receiver. "You don't seem terribly surprised," he said.

"Where did you find her?" Blankenship asked.

"I found her at Grand Central, just coming back into town. She went on a mini vacation, apparently," Harry said.

"She didn't mention a trip," Blankenship said.

"Neither here nor there," Harry said. "I can bring her by."

"Very well," Blankenship said. She gave Harry the address. It wasn't exactly mid-town, but it was close.

"We'll be there in half an hour, maybe more," Harry said.

Blankenship hung up. Harry stared at the phone for a moment and gently replaced the handset. "Your mother's kind of a bitch," he said.

Cecilia grinned. "Just figuring that out?"

"Let's just say my theory has been confirmed by some new data," he replied. "Let's get it over with."

Harry reflected that Mike wouldn't last much longer. This girl was overly fond of huge, dramatic scenes. Mike seemed like a pretty simple man. Sooner or later, he'll have had enough.

They went down to the street and Toni flagged a cab. Mike walked them down and he and Cecelia kissed several times. Toni took Harry's arm and smiled at them.

"I'll be back soon," Cecilia said.

"Hope so," Mike said.

They got in the cab and rode downtown to Cecilia's mother's apartment. Harry gave the driver the money and they went to the door. The doorman waved them inside.

They rode the elevator to the twenty-second floor and Cecilia walked them to her door. Cecilia used her key and they walked in. Mrs. Blankenship glared at her daughter. Cecilia smiled. "Hi, Mom. I heard you were looking for me."

"Young lady, I'm in no mood for your attitude," Mrs. Blankenship said. Harry raised a hand.

"You two have a lot to discuss, I'm sure. If you could just give me my fee-"

Blankenship glared at Harry. "I don't see that you've earned anything, Mr. DeMarko. My daughter would have come home on her own. Why should I pay you?"

"Why shouldn't you?" Harry countered. "You hired me and my associate to find your daughter, assuming she's been kidnapped or something. We found her. Where she was didn't matter. You didn't specify that I should only find her if she were in grave peril. She was missing, we found her. Case closed, and you're the lucky recipient of the news that nothing untoward happened to your daughter. Parents all over would kill for that kind of news. I did my job. Pay me."

Blankenship looked sour. "What do I owe you?"

"Three days, fifty bucks, two cab rides, a couple of hours work downtown... call it two hundred even," Harry said.

She eyed him for a long moment, the withering stare of a woman used to backing down the help. Harry smiled at her and refused to look away. Finally, the woman took a checkbook out of her desk the size of an accounting ledger and scribbled a check. She handed it to Harry who folded it without looking at it and put it in his pocket. He took a card out.

"If you ever need my services again, you get preferential treatment as a repeat customer. Please feel free to spread my name to any friends you might have with needs I can fill. Thank you very much, and have a pleasant day. Ms. Bennett, let's go." He turned on his heel and headed to the door. Toni followed him. They left with Cecilia and her mother glaring at one another like weasels, and Harry smiled, imagining the fight that was about to ensue. In the elevator, Toni said, "Well. That was fun."

"Eh. Everything I said was true. She's lucky. I knocked on doors for years looking for clues to a million kids who won't ever come home," he said.

"Huh." Toni seemed pensive.

"What's wrong?" he asked.

"Oh, nothing. Associate?"

"Well," Harry said. "You're my partner, right? That makes you an associate."

She smiled. "Do I get a gun?"

They left the elevator and hit the street. Harry flagged for a cab. "Are you kidding?"

"Nope," she said.

"Okay… have you ever even *held* a gun?"

"No," Toni said. "Seen a bunch, never held one."

"Okay, well, we'd have to find you a gun, and I'd have to take you to the range. You don't get to carry a gun until I'm *sure* you're not going to shoot me, or yourself. In that order. But before that… uh… Toni, are you a convicted felon?"

She shook her head. "Nope. I have a minor record, though. Soliciting, loitering. Penny-ante stuff. Why?"

Harry nodded. "As long as you're not a felon, you can get a permit. No point in going any further if you'd had a record."

"Come on… you wouldn't let me have a gun? I'm sure you could get one. Hell, *I* could get one this afternoon," she said.

"Not on your life," he said. "There's rules. We follow them. And if you want to really be my partner, we're going to have to get you licensed eventually. You can work for me and you'll fall under my license, because it's my business. And to get yours you'll have to work for me for three years. Then we can apply and you can be licensed."

A cab screeched to a halt and they climbed in. "Houston and Elizabeth."

"Sure thing, pal," the cabbie grunted.

"Ooh, do I get a badge?" she asked.

"You get an ID. It'll get you somewhere with civilians, less so with cops. It helps, though," Harry said. "Have to get you fingerprinted. A couple other things."

Toni studied him for a moment. "You're kind of… you're a professional, aren't you?" Toni asked.

"I may look like a bum and live in a decrepit building, but yes, I'm a professional. I renew my license soon. Every two years. It's not bad. I've done a few skip traces, too. There's a couple-"

"Skip traces?"

"Uh, people who get bailed and then run. Bounty hunting, really, but I'm licensed to do that. You usually get ten percent of the bond if you bring them back," Harry said. "I don't like it. Most criminals, when they jump bail, head for the hills. I don't like leaving the city."

Toni nodded. "There's a lot to this."

"There is. Of course, you don't *have* to be an investigator. I could use a secretary. I know you know how to make decent coffee-"

She hit him.

"Ow. So, not a secretary. Got it," Harry said, smiling.

"No, I'm not your secretary."

"Too bad. I could use another good looking girl around the office."

She snorted. "You're a pig."

He shrugged. "Maybe."

She smiled at him. "I'm a good-looking girl?"

Harry looked out the window. "You're gorgeous," he said quietly.

She smiled happily and put a hand on his leg. "Okay, forget the pig thing. You're a sweetie."

Harry chuckled. He remembered something. "Hey, I'm going to be out tonight. I have-"

He broke off and turned to her, a thoughtful expression on his face.

"What?" she asked.

"Do you play poker?" he asked.

"Uh… not for a while. Why?"

"Tonight's poker night. But… Porter's one of the players. Does that bother you?" he asked.

She considered it. "No… but it doesn't bother *you*?"

Harry looked at her. "No, it doesn't. Not if you're walking in on my arm and walking out the same way," he said.

She smiled so hard her dimples showed. "Keep it up, mister," she said, "and you won't be able to make that game."

He grinned. "Come on. I want you to meet my friends."

She stared at him in shock.

"What?" he asked.

"Nothing... just... you really don't hesitate when you make up your mind on something, do you?" Toni asked.

The cabbie turned onto Elizabeth. "Just up that way, on the right," Harry said.

The cab stopped at the corner and they got out. Harry gave him a five. "Keep it."

"You got it. Have a good one."

He waited by the door until Toni started to wonder what he was doing. He looked at the door and back at her. She caught her breath and realized what he was doing. She fished her key out and unlocked the door. It was silly and it was childish, maybe, but she flushed warm and couldn't stop grinning.

After giving Jasper a cup of coffee, he sat at the desk. "Go get a chair," he ordered in a businesslike tone. She blinked, and then did as he told her.

"Okay, this drawer's open cases," he said, and pulled out the single folder currently inside. He opened it. A piece of paper with a few handwritten notes lay inside. He jotted the outcome of the case and the fee.

"They go over here when you're done, alphabetically by client's last name." He opened a second drawer. It was full of folders. She stared.

"Harry..." Toni said. "How many cases have you solved?"

"Well, some of them aren't mysteries, really, so much as snoop jobs, the occasional bounty. There's a missing dog in there. But that's what I've been doing for the last couple of years," he said.

"Wow."

He shrugged and filed the folder.

"You... you don't have a folder for the murders?" Toni asked.

Harry shook his head. "It's not a case. I'm not getting paid. I started out just looking around for Porter because he figured the street girls would talk to me a little more readily than they would the cops. So, no folder. But I remember everything I need to. I told Porter I'd keep digging, and I will. So, next up: can you get in touch with your friends? Porter's still got two open murders. I said I'd try and help."

"Okay... let me think a minute." She ruminated. "Hand me the phone?"

He pushed the rotary handset within her reach and she tried a number. No dice. Second number. Same. A cheap motel. Not in. She tried number after number.

"How do you remember so many phone numbers?"

She shrugged. "I don't know. I like numbers. Phone numbers always stick. Same with addresses. Stuff like that just gets stuck in my head."

"Handy," he said. "I can't remember shit without a Rolodex."

She patted him on the leg. "Well, now you've got me. I make coffee, I ride in cabs well, and I remember all the phone numbers you could ever want."

"Adding you to the firm has been a smart move," he agreed. She laughed, and stopped short as someone answered her latest call.

"Hey, Mick, it's Toni. Are Taneesha, Tina, or Angie there? Put her on, okay? Thanks." She covered the handset. "Jackpot."

Harry gave her a thumbs-up.

"Angie? Hey, it's Toni. Of course I know. Girl, I know more than *you* do. Listen, I need- no, I know. I know. Shut up, blabbermouth. I need to talk to you guys. Get everyone together. Yes, everyone."

She looked at Harry and pantomimed a circle and pointed at the desk. Harry cocked his head, and then nodded.

"Here's what I need you to do. Get everyone and get in a cab. You're headed for 303 Elizabeth Street. No, I- Angie, just- will you fucking zip it? Do as I tell you. Because it's important, that's why! It has to do with Mr. Jay. Yeah, I know he is. And I want to introduce you to the guy who killed him. Just get the girls and get over here now. All right. All right. See you soon." She hung up.

"So…" Harry said.

"It was the only thing I could think of. She's going to round up everyone she can find, and they'll be here," Toni said.

Harry nodded. "Okay. Look, I'm hungry. Want me to run up to Dahli's and grab some stuff?"

Toni debated. "Yeah, okay. I could use a meatball hero."

"Got it. Anything else?"

Toni shook her head.

"All right. Be right back." Harry got up and headed for the door.

"Harry?"

He looked at her.

"Thank you," she said.

"What for?"

"The way you're treating me. The way you're just... the way I'm just all of a sudden part of your life. Your world," she said shyly. "You've been wonderful to me."

He studied her. "You deserve it, Toni. And I like having you around."

"Really?"

He nodded. "Really. I always have."

She blushed.

"I'll be right back."

"All right, hurry. I'm starved," she said.

He smiled. "You got it."

Chapter Twenty

By the time he got back, his office was filled with women. Anticipating this eventuality, he'd bought three bags of sandwiches. He walked in the door to find five women with coffee and big smiles staring at him. He stopped in his tracks.

"What?" he said cautiously.

Toni just grinned.

"What?" he insisted.

"Nothing," Toni said. "Gimme food. I'm starved."

Harry set the bags on his desk and rummaged until he found a meatball hero and handed it to her. He pulled a bottle of orange juice from a different bag and opened it for her. She took it with a smile.

"Thank you," she said. Turning to the room, she said, "See?"

Harry looked around in confusion. "What the-"

"Don't worry about it," Toni said.

"Uh, okay," Harry said. He passed the bags around. "There's plenty for everyone. Grab a bite. I got juice and milk."

Toni beamed at him. "So, I got them here. What now?"

"Now you get out of my chair," he said.

"Yes, boss," she said. She moved to the couch, between two other girls. Harry dropped into his chair and grabbed a sandwich.

"Okay, ladies, I have questions. First off, you might know that Mr. Jay was killed-"

Angie cut him off. "We know. We knew before Toni called."

"Oh. Okay, so-"

"She said you killed him because he backhanded her," Angie said.

"Uh…" Harry stammered. "Not- not exactly. But… yeah. I shot him. Him and his pal Marvin. So, there's that. I realize it's probably going to mess up your life a little, but-"

Angie laughed. "Oh, sure. We're all heartbroken. Listen, it couldn't have happened to a nicer guy. But… why are we here?"

Harry said, "Because Bebe's still dead. And Cheddar Cheeseborough across the way lost a girl too, named Katy. Anyone know her?"

The women all shook their heads.

"Crap. All right. Someone's making a mark, and I still want to find out why, and who," Harry said. "And I wouldn't mind seeing them put away for the rest of their natural. Do you ladies have anything, anything at all, that might help? A suspicious comment, a weird client-"

"All of them are weird," Tina chimed in. "you'd have to be way more specific."

Harry nodded. "Okay. Someone who likes to hurt the girls. Someone who might have been turned away for getting too rough?"

They all shook their heads. "Jay never let us turn down a john," Toni said.

Harry sighed morosely. "Shit. So you have nothing?"

"Not that I can think of. We kind of all thought it was Mr. Jay who killed Bebe anyhow. But you say he didn't?" Tina said.

"I just never got that impression," Harry said. "I could be wrong, but it seemed a little too far for him. He liked to think he was a badass, but it takes a push to finally cross that line. He didn't seem like he'd made that jump yet."

"So you think someone is still out there that might hurt one of us?" Toni asked.

Harry eyed her. He didn't like the way she included herself, but they'd all been together for a while. It was natural, he supposed, to phrase it like that.

"Maybe. I hope not, but unless I get something to go on, I can't say for certain. We'd… we'd kind of have to wait for the perp to leave another body in the street before we know for sure. If it was a turf war between Cheddar and Jay, then the bodies will stop. But I'm not really happy with that choice. I'd rather find the son of a bitch and get an answer."

The black girl, Taneesha, spoke up for the first time. "If you do, you gonna arrest him?"

"I'm not a cop anymore," Harry said. "But believe me, I'd have the cops on him in a heartbeat."

They looked at each other. Even Toni looked less than satisfied with that answer.

"What?" Harry asked.

"We don't want the bastard in jail, honey," Taneesha said. "We want to know you'd drop him."

Harry looked at Toni is surprise. She shrugged a little.

"Look, I'm not in the habit of going around shooting people-"

"You killed Jay's ass good enough," Angie said.

"Well, yes, but-"

"And he was just layin down a beating on Tone here," Taneesha said. "So you'd shoot him for a beatin, but you wouldn't kill someone for stabbing a girl and leaving her in the snow to bleed to death?"

Harry raised a hand. "Look, I shot Jay because the situation was different. His pal had a gun and he pulled. Jay was fixing to beat Toni within an inch of her life. All those factors added up to the conclusion that I *had* to shoot him. I don't think he was going to let Toni off with a couple of black eyes and a bruised lip. And chances are they would have put one through me because I'm an ex-cop and a witness. But if I did figure out who it was killed Bebe and Katy, and they *didn't* come quietly, or pulled on me, then yes, I'd put them down like a rabid fucking animal."

He set his jaw and looked around at the women.

"The mindset here is, you're just... just *things*. Just objects to be discarded. I don't care for that. Not... one... *bit*," Harry's hand came down on the desk hard. Toni and Angie jumped at the noise. "You're people. You deserve more than what Bebe and Katy got- dumped in an alley with a hole in your chest. I've got a problem with that, and if I can stop this, I will. I could use your help, though. But either way, I'm going to stop it."

The women looked around at each other, seemed to talk without speaking, and all nodded. Angie reached into her cleavage and took out a roll of cash. She laid it on the desk.

"What's this?" Harry asked.

"You're hired," Angie said.

"Look-"

"Toni told us you've been poking around for your cop friend. Well, the cops haven't done jack shit for us. The cops haven't even bothered to question us. Bebe's getting cremated because she's got no relatives to claim her. We don't trust the cops. But we trust you. And we want your help. Toni says you're a good man, and a good detective. So we want to hire you. There. It's not just a favor for a friend. It's a job," Angie said.

Harry studied Angie for a moment, and looked at each woman in turn. His eyes settled on Toni, who bit her lower lip and nodded.

Harry pulled open the center drawer of his desk and took out a manila folder. He carefully lettered the label along the side, flipped it open, and pulled a fresh, blank sheet of paper out of the drawer. Sliding it into the folder, he picked up his pen.

"All right," he said. "I'll take the case. I've got questions."

Chapter Twenty-One

Two hours later, they finished and Harry called the girls a cab while Toni cleaned up. As Harry handed Jasper a cup and locked the door, Toni slid up behind him and put her arms around his waist. She pressed her head against his back and they stood there for a moment, just touching. He turned in her arms and smiled, putting his arms around her.

"Thank you, Harry," she said.

"For what?"

"Agreeing to look out for the girls."

"I didn't need to be hired, but this way I have a reason to be a pain in the ass. And I'm going to have to be, otherwise nothing's going to get done. I need to track down Eugene at the morgue, I have to coordinate with Porter, I need to see if we can find a witness, I want to talk to that Cassandra chick again. She seemed to know more than she was letting on." Harry bent down and kissed Toni quickly. She lifted her face and responded with a smile. "If you're going to learn, you need to pay attention and ask a lot of questions."

"Okay."

"That was lesson two," he said. "Not just to me. In an investigation. You need to be a pest. You can't let any detail go. If you need a notebook, we'll get one. You have to become really detail-oriented, Toni."

"Yes, boss," she said.

"For now... well... I think we'll head over to Beckett's and see if Darius is around. I want to ask him about Katy," Harry said.

Toni nodded. "Makes sense."

Harry shook his head. "Not really. In fact, nothing about this makes sense. If it's random, why two hookers? If it's a serial, why two hookers from different pimps? If it's darker than that, we're missing a piece. I need more information. I need-"

He broke off and looked at Toni, who cocked her head. "What?"

"What crew was Jay working with?"

"Huh?"

"Crew. Outfit. Who ran him?" Harry asked.

Toni shrugged. "I don't understand."

"Nothing in this town happens without mob say-so. You worked for Jay. Jay worked for someone else. Or at least, he paid for the privilege of running his girls. There aren't any independent operators in this city. Like Delmonico's. Someone owns Delmonico's, and someone owns them. The Bonanno family. Jay works for someone, kicks money up for the privilege. That money ends up with one of the outfits. That's who runs Jay, when you get down to it. .Say... I wonder if that's it? Maybe Jay stopped paying? But no, then why would they kill one of *Cheddar's* girls?"

Toni watched him pace back and forth. "All right. Let me make a call, and then we'll go," he said.

He dialed the desk sergeant by memory. "Vice, please," Harry said. A click and a buzz and he was transferred.

"Vice," a woman said. "Bowdler."

"Hey, Fatso," Harry said happily. "How they hanging?"

"Harry?" Clara Bowdler said. "Harry DeMarko? What the hell are you up to, you jerk?"

Harry pictured the skinny woman. She was a legend around the 9th Precinct for her ability to eat endless amounts of food. No one had ever seen her get full, or sick, or stop until everything in sight was demolished. She never gained a pound, and in fact had to work hard to maintain her body weight. Her passion was crullers.

"Oh, not much, not much," he said. "I'm working a case and I could use some help."

"Please. You still owe me lunch, Harry," Clara said. "Why would I let you slide any deeper in debt?"

"I can't afford to feed you, Clara," Harry said. "Take pity on a friend?"

"A friend who bet on the Cubs," Clara said loftily, "is not a friend I'm going to do anything for without cash on the barrel."

"Fair enough, fair enough. All right, I'm your slave for life starting, oh, next Tuesday. How'd that be?"

Toni watching him talking, fascinated by the animation in his face. She'd never seen him look so… human. She realized she'd never seen him talk to anyone he considered a friend. Never seen him comfortable with someone who knew him. Porter was the first one. Were all his friends cops? She wondered what else he'd left behind when he left the force. Friends? Lovers? He was a part of their gang, and then he wasn't. That had to be…

She suddenly remembered earlier when the girls had arrived. They were closed-mouthed and reluctant to talk to her at first, and she realized it was because she, too, was an outsider. The girls she'd known for years were all of a sudden distanced. A gulf had opened between them. It had gotten better after a few minutes of gossip and shop talk, but it had surprised and hurt her. She wondered what it would be like to work with someone for twenty years and suddenly be on the outside. She realized Harry looked happy because it was like he'd come home for a visit.

"It'll have to do, DeMarko. What do you need?" Clara asked.

"I've been retained," Harry said, "by a consortium of clients who want me to look into a couple of DBs turned up near the Village. Couple of working girls. Porter Rockwell's got the cases. You know the ones?"

"Yeah, I know them," Clara said. "Why don't you ask Porter?"

"Because you probably know what I'm looking for faster than me asking him, him asking you, you telling him, and him getting back to me. Figured I would just go to the one with the answers," Harry said.

"Flattery gets you everywhere, DeMarko. What do you need?"

"What I've gathered so far is, the two girls each worked for different pimps. One was working with a guy, his street name's Mr. Jay, and the other working for Cheddar Cheeseborough. What I need to know is, what crew runs them? Or crews," Harry said.

Clara didn't say anything at first.

"Clara?" Harry asked.

"I'm here," she said. "You're working this? Does Porter know?"

"He asked me to look into it, and I asked around a bit. But I've been hired to dig, so I'm digging."

"I see," Clara said. "All right, it's no secret. They're both running under the Gambino banner."

"You have an idea which crew they answer to?" Harry asked.

"Harry… you're not going to go have a chat with them. You have any idea what kind of trouble you're letting yourself in for?"

Harry said, "Clara, it feels like a turf war. I thought it was a beef between Mr. Jay and Cheddar at first, but then I thought maybe it was a higher-up beef. Now it turns out they were both working for the same people. So maybe someone's going after the higher-ups. I just want to dig a little, that's all. Nothing heavy."

"You don't think those guys will talk to you, do you?"

"The big guys, of course not. But a street crew? Maybe. Especially if they can turn some heat onto a crew giving them shit. You know what it's like for these guys: they can't afford to lose face. They're going to be looking for payback, if it's what I think it is. That means more bodies are going to drop in the streets. I might be able to head that off. Come on. I'm not asking you for anything that's not public record. I could dig out the answer with a couple hours of research, a few calls to the Daily News, but I don't have time for that. Clara, two girls who didn't do anything are dead. Come on."

Clara sighed. "You always have a way of making unreasonable shit sound like perfect logic, Harry," she said. "All right, all right. But now you owe me two lunches."

"I'll take out a loan first thing tomorrow," he said.

"There's a jewelry store on 39th and 47th over in Queens. Called the Four Aces. That's where they're out of. Skinny Sally D'Amico and his boys. They're fronting the tail-runners over here for the Gambinos.

You know the drill, Harry. You walk in, you're going to be bird-dogged by the Feds."

"They're staking it?" Harry asked.

"They're staking *all* the Families' operations. Not just the G's, but *all* the five. You know how RICO works, Harry. They're trying everything to shut them down," Clara said. "Trying to clean up New York."

"This city," Harry said, "wants to stay dirty."

"The Feds are gonna drag it into the light eventually. Clean up the Square, make the whole town a tourist trap. They'll grab you the minute you walk into the Aces."

"Yeah," Harry said. "Can't be helped, can be explained. I'm not worried about the Feds. I'm just getting tired of bodies dropping on my streets. Look, I'll fill Porter in when I get something. You want me to drop a dime?"

"If you find something you think is worth sharing, yeah, give me a call," Clara said. "Otherwise, this never happened. We never spoke."

"It's like that, huh?" Harry asked.

"Yeah. Captain Wells is coming down hard on internal leaks. Even when they're not leaks. People talk, you know? Nature of the business," Clara said.

"Got it. Thanks, Clara. I owe you one."

"Just one?" Clara said.

"All right, two. Two and a half," Harry said.

"That's better. Stop by some time, Harry," Clara said. "Visit. Bring food."

Harry laughed. "You got it. Thanks, Fatso."

"Welcome." Clara hung up.

Harry put the phone down. He thought about what he'd just learned.

"So Jay and Cheddar," Toni said, "They're… what? Mob guys?"

Harry snorted. "They wish. No, they're just worker bees. But leaning on Cheddar might still give us something."

"What about… who did you say? The Gambinos? What about them?" she asked.

"No, the street crew *running* the pimps is who we talk to. Accuse a higher up guy of penny-ante shit and you'll wind up in a landfill over in Jersey. Might still, just talking to that crew. But it's a lead. So I'll check it out," Harry said. He jotted notes.

"You mean *we'll* check it out," Toni said.

"No. I do this one alone. That's heavier than you're ready for. I don't want you exposed."

"Harry, I-"

"Toni, a couple days ago you were a hooker working for the guys who work for these guys. You really think it's smart to let them know you decided to quit? You think they'll just nod, smile, and say, 'well, do you want a reference for your next employer?'" Harry asked.

Toni looked chagrined. "Well, no."

"No. So we keep you away from anyone who might have a vested interest in putting you back out there," Harry said. "Until you're completely broken away and standing on your own you're at risk. You know that."

Toni nodded. "I know. I don't like it, but I know."

"We'll get you there. It'll take a little time, that's all," he said. He looked at the clock. Almost five. "So let's go see Cheddar."

Chapter Twenty-Two

They pulled up to the bar and looked around. Harry told the cabbie to wait and looked around. The Eldorado was gone. Inside, the music was too loud and the bar was too empty, but over in the corner by the pool tables sat Cheddar and a group of his guys.

Harry went to the bar. He took out a ten. "Round of drinks for the guys in the corner, okay?"

The bartender nodded and set about getting beers and shots ready. He took them over and pointed at Harry and Toni. Cheddar stared at him for a while and then raised his beer in salute. Harry touched Toni on the arm and walked over. She trailed after him. Cheddar didn't get up, and Harry didn't expect that he would.

"Cheddar. Good to see you again," he said.

Cheddar said nothing.

"Would you answer some questions for me, please?" Harry asked, figuring politeness would help, or at least couldn't hurt.

Cheddar raised his beer. "This buys you one answer."

Harry nodded. "All right. Do you have any idea who killed Katy?"

"Nope," Cheddar said. He finished his beer and tossed the bottle at Harry, who caught it and set it on the table next to him. Harry signaled the bartender, who came back with another beer. Harry gave him another ten.

"Keep them coming," Harry said to him. To Cheddar he said, "I have more questions."

Cheddar shrugged, but grinned.

After he popped the top off his beer, Cheddar took a long swallow and then said, "Ask."

"Have you heard any rumors about payback for Bebe, from Jay's crew?"

"Nope. Heard you killed old Jay, though," Cheddar said.

"Yeah," Harry said. "He pissed me off."

Cheddar smiled. "Who's the fluff?"

Harry looked at Toni. "She's my partner. We're looking into the murders."

"I thought you were already doing that," Cheddar said. "You sure made noise like that when you were here before."

"I was asking around for a friend. This is different. I've been hired to find the killer and make sure it's done right."

"Oh?" Cheddar said. "And who you working for, man?"

"You didn't buy me a drink," Harry said.

Cheddar laughed out loud. "That's good. You're quick. As for the other, it wasn't me. First Bebe, and now Katy. She wasn't my best girl, but she was *mine*. Believe me, if I knew who did it, I'd already have holes in him."

Harry nodded. "I figured that too, except if it was someone muscling in on D'Amico."

Cheddar went silent as Harry dropped the name.

"Well?" Harry asked. "Someone pushing on your boss? I'll buy you a shot."

Cheddar shook his head. "No idea what you're talking about, man."

"Come on, Cheddar. You know how this works. You give me a name to go off yelping after like the braying hound I am, and you get a problem solved. I don't get any dead bodies, and you get to keep doing business."

"And if I don't give you a name?" Cheddar asked.

"It'll piss me off," Harry said evenly. Toni stopped breathing. Cheddar's eyes roved over Harry.

"Huh," he said.

He and Harry locked eyes for a while. Finally, Cheddar shook his head. "Look, man, I wish I could help you. I *really* do. I don't like the idea of anyone fronting my turf or hurting my girls." He looked at Toni and smiled a lazy, gapped grin. "I prefer to do that kind of thing myself. But I don't know. I've had feelers out for a while now, but nothing. I'd be happy to dump you on someone else's doorstep, but I got no address. I'm still looking, though, and if it'd keep you from coming in here and harassing me, I'd gladly sic you on them. Whoever they are. As for someone feuding with the higher-ups? No dice, man. I don't say their names. Not to a pig. Not even an ex-pig."

Harry nodded. "I get that. I really do."

"Good for you." Cheddar turned his attention to Toni. "You look familiar. I know you?"

Toni shook her head. "No. Nice to meet you."

"Charmed," Cheddar said. He looked at Harry. "Anything else?"

"Not unless you can think of anything, anything at all, that might help me find the asshole that killed your girl," Harry said.

"Nope. Your tab's run out," Cheddar said. "Time to go."

"Come on, Toni," Harry said. "Let's get going."

"You can stay," Cheddar said to Toni. She smiled sweetly at him.

"That's a lovely invitation, but I only spend time with men." She took Harry's arm and waited.

Harry struggled not to laugh. Cheddar beat him to it, letting out a huge belly laugh.

"She's all right," Cheddar said. "I'd make you my number one girl."

"Sorry, Cheddar," Toni said. "You can't afford me."

He snickered. "Maybe not. Maybe not."

Harry and Toni left. Out in front, the cabbie was arguing with a beat cop. He saw Harry and pointed. Harry and Toni got in.

"Sorry, officer," Harry said. "I called for the cab, and we got held up."

"Well, you kept your man here double-parked," the officer said. "You can't do that."

"I'm sorry," Harry said again. "We won't do it again."

"All right, all right, get outta here," the officer said.

"Bleecker and Elizabeth," Harry told the cabbie.

"So," Toni said. "Cheddar seemed nice."

Harry snorted.

"Did you learn anything useful?"

"I don't know. He didn't seem terribly upset. Not until I mentioned his bosses," Harry said.

"What does that mean?"

"I haven't the slightest idea," Harry said. "I can't put the pieces together until I know what they all are. I need more information. We'll talk to Porter tonight, see if he has anything. Tomorrow I'll go see the Gambino crew over in Brooklyn. Maybe that'll turn up something. Otherwise…"

"Otherwise what?" She asked.

"Otherwise we'll have to wait until another body hits the ground," Harry said. "I don't want that to happen, but it might be the only way we ever get a handle on this asshole," he said.

"Harry, we have to do something before that," Toni said.

"I want to, but you have to remember… hundreds of murders a year are essentially unsolvable. No evidence, bad evidence, no witnesses, no body… it's not easy. That's why Porter and the other guys in Homicide are so cranky. No one likes being responsible for letting a killer go free, but every detective everywhere with a thousand unsolved cases in his docket. It's the nature of the business. Cops can't do everything," Harry said. "But if there's any chance of getting this guy, I'm going to take it. If he can be got, I'll get him."

She squeezed his hand. "I know you will."

"It's more than I know," Harry said, staring morosely out the window at the snow and ice and cars. "Until you get a collar, everything's up in the air."

Back at the apartment, Harry jotted a couple more notes in the file and they went inside and relaxed on the bed. Harry lay with his hands behind his head, staring up at the ceiling and thinking about the case. Toni curled up next to him and rested her head on his chest. She looked up at him and smiled. "Your raccoon mask is starting to go away," she said, reaching up to gingerly touch his nose.

He nodded. "Yeah. I only look like I lost a little fight instead of a big one."

"I think it makes you look dark and dangerous," she said. "Not at all like the big softie you really are."

He glanced down at her. "Softie?"

She put her head back down and snuggled closer. "You heard me."

"I should tickle you for that," he said.

"You wouldn't dare."

"Don't bet on it, woman."

They lay in companionable silence for a while. Harry broke it with a question.

"Doesn't it bother you I'm twice your age?" he asked.

She shook her head, eyes closed. "No."

"Huh."

"Does it bother you that I'm half yours?" she asked.

"I thought you were all mine," he said.

"Tease. You know what I mean," Toni told him.

"Yeah. And no, it doesn't bother me. I'm getting the better of the deal. Why would I complain?"

"You think your friends are going to give you shit for me being so young?" she asked.

"Oh, probably. But so what? It's all in fun. They either tease because they're friends, or they tease because they're jealous. Either way, no sweat off my nose."

"Jealous?" Toni asked.

"Well of course," Harry said. "You're pretty adorable."

"Pretty adorable?"

"Well, kind of. Sort of adorable? Fairly adorable? More or less adorable? Somewhat- ouch!"

Toni pinched his nipple hard.

"Okay, okay. Very, utterly, amazingly, completely adorable," Harry said.

"That's better."

"Also ruthless," Harry said. He fended off another pinch. "Which, as it happens, isn't exactly a bad quality in a woman."

She smiled up at him. "I'm glad you appreciate my complexities."

"Oh, sure," he said. "Just stop pinching me, I'll appreciate all your qualities."

"Tease," she said.

"A tease promises and never delivers. I intend to deliver."

Toni looked up at him hopefully. "You got an ETA on that delivery, Harry?"

He shook his head. "Nope. But it's coming."

"Me too, I hope," she said with a grin. He blushed, and then laughed. He looked over at the clock on the wall.

"I guess we better wander over," he said.

"Okay. What do you want me to wear?" Toni asked.

"Well, I'm introducing you to the only friends I have in the world. I've never brought a girl around. I haven't had a girlfriend for years. Or a date, for that matter. So... I don't know. Something really gorgeous? Do you have something that will make everyone jealous?" Harry asked.

She craned to look at him again.

"Why?"

"Uh... because I want to make a great first impression?"

"No, why won't you fuck me? And why weren't there any other girls?" she asked.

He didn't speak for a while. Finally, he sighed. "As for the second question... a whole bunch of... of bullshit, really. I was ambitious. I wanted to make

238

detective. I wanted to make lieutenant. I wanted to make Chief someday. I worked day and night. Weekends. I put in so many extra hours, they actually ordered me to stop. It wasn't overtime, it was my intensity. I was driving everyone up the wall. My Captain actually ordered me to find a hobby. He threatened to fire me if I didn't find an outlet. He actually told *everyone* to find me a hobby. Porter used to make me go bowling. One night I went over to Brandt's for a bottle, and stopped a robbery. He invited me to play poker and we've been playing for a decade now. But aside from twice-weekly poker nights, I was a workhorse. It didn't matter. I went after chain snatchers, rapists, Monte dealers, everyone. I was a holy terror. Twice the arrests of any portable on the street. But I was so single-minded I didn't make any time for anyone. So I was alone. When I was in the hospital, no one came to see me except work friends. Now that I'm not a cop, no one comes to see me. I still go to the games, but I have the feeling that if I didn't, no one would say anything."

Harry looked at her. "As for why I won't fuck you… first there was your job. And now… you're the best friend I've ever had and I don't want to screw all that up."

He sighed. "So, I was a workhorse. Never a girlfriend. Never a wife. Never… anything," Harry said. "I put everything into the job. And one night, I chased a suspected rapist into an alley, got shot, and that was that. No more cop. No more promotion track. No more life. And when I was out, I discovered I still had no life. Except for this shitty shop, my half-assed PI company, and… and you."

She smiled up at him. "You didn't just get shot. You saved the girl, Harry."

He shrugged. "That's what I was supposed to do."

"Harry, all you had to do was let him go," she said.

He looked at her as though she'd gone mad. "Let him go?"

She shrugged. "You wouldn't have gotten shot. He wouldn't have killed me. He wasn't a killer."

Harry's jaw set, and he got that look on his face. That one she'd seen when he really put his feet down and resisted, even against the whole world. He said quietly, "It doesn't work like that, Toni. You don't let someone like that get away. They don't get to bargain. And you don't know what he was capable of. Just because we didn't find any bodies doesn't mean he wasn't a killer. And besides, a rapist is bad enough. You telling me you wouldn't have minded getting raped?"

She shrugged. "Harry, it's not like I'm a stranger to all kinds of shit. If he had raped me, it wouldn't have been the end of the world."

"*Jesus*, the life you lead…" Harry said. "Led. Whatever. The fact that you can be so… so *casual* about this… it just reinforces my point of view. Shit like that cannot *stand*. It's got to be fought. That's what I… did."

She patted him. "And I'm grateful. You saved my virtue. My knight in shining blue armor."

"Don't be cynical," he said.

"I'm not," she replied. "Maybe I didn't have much virtue, but even if I know it wouldn't have killed me, that doesn't mean I was looking forward to it. That kind of thing… half the girls on the street have been forced. It… it makes you… when it happens, it makes you feel like… like you *deserve* it, somehow. Like you *asked* for it. And if you're a hooker, then you *did* ask for it. Didn't you? It wouldn't have happened if you weren't trolling. Right? And if it wouldn't have happened if you weren't turning tricks, then you *wanted* it to happen. You practically begged for it. And that means you deserve it. It makes you feel less than… less than *human*. So why fight it? But then a guy like you comes along and says that it isn't her fault, and it's not something she should expect. And then you get hurt. You bet your life for me. For a girl you never *met*. You can imagine what that kind of… of *gesture*… tells a girl about herself. That night-"

Chapter Twenty-Three

Harry could remember every detail of that night. June, it had been. Hot as hell, even though it was two in the morning. He'd been slowly making his way, heading home. He was off the clock after a long double shift. Still in uniform. The girls on the street were working hard, getting plenty of action. They eyed him warily, but he didn't hassle the girls. They had it hard enough, and he wasn't Vice anyhow. As he came to the end of the block, he saw a man under a street light, just watching the girls. It was his predator's eye that got Harry's attention. He was watching the street like a lion watching a herd of antelope. He looked closer at the man's face. He realized he knew who the man was because he'd seen the posters at the Precinct. McRainey was wanted for a dozen assaults. No one seemed to want to press charges. The girls he'd had were all scared of him. Harry could understand that. They'd been hoping to catch him in the act, but so far he was too canny. Harry slowed to see what was what. McRainey hadn't seen him, so Harry faded into the shadows on the side of the street.

He watched McRainey for most of an hour. The man talked a lot, yelling at the girls, but he didn't seem to want to make up his mind. He wandered around a bit, up and down the street.

Harry didn't like it; he had the look of a predator trying to flush prey. He leaned against the building in the shadows and just watched. McRainey crossed the street, and headed up toward the alley. Suddenly, he vanished into the shadows much like Harry had. Harry was about to cross the street when a young girl, a working girl judging from her outfit, crossed in front of the alley. She wasn't paying attention and suddenly she vanished into the darkness with not even a yelp of surprise. Harry bolted across the road, almost getting hit by a car. He drew his .38 and ran into the alley. He ran down blind, until he came to a corner. He peeked around it and McRainey had the girl by the front of her halter and a gun pressed to her forehead.

"Drop it!" Harry yelled. McRainey was startled enough that he almost dropped his gun.

"Jesus!" he yelled. He spun to put the girl between them.

"I said drop it! Police! Hands up, asshole! Let the girl go," Harry barked.

McRainey pulled the girl against him with an arm snaked around her neck. He jammed the gun harder against the girl's head. Harry remembered thinking that she couldn't have been seventeen. She looked terrified. She shook like a leaf. Her eyes were saucers and her teeth had caught her lower lip.

"Let the girl go," Harry said again.

"Like fun," McRainey said. "Tell you what- let me walk, and I'll let her go. We'll just move to the street, and I'll let her go. I'll be gone, and she'll be fine, eh, pig?"

"No chance, McRainey," Harry said, and realized it was the wrong thing to say. Now he wasn't anonymous. Now he had nothing to lose. Harry cursed himself.

"Oh, you dirty bastard," McRainey breathed. He snapped a shot off at Harry but the bullet whined off the brick as Harry ducked back.

Harry knew the score: McRainey *had* to kill him. Him and the girl both, if he wanted to walk away. More, he could see McRainey knew it, too. Harry peeked around the edge of the wall and chips from McRainey's second shot flew. One of them sliced Harry's cheek and made a small cut.

"You shoot at me one more time and I'll kill you," Harry said. "Drop the gun, let her go, and it's just assault. I won't report you shooting at a cop. I give you my word. You don't drop it, I'm not arresting you, pal, I'm putting you in a bag."

McRainey's eyes darted to the left and right. The cul-de-sac he'd found for his playtime was inopportune for a fugitive. Nowhere to run.

Harry held up his hand. "Listen, I don't want to shoot you. I don't want you to shoot me. And that girl sure as hell doesn't want to be caught between us doing it. But you *are* going down. As I said, toss the gun, let her go, and it'll be assault. I won't even do you for the gun. Plead it down to battery, you pay a fine. No time, aside from the overnight in the tombs. You don't comply, it'll go bad for you. Assault, attempted rape, unlicensed firearm, attempted murder of a police officer. You're gone for a minimum of twenty. That's a lot longer than one night in lockup. What do you say? I've had a shit day. Don't make it worse. I'll call a car, we'll be done up in under an hour. We both get some sleep, come back fresh tomorrow."

McRainey seemed to consider it, but his eyes shifted in a way Harry'd seen a thousand times. He cursed under his breath. McRainey was making that final decision. He'd kill the girl and shoot it out with Harry, hoping to make a good shot.

"Don't do it, McRainey!" Harry yelled. The man hesitated, and that was what Harry was waiting for. He had to aim wide. Go for a good wound. He couldn't make the shot without stepping out, though. He was a righty.

He darted left into the open, .38 held in a good Weaver stance. They fired at the same time. Harry's shot took McRainey low in the chest, just missing the girl, who had squirmed away from McRainey's gun. McRainey's bullet slammed into Harry's left shoulder. He stumbled back as a sledgehammer hit him in the chest and knocked him backward, threw him off his feet and slammed him into the wall of the alley. He slid down the brick with his legs splayed in front of him in a V.

His left arm dropped uselessly to his lap, but he held his gun in his right hand. He kept it aimed at McRainey, who lay on his back blowing blood into the still, hot air with racking coughs. The girl watched him from a few feet away, curled against a trash can, eyes like saucers. Harry's gun was suddenly too heavy to hold up and it dragged his hand down into his lap.

One last choking cough, and McRainey was gone.

Harry shivered. He wondered why he was cold. It was cold. In June. Early winter, maybe. It was late. He needed to get home. He was so tired.

The girl scrambled to his side, dropping to her knees. She accidentally pressed against his shoulder and he cried out weakly. She winced and grabbed at her purse. She pulled out a long silk scarf. She wadded it up and pressed it against Harry's shoulder, and he screamed. She poked it into the hole, pressing hard. He squirmed and tried to push her away, but his strength had gone. He only vaguely realized she had pulled his bulky Motorola radio from his belt and was yelling into it for help. She told the emergency operator where they were and that Harry had been shot. The operator gave her instructions on what to do, and she agreed.

Dropping the radio, the girl moved him away from the wall a little and felt behind his shoulder. Her hand came away clean. She nodded to herself, and pulled him over, drawing another scream from him. She had him prone on the filthy alley floor, and she made him scream again. She pressed hard on the wound and kept pressure on it.

He tried to reassure her. "D-don't worry," he stammered, "just a-a little pain… and some b-blood. No big deal."

"Sure, sure," she said, and pressed harder. A bolt of lightning seemed to fork through him and he screamed again. Harry scrabbled against her, trying to push her off, but he was too far gone. Ears ringing, vision fading black, he tried to reassure the girl again, but it was too hard to speak. He blacked out trying to tell her it would be all right. That it was just a little blood.

When the squad cars and the ambulance arrived, she backed off as they took him out of the alley but insisted on riding to the hospital with him. She went with him all the way to the doors when they stopped her. The nurses looked her up and down, cast disapproving stares at her, but led her to a waiting room and gave her coffee. She waited for six hours while doctors took the shrapnel out of him, set his clavicle, and repaired what they could. The doctors came out to speak to the police and to Toni, who listened solemnly as they explained that Harry would probably lose feeling and function, that his shoulder would never be the same. That he would need help, rehabilitation, and time. That he might not be able to be a cop anymore. While the doctors spoke to Harry's friends, two patrolmen took her statement, and had her sign her name. Her scribbles were hard to read, and one of them had to ask for her name.

"Toni B," she said.

She waited until they told her he was out of danger. They gave her his room number. She didn't go up, but in the coming weeks, she would drop by three or four times a week. She peeked into his room but never went in. He didn't even know she'd been there until the day before he left, when the nurse told him about the girl that kept coming around. About the girl that had saved his life.

Chapter Twenty-Four

"…you made me feel better about myself than anyone had. What you did, Harry, was the… was the opposite of rape. If rape makes you feel horrible and less than human, what you did raised me up and told me I was *worth* something. You almost died for me. You risked your life to protect me. You've been doing it ever since. You know I watched you come home. I wanted to show you a good time, because you'd been so good to me. You couldn't even get the door open. You dropped the key. So I picked it up. I wanted to come in and make you feel good." She sat up and looked at him solemnly. "But you wouldn't. You never would."

Harry said, "I don't know why you kept putting up with me. And I told you before-"

"I *know* what you said, Harry. As for putting up with you… if what you did was the opposite of rape, how do you think it felt for you to refuse to fuck me? Not because I was *dirty*, but because you wanted me to be *clean*. Because you *did* want me. How could I *not* love you for that? I put up with you, because you put up with me. With my bullshit. With my life. With my job. And you're my knight for that."

"You deserve better than you've had. Better than I have," Harry said.

"*Harry,*" she chided, "You don't get to decide that. That's for me to decide. Right?"

He shrugged. "I guess so."

"You wouldn't let McRainey go. And you wouldn't let me get raped or killed. You wouldn't budge. You never *do*. You know what's right, and *I* know what's right by watching you. So if you tell me it's not time, then I know it's not time. And when you *do* tell me, I'll know it's *right*. That's why I put up with you. That's why I keep coming back. That's why I'll wait forever, if I have to." She stretched up and kissed him softly and sweetly. "Long as I have to."

Chapter Twenty-Five

They walked over to Beckett's, stopping into Dahli's to pick up some food. Harry held the door for Toni, and Sandy greeted her in a chirpy tone before Harry entered.

"What can I get you, hon?" Sandy asked Toni. Harry came in after. "Oh, hey, Harry. Be right with you," Sandy said.

"She's with me, Sandy. Toni, this is Sandy. Sandy, Toni. Sandy's the brains behind the operation."

Sandy was silent. Toni stuck out a hand and Sandy had to actually shake herself to break the spell. She looked at Harry and took Toni's hand.

"Uh, pleased to meet you?" she said hesitantly.

"Likewise," Toni said.

"Who's here?" Harry asked.

"Uh, you're the first. Grab a bottle," Sandy said, staring at Toni.

"You got it. We brought stuff for sandwiches and things," Harry said. "Come on, Toni."

Sandy watched them go as Harry and Toni headed back to the room. Harry looked at Toni. "What do you fancy?"

Toni looked around. "What... anything?"

Harry nodded.

"Uh... I like Black Velvet and ginger," Toni said.

"Really? I didn't know that. Good choice." Harry grabbed a bottle and led Toni to the back room. They set up the table and put out chairs. Harry counted, and went to the back to get another chair.

"She seemed… surprised," Toni said.

"No doubt," Harry said. "I've never brought anyone here. Never had anyone to bring."

He stopped what he was doing and went to her. He put his arms around her and kissed her. "I like having someone to bring."

She smiled. "I like being brought."

"Want to lay out the food while I get glasses?" he asked.

"Sure," she said.

Soon enough, the door opened and Mitch Abso wandered in. He froze at the door, at the sight of Harry and Toni sitting quietly. They smiled.

"Mitch, Toni. Toni, this is Mitch. If you had a car, he'd be fixing your parking tickets," Harry said.

"You wish," Mitch said. He covered his hesitation by going to the sideboard, picking up a slice of cheese, and munching it. He eyed Toni speculatively. Harry waited for it. He knew it was coming.

Mitch said, "So, Toni… who do you like in the Super bowl?"

Harry laughed, and Mitch smiled.

Toni said, "Who cares? Jets and Giants are out. If I had to pick, Philly. But only because they're so close to New York. Oakland? Who even knows where that is? It sounds like South Jersey."

Mitch gawped and then threw his head back, laughing. Toni smiled and Harry grinned. They sat and chatted for a while until more of the crowd shuffled in. Harry introduced Mike, the owner of the store, and Cathy Michaels to Toni. Finally, Sandy closed down the store and came back. She started to say something, and a hammering knock on the front door interrupted. She went back out and came in with Porter.

"Sorry I'm late," he said "I-"

He broke off as he saw Toni. Harry waited for his inevitable scathing comment, but Porter merely ducked his chin.

"What's up?" he asked her.

"Hi," she said.

They each looked away at the same time. Harry smiled in amusement. Everyone stood around for a moment, just being uncomfortable.

"So," Harry finally said. "I brought a friend. Hope that's okay."

They all chuckled.

"And yes, she's a girl. And my friend. Put them together and you get-"

"A complete *mystery* why she'd like you," Porter said.

Toni put her hand on Harry's arm. "I do, though. And it's no mystery. A real gentleman has-"

"What," Porter asked. "Enough cash for a good time?"

The room went quiet as Harry's right fist clenched. Everyone looked back and forth between Harry and Porter. The crack of Harry's knuckles echoed in the small room. Toni just smiled again.

"Actually, I'd be paying *him*, but he won't take the money," she said. "He's a gentleman that way."

Porter stared at her for a moment, and then barked a laugh.

"Yeah, he's too good for his own good," Porter said. "You're Toni, right?"

"That's right," she said.

"So..." Porter said. "We playing, or what?"

Harry relaxed a little, and Toni put a hand on his. Staring at Porter, Harry touched her hand with his own. Porter shrugged and picked up the bottle.

"BV?"

"I like it," Toni said. "But if it's too much for you-"

"Oooh," Sandy crooned. "Get him, Toni!"

Porter cocked an eye at Toni and grinned. "I'll drink you under the table, darling," he said.

"I go under the table, it won't be for you," Toni countered. This time it was Cathy who laughed out loud.

"You've been here, like, five seconds, and you fit right in," she said. She poured a drink and handed it to Toni. "It's your deal, honey."

Everyone sat down at the table and they started playing. Porter kept looking at Harry and Toni, who were sitting across from one another.

"Hey, Harry," he said. "I meant to tell you… I really need you to back off now. The Captain heard you were at Cheddar's again. I appreciate the help, but I need you to knock it off. I'm going to get in trouble if you don't stop pushing for me."

Harry nodded. "I bet. There's a problem with that."

"I don't see the problem," Porter said, "just stop doing anything."

Harry dropped a couple cards. "I'll take two, Toni. The problem, Porter, is I'm not doing it for you anymore. I've been hired."

Porter dropped his cards on the table. "I'm out. What the fuck do you mean, 'you've been hired'?"

"I have a client. Several clients. They hired me to do the same thing you asked. To look into it." Harry sipped his drink.

Mitch and Cathy looked at one another and grimaced.

"Harry," Porter started.

"Don't bother, Porter," Harry told him with finality. "It's done."

"*Un*do it," Porter said. "I need you to back off this."

"Conversation's over, Porter."

"Bullshit. Who's the client?"

"Clients. Why do you care?" Harry asked.

"I care because it's my neck," Porter said. "I'm the one let you off the leash."

Harry stopped tapping his cards together and looked up at Porter. "Excuse me?"

"Hill knows I'm the one who told you to poke around."

"You don't own me, Porter. And you don't run me. And you sure as hell don't control me. And it doesn't matter. My client calls the shots. And they want someone found. We can work together, if you like. The fact that I'm a PI with a client will calm Hill down. I can do anything I want," Harry said.

"Harry, Hill's going to give me shit for this. You *know* that," Porter said.

"That's unfortunate," Harry said. "But it doesn't change anything. And it's not your fault. Tell him that. Hell, give him my number."

"Well, who're these clients?" Porter asked. "Maybe I can talk to 'em."

"They won't talk to you," Toni said.

Porter glared at her. "I didn't ask you a fucking thing," he snarled.

"Hey," Harry said mildly. "No call for that, Porter. Keep a civil tongue."

Porter stood up. He poured more whiskey. "Just because you're dotty over some whore is no reason-"

"I said. That's. *Enough*." Harry grated. "Toni's got nothing to do with it."

The looks went around the table, but both Harry and Toni had been expecting it sooner or later. Toni shrugged. "I was a hooker. I'm not anymore. Now I work with Harry."

Cathy looked at Harry with raised eyebrows. Harry nodded. "She wants to be a private investigator. She's my assistant."

"She's a fucking whore," Porter said. "And the clients are what, the rest of the whores?"

Michael spoke up this time. "Porter. You want to cool it a little?"

Porter looked at Mike as though he'd never seen the man before that moment. "*What* did you say?"

"He said keep a civil tongue," Cathy said. "We're all friends here."

"She's a hooker!" Porter said, jabbing a finger at Toni. Toni stared impassively back at him.

"And you're a cop," Sandy said. "Nobody's perfect."

Porter looked around the table in disbelief. "Are you seriously-"

"Seriously what, Porter?" Harry asked. "Human? Decent? So what if she used to be a hooker. So what if my clients are the friends of the hooker who got killed? Can you think of anything better-"

"You're working for a bunch of whores? And *with* a whore?" Porter hooted.

"That's enough, Porter!" Cathy said. "Knock it off."

Porter stared evenly at Cathy. "Aren't we just one big happy family. Well, maybe you haven't realized this, but her and her friends used to work for the same guy Harry here put down in the street."

Cathy, Mitch, Mike, and Sandy looked from Toni to Harry.

"That true?" Mitch Abso said.

"Yeah," Harry said. "He tried to beat the shit out of Toni in front of me. His muscle had a gun. I had to do it."

"See? He doesn't even try to hide the fact that he killed a pimp for his string," Porter snarled. "He's probably setting up shop on the same corners!"

Toni finished her own drink and slammed the glass down. They all stared at her. "I'm not a hooker anymore, Porter. And I was *never* a whore. Don't call me that again. And yes, Harry killed Mr. Jay. Killed his hired gun, too. And *yes*, the clients are all Mr. Jay's girls. But that doesn't mean Harry's setting up a new string. In fact, the girls asked if he wanted to, and he got very angry at them."

Harry shrugged. "I'm not a pimp."

"Harry's a friend. He's been helping me out for years," Toni said. "He's been there when no one else would have helped me. I owe him a lot. I don't appreciate you giving him a hard time about me."

Porter stared at her in shock. He shook himself. "Did... did you just warn *me*, you bitch?"

Michael stood up. "That's it. Porter, leave."

"Now wait a minute-"

"No, you wait a minute," Michael said. "You come into my place, start causing trouble, and insult one of my guests-"

"Guest?" Porter snorted.

"Yes, *guest*. Just like you're a guest. There's a sign out front says I reserve the right to refuse service to any asshole," Mike said. "Quit being an asshole."

Porter looked about to argue, but Toni said, "Isn't the whole point of this to find whoever who killed Bebe? And that other girl? Who cares who hires Harry? Why does that even matter? And you *know* no one on the street is going to talk to you. But us? Us they'll talk to. So, we work together. Logical, right?"

"No it's not logical. It's not fucking logical, because cops don't work with half-assed civilians. Especially whores who-"

Harry stood up and punched Porter in the mouth. It was an awkward shot, him half-leaning over the poker table like he was, but he got a good solid connection anyhow. Porter pitched backward over his chair, slamming his head against the floor. He blinked stars out of his eyes, dazed, and realized Harry had come around the table and was on top of him. Harry's hand clenched Porter's hair. Harry shook the man's head once.

"You need to watch your fucking mouth, Porter," Harry said.

"Harry, come on, this bitch- Ow!" Harry slammed his head on the concrete.

"I said, you need to watch your fucking mouth, Porter," Harry said.

Porter blinked away the spots in his eyes and stared at Harry. "Are you insane? I could-"

"Could what?" Harry asked. "Arrest me? You're not on duty. Besides, you gonna let word get around that a one-armed ex-cop got the drop on you?"

"No one's would believe-"

"They'd believe it, Porter," Cathy said.

"Damned right," Mitch said.

"Why don't you shut your mouth and sit back down before you get your smart ass kicked, Porter?" Mike said. "We want to play cards. If you're not gonna let us do that, we can do the other thing."

Porter's gaze went around the room. The only two people he would have expected to back him up, being cops themselves, were against him. He sighed.

"All right, all right. Harry, get the fuck off me. I promise I won't call her names. Happy?" Porter griped.

Harry let go of Porter's hair and stepped off him. He went to his chair as Porter came off the ground. With alarming speed, Porter drew his gun. Before Harry, Cathy, or Mitch could do anything, a glass crashed into the bridge of Porter's nose. He screeched and dropped his pistol. Cathy scooped it up quickly. They all looked at Toni. She sat there with a smug grin on her face.

Porter had a streamer of blood running from a cut in the center of his forehead. His eyes blazed, but he took a deep breath and let it out. Cathy put the gun on the shelf behind her and put herself between it and Porter. Porter cleared his throat and actually looked embarrassed.

"I'm sorry," he said to Toni, looking her right in the eyes. He turned to look at Harry. "I'm really sorry. I guess I didn't realize how close you and the girl are. I won't forget again."

Harry didn't look impressed. "What's with the gun, Porter? You pulled a *gun* on me."

"Reflex. I was really, really pissed." He turned to Toni again. "Seriously, thank you. You kept me from doing something incredibly stupid." He looked around at the rest of them. "I'm sorry."

Cathy picked up his gun and she and Porter eyed each other. Cathy checked the safety and shoved Porter's gun into the waistband of her jeans. "You get this back when we leave, Porter," she said.

Porter nodded. He looked at Mike and stuck out a hand. "Mike, I'm sorry. You're right, I'm a shitty guest, I'm sorry. Let me make it up to you. Drinks are on me from now on."

Mike seemed hesitant, but Harry, to their surprise, spoke up. "Porter, I'll do what I can about keeping Hill off your back," he said. He grinned. "And it's your deal, you fucking asshole."

They all laughed as much with the release of tension as the jape. Porter nodded. "Yeah. Lemme get some food in me first. Too much booze, not enough food."

They all watched him go to the side table and make a sloppy sandwich. He carried it back to the table and sat down, taking a bite of wheat and turkey with mustard. He chewed thoughtfully, and picked up the cards.

"Okay, let's do this thing," he said.

They all finally settled down and began to play. After three hands, Porter said, "So, you and your… friends got together and hired Harry, huh?"

"I introduced them, and they hired Harry and me. I'm working with *him*."

Porter snorted, and shot a glance at Harry, who didn't say a word. "Working with him how?"

"He's teaching me," Toni said.

"Teaching you what?" Porter asked.

"Well, yesterday he taught me how to get past building security, how to fake out a scared boyfriend, and how to talk a runaway into going home," she said.

"Huh."

"He taught you how to use a gun yet?" Cathy asked.

"No. He says that I'm not ready," Toni said.

"Well, you aren't," Harry said.

"When he says you're ready, listen to him," Cathy said. "He knows what he's doing. He taught me."

Harry shrugged. "You were dropping your shoulder, that's all. You just needed a stance adjustment."

"I wouldn't have passed the exam if you hadn't helped me," she told him. "Don't be modest."

"What else can I be?" he asked. "It wasn't a big deal."

Toni smiled around Harry at the woman. "He's always like that."

"The good ones usually are," Cathy said.

"You know he's saved my life twice?" Toni asked.

Cathy studied Harry's face as he slowly turned pink. "No kidding."

"Yeah, he… Harry? Can I tell it?" Toni asked.

He looked at her. "If you have to," he said quietly.

Cathy put her hands on the cards in the center of the table. "You have to," she said.

"Well, it's true that Mr. Jay was beating the shit out of me. Harry shot them both, Jay and his enforcer,

Marvin. But… he saved my life when he was a cop, too. It was when he got shot," Toni said.

They all looked at Harry. Harry sipped his liquor. Porter studied Harry's face carefully while Toni talked. She told them about being grabbed and pulled into the alley. How Harry wouldn't let him hurt her. How he got shot rather than let her get taken. How he almost died for her, but she saved him. Sandy whistled. Cathy nodded and pointed at her. "What she said."

Sandy said, "That's the most romantic thing I've ever heard."

"Oh, come *on*," Porter said. "You didn't tell me she was the girl from *that* night, Harry."

"I didn't see it as relevant at the time, and I don't see it now," Harry said. "Had nothing to do with the shooting. No point in telling old war stories."

Cathy threw a thumb at Harry. "Romantic, like I said."

Toni refilled Harry's glass, and then offered the bottle around. Porter held his out, Mike covered his. He didn't trust Porter and didn't want to get drunk. Porter seemed to be enjoying himself, though, despite the lumps he'd taken.

"So this is why she's so rabid about sticking up for you," Porter said. "She's paying off a debt."

Harry looked at him coldly. "It's not a debt. It's a friendship. Learn the difference."

"A friendship?" Sandy asked. "You sure? Saw your eyes when Porter called her a name, Harry. You're in looo-oove."

Cathy grinned. Toni blushed and looked at the floor. Harry took a swallow of the whiskey. Porter studied Harry carefully.

261

"That true, old buddy? Is it love between you and the- the girl here?" he asked, still with that sardonic grin.

Harry rearranged his cards and tapped them closed. He looked up at Porter. "Call."

Porter grinned. "I'll be damned. It's about time, pal."

Harry shrugged. "Time's got nothing to do with it."

"You've had her stashed at your place for the last two years?" Mike asked. "You should have brought her sooner."

Toni spoke up, not realizing she was making a mistake until it was too late. "Oh, Harry wouldn't let anything happen. Not until I was out of the old life. That's why he wouldn't bring me. Or mention it. I didn't exist until I wasn't a hooker."

Harry looked over at her, his melancholy eyes settling on her with a weight she could feel.

"Harry, you're kind of a jerk," Cathy said.

He didn't respond.

"No, no, it's not like that," Toni insisted. "He just- he just didn't want to take a chance on me until…" she trailed off, finally seeing the look on Harry's face. "I just… never mind."

Harry reached over and took her hand so she wouldn't think he was upset at her. "I wasn't ready, that's all. It was my deal, not hers."

They looked at each other with identical smiles. Cathy grinned at her friend. And then Porter opened his mouth again.

"The sex must be pretty spectacular, right? I mean… given her former line of work, she's gotta-"

Cathy backhanded Porter. The flat smack of her hand against his cheek didn't echo. At the same time, Mike said, "Fucking asshole."

Mitch echoed the sentiment. "You're a *dick*, Porter."

Sandy's looked at Toni, whose downward-cast gaze told her everything. She stood up.

"I'm not staying here if *he* does," she said. She put a hand on Toni's shoulder. "And neither is Toni."

"So leave," Porter said.

Sandy crossed her arms in front of her. "Guess again, shmuck."

"Oh, come on-" Porter started. Michael cut him off.

"She's right. That's it. Get the fuck out of my store," he growled. "Cathy, walk him out, give him his fucking gun, and lock it behind him, would you?"

"Damned right. Let's go, Porter," she said, rising.

"Porter looked from face to face. "Are you kidding me? Over *her*? She's a fucking hooker! What's the big deal?"

Cathy put a hand on Porter's chair. "Not telling you again, Porter."

He looked up at her. "What are you going to do, Cathy? Arrest me? Shoot me? Huh?"

"I will fucking pistol-whip you unconscious, drag your sorry ass out into the street, and handcuff you to a railing, *so help me God*. You're being a shit. You're being *rude*, you're being intentionally shitty to her, and you've worn out everyone's patience. We're going to have a better time when you get gone. Now get up, grab your coat, and let's *go*."

She actually put a hand on his arm and started hauling him up. He looked around and saw that no

263

one was looking at him. Harry was examining his cards, Toni was staring at the floor, Mitch was making himself a sandwich, Mike studied his drink, and Sandy was looking at Toni. Porter snorted.

"Fine. Buncha assholes." He stood up, swayed, and caught himself on the edge of the table.

"You're drunk, Porter," Mike said. "But you better shut up before we stop taking that excuse."

"Come on, Porter," Cathy said. "Let's go. Right now."

She led Porter to the front of the store, pulled his pistol out of her jeans. She dropped the magazine out of the grip, caught it, and racked the slide with the same hand in one smooth motion. She caught the popped round out of the air, and handed all three to Porter. She shut the door in his face and locked it pointedly. She turned her back on him and went into the back room. She tried to ignore the crawling, nape-of-the-neck feeling of leaving him with a weapon behind her. But he was a cop, drunk or not, and she wouldn't believe him capable of insanity like that. She joined the group in the back room. Mike and Sandy were reassuring Toni that Porter wasn't normally like that.

"He's not what you'd call a *nice* guy," Sandy was saying, "but he's normally not such an asshole, either."

Cathy slid into her seat, listening. Harry spoke up. "He's wound up about something. It's not just Hill. It's not just the murders. Something's tweaking him," he said softly.

Mike blew air through his pursed lips. "Nothing gives him the right to be such a prick," he said.

Toni said, "He really doesn't like me, does he?"

Cathy spoke up finally. "This doesn't matter, not one bit. What he said was out of line. But… Francine left him a while ago."

Harry looked up, shocked.

Toni looked form Harry to Cathy. "Francine… his wife?"

"Yeah," Harry said.

"That doesn't give him any reason to come down so hard on you. You two… being happy… sure, it had to sting, but that doesn't give him the right to treat you like crap, Toni. I apologize. For him, for everything he said. I'm sorry," Cathy said.

Toni shook her head. "If ever I worried about what people thought about me, I'd crawl in a hole and never come out. Harry's opinion matters. And all of you, because you're his friends, and you've been nice to me. But Porter doesn't bother me."

Mike patted her hand. "Doesn't mean we're not embarrassed by him."

"I don't blame *you*," Toni said. "That's stupid. That would be stupid."

"*Porter's* stupid," Sandy said. "He's always been rough, but tonight he was so far over the line."

Cathy said, "You really don't understand what just happened, do you?"

"What do you mean?" Toni asked.

"Sometimes when you're not happy, seeing someone who *is* can make you crazy. Make you just completely insane. I don't think Porter's necessarily angry at you *or* Harry. I think he's just really upset because he lost what you've got."

Harry looked at Cathy thoughtfully. "Interesting."

"I'm sorry that happened to him," Toni said. "But that's no reason to be a jerk. And being a jerk is every reason for her to leave him."

"He never mentioned any trouble to me," Harry said. "You'd think he would have said…"

Cathy and Sandy looked at him and looked away.

"What is it?" he asked.

Sandy bit her lip, but being a fellow cop, Cathy saw no reason to hold back. "Harry, I'm surprised you don't know, but… Porter doesn't actually like you all that much."

Harry looked blank. "No, that… that's… why do you say that?"

Mike nodded along with them. "They're right, Harry. He doesn't, like, go off on you or anything, but he's not your biggest fan. He's never said why, but he definitely doesn't think highly of you. He… you know… he's brought it up a couple times why you're even still invited to these games."

Mitch said, "We told him to go fuck himself. You never did anything to get kicked out, and you're always nice. A little distant, sometimes, but always nice. Porter just turned into a dick. So, we all figured he'd be the one to get kicked out if anyone did."

"If he's really having a rough time, then maybe he just needs someone to talk to?" Toni asked. "A friend? I know what it's like to have one friend who won't let you down."

She looked at Harry with a very sweet smile. Everyone grinned as Harry flushed.

"Maybe, but the one person in this room who considered himself a friend of Porter's is the same one who gets to be the target when something good finally happens in his life, and Porter doesn't feel the same," Cathy said. "As far as I'm concerned, fuck Porter Rockwell. And you shouldn't waste your time, Harry. He's not worth it."

Harry didn't say anything for a while, and they all just sat there. Finally, he shrugged. "It is what it is. He wants to talk, I'm around."

"You're too good for the likes of him, Harry," Cathy said. She looked around him at Toni. "He might be good enough for you, though, hon."

Toni laughed. "He'll do."

Harry scooped up the cards and shuffled. "You guys want to play, or are we done?"

"Fuck that," Cathy said. "I came here to have a good time, some booze, and some food. I'm not leaving until I'm bloated, drunk, and rich."

Harry chuckled, and Mitch laughed out loud. "You might get drunk, and you can out-eat any three of us, but I'm taking you to school, babe."

"Bring it, big-mouth," Cathy said with a snide grin.

"Pour it, baby," Sandy said to Mike, holding out her glass. Mike killed the bottle, tossed it into a box nearby, and stood up.

"I'll go grab some more," Mike said. He ran out to the store and pulled down another bottle.

They played for two more hours. Despite the rocky start, they actually began having a good time. Laughing and joking, they sat and played and got to know Toni and surprisingly, Harry. They had always known Harry was a decent person, but seeing him with Toni opened up an entire part of his personality none of them had ever seen before. They discovered that they liked Harry a little more now. Toni was full of laughter and Harry couldn't help but smile every time she laughed out loud at a rude comment or a crude joke. She made many of them on her own and Harry didn't seem to mind being the butt of them. Cathy reflected privately that if she'd known Harry was such a man, she'd have made a move on him long ago. *You never can tell*, she thought. Now, though, even if she were inclined to be a bitch to Toni and try and swipe Harry away, she could see in his eyes that there weren't any women in the world aside from Toni. All the other women were just people. For Harry, *she* was the only woman that existed. Gave you hope, she mused.

They broke up around two and Toni helped clean up the food and dishes while Harry put the chairs and table away. They all walked to the door and Harry found himself disappointed for the first time that poker night was over. He shook hands with Mitch and Mike and hugged Cathy and Sandy. Toni gave everyone a great big hug and a kiss on the cheek, and she and Harry left hand-in-hand. The group watched them head for Bleecker.

"That," said Cathy, "is so weird."

"I think it's sweet," Sandy said.

"Sure it is," Mike said. "But also strange. I'm glad he found someone. Even a hooker."

Sandy and Cathy both looked at him. "*Even?*"

"What?" Mike asked.

"She's not some… lower class, Mike," Sandy said.

"I didn't mean that. Just… you know… a hooker?" he said plaintively.

The women looked at each other, and then at Mitch, who put up his hands and said, "I have no opinion at all. I don't care about anything enough to criticize it."

Mike laughed, and stopped as the women turned on him. "You think you're so much better?"

"Than a hooker?" Mike asked. "Little, maybe."

"Ex-hooker," Sandy said.

"Yeah, for about twenty minutes," Mike said.

"I didn't hear you speaking up in there," Cathy said. "You had plenty of opportunity."

"Look, just because I think it's a little sketchy doesn't mean I'm gonna step all over his happiness. I'm a jerk, not an asshole," Mike said. "Not like Porter."

Cathy nodded. "Yeah. I don't know what they hell got up his ass tonight, but he was out of line. Harry should have knocked his teeth down his throat."

Mitch nodded. "He's starting to lose control more and more. I hear the Captain's had to step on a couple of complaints. Sooner or later Porter's going to go too far."

"Is it true about Francine?" Mike asked.

"Yeah," Cathay said. "Kicked him out of his place. No idea where he's living right now."

"That's rough," Mitch said, as he zipped up his coat against the weather. "But I'm not going to lose sleep over it. Good night."

Mitch walked away toward the subway. Sandy linked her arm through Mike's. "Walk me home?"

"You got it," Mike said.

"Good night, you two," Cathy said, and headed toward Houston to grab a cab that would take her to the Bronx.

Chapter Twenty-Six

Jasper was gone and his spot was snowed over. Harry checked the messages. Nothing important. A thank-you from Cecilia Blankenship. Three calls for Chinese takeout. Nothing else. Toni kissed Harry on the cheek and went into the bathroom. Harry shucked his jacket and shoes and sat on the edge of the bed. The look of anger and hurt on Porter's face came back to him and he leaned forward, elbows on his knees, hands dangling between them.

What the hell was Porter's problem? And since when did Porter not like him? Was he that much of a downer that Porter didn't want him in the game? He and Porter had never been partners, but they'd worked together a number of times. Porter made detective early, and Harry had never had a chance to carry the gold shield. But as a patrolman, Harry had canvassed for Porter on numerous scenes, brought in witnesses, and helped him make two arrests. Harry had looked forward to the day he got his badge and moved up to homicide, but it wasn't to be. After his wound, Harry couldn't pull the trigger on the gun enough times, couldn't hold it aloft, couldn't do pushups. He lost a lot of motion and feeling, and it ended his career. He'd been very angry at first, angry all the time, but that had gradually given way. You can't stay angry forever, he discovered.

He pulled off his socks. His head had cleared as the whiskey slowly wore off. He unbuttoned his shirt and took it off, just to look at his scar in the mirror.

He was still standing there, prodding and manipulating the stiff patch of scar tissue when Toni came out of the bathroom. She was naked, her hair was slicked back, and she had a smile on her face. He looked at her.

"What are you doing, Harry?" she asked.

"Nothing. Just looking," he said. He looked back at the mirror and rotated his arm. As usual, he had a catch at the top of the windmill. He followed his collarbone from the hollow of his throat outward, stopping as he always did at the thickened part of the bone, where it had healed from the break. Just beyond that was the scar. He pressed it and winced. It still hurt if he put pressure on it. Toni came over to him and ran her fingers over the same trail, stopping at the scar. She gently massaged it. Then she bent to kiss it.

He tingled as her lips touched the scar tissue, even though he couldn't really feel it. She kissed along his collar bone, and to his neck. She kissed him in a line up his neck and down his jaw line. He closed his eyes and put an arm around her.

She kissed his lips and he responded. Kiss after kiss, they enjoyed the feel of one another. She lifted her face to him and whispered, "Tonight?"

He debated for what seemed like an eternity. Finally, he sighed. "I… I just… I don't-"

She put a finger on his lips, stopping his words. "It's okay. It's okay."

"It's not," he said angrily. "I don't know what I'm waiting for. I don't know *why* it doesn't feel right yet. Why it… it isn't *time* yet," he said. He looked into her eyes. "I will, though. I *will* know, and the second I do, I'll tell you."

"You'd better," she said. She disengaged and crawled into the bed. Into *their* bed. "Come hold me?"

He nodded. He stripped off his pants and turned out the light. "Give me a second."

In the bathroom he examined himself closely in the mirror, angrily berating himself. *Moron,* he thought. *Idiot,* he thought. *Ridiculous. Stupid. Unnecessary. What the hell is wrong with you?* He didn't know the answer. But he knew in his heart it didn't feel right yet. He was oddly heartened by that. For two years he'd refused to touch her. Now he was holding her, and kissing her, and thinking *yet* instead of *if.* Progress? *Of a kind,* he admitted. *It would be a hell of a lot easier if I understood myself.*

He brushed his teeth and finished his ablutions, and turned out the light. He went to the bedside and climbed under the covers. Her body was still cold from the shower, and he wrapped her in his arms to warm her.

"What are we doing tomorrow?" she asked.

"Tomorrow I go over to Brooklyn and see the D'Amico crew. After that, I thought I might go find Porter and have a talk with him. Or a fight. I haven't decided which yet," Harry said.

"You don't have to get into it over me, Harry," she said. "It doesn't mean a thing to me, what he thinks."

Harry said, "I know. But you're my girl, and I don't take that kind of shit from anyone. If I-"

"Your girl?" Toni asked.

"Aren't you?"

She smiled widely. "Since *forever,* Harry."

"Well, then. I'm not going to let anyone trash-talk my girl. That's not on your account, but on *mine.* No man would allow that," he said, a little self-consciously. "No matter what."

She pressed back against him and hugged his arms more tightly around her tiny body. "Your girl."

"Yep," he said.

She sighed and said with a smile, "Do I get a letterman sweater, Harry? Or a class ring to wear?"

"No, but I'll get you a gun."

"Sold, honey," she said. "Do they come in pink?"

"I doubt it."

"Nuts," she said. "So while you're off talking to mobsters and fighting cops, what am I supposed to do?"

"I want you to call the morgue and see if you can find anything out about the girls," Harry said. "Eugene should have finished them by now, and he might know something about them. Some clue he might have turned up."

"Eugene?"

"Kaminski, the head coroner. He'll be the one you need to talk to. I'll write down the information before I go. See if you can get him to make you copies of the files. Technically, we're not supposed to-" he broke off. "Uh, technically, the *police* aren't supposed to let civilians see the files, much less make copies, but Eugene likes me. Tell him I said he throws a baseball like Thurman Munson. He'll know it's me sent you then."

"Who's Thurman Munson?"

"He used to catch for the Yanks. He died last year. Eugene has every card they ever made for Munson. He was a huge fan," Harry said.

"Oh. Is Eugene good at throwing a baseball?" Toni asked.

"God no," Harry said. "He couldn't hit the broad side of a barn if he were inside it."

She laughed. He chuckled against her neck, sending shivers down her spine. They lay in darkness for a while before she said, "Thank you for standing up for me."

"You're welcome," he said.

Chapter Twenty-Seven

Harry awoke the next morning to the smell of eggs and bacon. He rolled over and smiled as he watched Toni working on one corner of the huge flat grill.

"Good morning!" she called, stabbing at the eggs with a metal spatula she'd found God alone knew where.

"Morning," he said.

She took time out from grill duty to bring him a glass of orange juice. He rolled over and sat up, legs dangling off the bed, sipping the cold, tart juice.

"I ran over to Dahli's. We didn't have anything for breakfast aside from tomato juice. Surprise," she said.

"Yeah, I haven't bought groceries for a while," Harry agreed.

"Like forever," she said.

"Not forever," Harry protested, "just a season or two."

They ate breakfast in companionable silence. The heavy feel of the whiskey was gone from between his eyes by the time Harry finished. "Good eggs," he said. "Thank you."

"You're welcome. I haven't cooked in ages. Not since I- not since I was little," she said, stumbling over her words. He pretended not to notice. She'd never told him where she came from, and he wasn't going to ask. Either she'd tell him or she wouldn't.

After a hot shower, Harry dressed for the day. He wrote down the information she'd need to try and track down the autopsies from the dead girls. He gave her a kiss and headed out the door.

An hour later he was in Brooklyn, watching the Four Aces Jewelry outlet from a food cart down the street. He slowly chewed his hot dog while watching the traffic. There didn't seem to be anyone watching the store from any obvious vantage, aside from him. No unmarked vans, no suspiciously unsuspicious vagabonds. If the Feds were watching, they were either taking a break, or more likely, had rented an apartment on one of the buildings nearby from which to watch unobserved.

The Gambino Family had a lock on the greater part of New York City, but the Feds were barking closer every year. The broad sweep of the RICO statutes allowed the Feds to scoop up gangsters like a whale scooping krill. Any crime they had proof of could be applied to anyone known to be associated with the perpetrators. Prosecutions had risen, crime had fallen, and everyone was happy except the criminals.

As Harry finished the hot dog he hadn't really wanted and had only bought for a reason to stand and watch, a Cadillac pulled up on front of the Aces, and four men got out, looked around in a laughably shift manner, and went inside. Sal D'Amico waited for one of his men to open the door. Harry tried not to smile. The Old World bullshit. They loved their stereotypes.

He thought about how to play it, how they'd accept it from him. It was a crapshoot either way, but he didn't think soft was the way to go. At the same time, he realized he was walking into a dangerous situation. They might not have the pure power and fear they'd commanded for decades, but they were still gangsters. Still dangerous. Still Mafia, despite the thinning of that once-great herd.

He sauntered to the door, looked around slowly to give any Federals taking pictures time to get some good shots, and went inside. It looked like every jewelry store he'd been in with a huge horseshoe counter and a couple of smaller island display cases. There were two clerks, one male and one female, behind the counter. The man scowled and the woman smiled. The four men from the car weren't in the store proper.

He walked up to the scowling man and smiled. "Hey, how you doin?"

"Good morning, sir," he said.

"Tell Sal that Harry DeMarko's here to see him."

Harry turned his back on the guy and leaned against the counter.

"Sir, I-"

"Just tell him," Harry said in a tone of finality.

The guy looked at the girl and motioned. She went into the back room. A moment later, one of Sal's bruisers came out. He cleared his throat, but Harry didn't turn.

"Hey, pal," the flunky said.

"What?" Harry asked.

"Who the hell are you?"

"I told your dummy here. Harry DeMarko. I'm here to see Sal. Run along." Harry stared at the street.

The bruiser stared at him for a minute. He went in the back. After a long moment, Sal came out.

"Who the hell are you?" he said in a nasal voice.

Harry turned around with a big smile on his face. "Sal D'Amico. Don't tell me you don't remember me."

D'Amico searched Harry's face. He shrugged. "Never seen you before, pal."

"Sure you have. Picture me in blues. Gun, badge. Maybe that'd jog your memory," Harry said.

Sal shook his head. "You're a cop. Cops all look alike to me. Why do I know you?"

"You don't. Somewhere private we can talk?" Harry asked.

Sal blinked, caught off-guard by the mysterious act. "What do you want?"

"To talk, like I said. Won't cost you a thing. Might even benefit you. What do you say?" Harry asked.

"Talk about what?"

Harry looked at the counter and shrugged. Sal debated, and finally motioned Harry into the back room. Harry slid around the counter and past the muscle.

The back room was bigger than he expected. A card table was set up under the central light, and the other two bruisers were setting up for pinochle. Harry nodded at them. They remained impassive. Sal walked to the table and sat down. "Spill it and get out, pig," he said.

"First of all, you need to know I'm not a cop anymore. I was, I'm not now. Got shot. I'm retired."

"So?" D'Amico said. "I didn't do it. I gotta alibi."

"I never said you did. I just wanted you to know I'm not a cop," Harry said. D'Amico studied him. He didn't say a word, but Harry could see him thinking it over.

"I'm a private investigator now," Harry said. "I get hired to do things the cops can't or won't take care of."

"Like what?" D'Amico asked, almost out of reflex.

"Like dead hookers, for instance."

D'Amico looked perplexed. Harry took note of that. He didn't look shifty, he didn't look cagey, he didn't look angry or amused. He just looked confused.

"Come on, Sal," Harry said. "You're not gonna tell me you don't know about Mr. Jay's girl Bebe, or Cheddar's girl Katy. Both of them turned up with unnecessary holes in them in the last two weeks."

D'Amico shrugged. "No idea what you're talking about."

Harry frowned. As unlikely as it was, Harry believed him. He sounded sincere.

"Besides," D'Amico said. "Mr. Jay went and got himself erased anyhow. Probably the guy you're looking for's the same one whacked him out."

"Naah," Harry said casually. "I'm the one did *that*."

All four sets of eyes were on him now. D'Amico's eyebrows climbed. "Say what?"

Harry said pleasantly, "It's not like that, Sal. He jumped me. Him and his boy Marvin tried to strong-arm me outside my place. I'm the one shut them down. And I know *I* didn't kill those girls. And neither did Jay. So, just out of curiosity, whose crew did you piss off?"

D'Amico licked his lips. "You're saying you put down two of my employees?"

"I'm saying they went off the reservation. A cop, even a retired one, is off limits. You *know* that," Harry said, giving him a flat look.

D'Amico didn't nod, but he came close. And it was true. Nothing brought down the heat like a dead cop. Even when they were dirty, it pissed off the public, made life on the streets hard, and did nobody any good. Despite the bravura, the bullshit, and the violence, the OC, Organized Crime, was at its heart a business. They were in the business of making money. As much as they could, for as little effort as they could. Dead cops made it hard, sometimes impossible, to make a living.

Harry knew, like every cop knew, that crime didn't pay much. Oh, sure, a street crew might make a grand a week. They didn't *keep* a grand a week. At least half went to the crew runner, maybe more. No matter what Jay had been making, he gave the lion's share to D'Amico.

D'Amico didn't keep it either. He had to pass it up the rope. And so on, until you got to the top guys. They had money coming in from all over, in dribs and drabs. They worked their asses off, the guys at the bottom, but they didn't exactly make gravy.

Most of the time, it was the perks that kept them in the life. A connected guy goes into a restaurant, he doesn't pay. Not if the owner's smart. No bar charged them. They didn't pay for clothes. Or cars. So the money they earned, even though it wasn't glamorous, was all frosting. Throw-away money. Play money. That's why they kept doing what they did. They got used to the life.

"I didn't kill him because of some stupid turf war and I didn't do it to muscle in on you. I'm not making moves. With all due respect to you, I am *not* a threat, Sal. If he hadn't been fucking stupid, he'd still be alive and earning for you. And when you find someone else to take over for him, I won't have a problem with them just because of what they do, or who they work for. But that's not why I'm here. Why I'm here is, someone killed a couple girls on my streets, and I won't have it."

"You won't have it?" Sal asked with a snide smile. "Who died and made you king?"

"Fucking Jay Leslie, for one," Harry countered. "Marvin Salano, for another."

Sal blinked first, and then let out a barking laugh. His guys chuckled.

"Look, helping me is in your best interest. Right now, someone's laughing at you, Sal," Harry said. Sal D'Amico scowled. "Someone put down a couple of your moneymakers. Hit you right in the wallet. That'd be enough to piss me off."

"Not as bad as you making me find someone to take over Jay's string," D'Amico said with a warm smile that Harry didn't trust for a second.

"That's not business, that was personal, and had nothing to do with you. Jay was a little smarter, he'd still be alive. He'd been a little smarter, he wouldn't have started a personal beef on your time. You don't want a guy that dumb working for you, do you? What would you have told him, if he'd come to *you* about it? You'd have told him to let it go. Doesn't pay to mess with the cops, does it? And I *know* he was on his own. If I thought for a single second that you'd authorized a hit on me, Sal, this would be a much different, and much louder, conversation," Harry said, and he patted his hip where his gun usually lay under the jacket. In point of actual fact, he wasn't armed today. There were better than even odds that he would be searched at some point, either by D'Amico's thugs or by the Feds when they scooped him up to find out who the hell he was, and he didn't want the hassle of carrying a gun in either situation.

Sal's thin face had lost its smile. "Oh, you think so?"

"You *don't?*" Harry asked.

"You don't look like much," Sal pointed out.

Harry grinned. "I'll bet Mr. Jay thought that very same thing. It might even have been his last thought."

They stared at each other for a minute, and Sal coughed out a grudging laugh. "You're not bad under pressure," he allowed.

"I'm not *under* pressure," Harry said. "But I've got very little patience today. What are you going to give me about the hookers?"

Sal looked at his guys. "Any of you heard anything about the broads you haven't told me yet?"

All three shook their huge heads. Harry guessed Sal had had a height and weight requirement when picking his muscle. Her knew for damned sure they didn't go by SAT scores.

"They don't know shit, and neither do I," Sal said. "It ain't a crew beef. If it were, there'd be way more than two. You find out different, maybe you drop me a line. Other than that, how about you go screw?"

Harry didn't take offense. It was a predictable fact of life that crooks postured to cops, and cops sat on crooks. It didn't mean anything except the forms of conduct was being obeyed by all involved.

"You want me to believe if you could help me, you would?" Harry asked. "That don't sound like Skinny Sal to me."

Sal bristled at Harry's familiar tone and his nickname being casually cast around.

"I'll let you know the very instant anything you think becomes of interest to me," Sal said in a snotty tone. "The very instant. Now if you don't mind, my associates and I have other, important business to attend to."

"No problem," Harry said. "I'll show myself out."

At the door to the front of the store, Harry stopped and asked, "What about the cop?"

Sal looked up at him. "What cop?"

"The undercover in your crew. What about them? You heard anything?" Harry asked casually.

Sal's eyes narrowed and he stared hard at Harry, brow furrowed with thought. Finally he shrugged.

"You're fishing, *ex*-cop," he said. "There was an undercover in my crew, you'd die before mentioning it."

Harry grinned. "But now you're wondering, aren't you? Maybe you better take a harder look at everything up on Bleecker. Maybe check out *all* your guys a little more thoroughly. Put some attention there. Just to be sure."

Harry let Sal stew about that as he left the back room. Of course he'd been fishing, but that didn't mean it wasn't true. And any chance to sow discontent was a good chance to take. Whenever the OC thought they had a mole, business slowed to a crawl while they hunted around. Nine times out of ten, there wasn't a mole. They would probably find one anyhow, some poor unlucky sap who skimmed too much, or mouthed off too much. He'd vanish and everyone would feel good about it and business would get back to normal. But it cut down on crime for a couple three weeks while they made sure.

Harry browsed the jewels for a minute or two in case Sal sent a guy after him for a 'one more thing' chat, but no one came out so Harry flipped up his collar. The wind was really bad today. He was pissed

Sal had been another dry well. And worried. If it wasn't a gang beef, and it wasn't a pimp beef, that left only one other choice, and Harry didn't want it to be that choice.

Someone was targeting hookers specifically to kill them. If it wasn't business, it was personal. And if it was personal, that meant crazy. Berkowitz had left a bad taste in everyone's mouth, and that fear still bubbled below the business-as-usual surface of New York. Harry thought about it as he stood out in the street. The wind whipped his coat tails around like flags, and he trudged through the new inches of snow toward the corner. He waited, and turned left on impulse. Once out of sight of the Aces, he stopped and waited. Several taxis passed him with their lights on, but he didn't flag them down. He waited for most of an hour and considered giving up when a white panel van pulled up in front of him. Harry nodded amiably at the driver. The side door rolled open and two suits wearing nondescript men climbed out. The driver got out, and they took up a three-cornered stand around him, two of them out of the line of even his peripheral vision.

"About time," Harry said. "I'm freezing."

"Sorry to keep you waiting," the lead agent said.

"In the van?" Harry asked.

"In the van," the lead agent confirmed. "*After* you grab some door."

Harry took up a stance against the van, feet spread wide and far back behind him, putting him off balance and at a severe disadvantage. The lead agent noted this.

"Been frisked a lot? You in the system, friend?" he asked Harry.

"Sort of. Usually I'm on the other side," Harry told him casually.

All three paused at that. The lead said, "You're doing the frisking?"

"Used to. Worked out of the Ninth, across the way. Used to beat the Village," Harry offered.

"You're a cop?" the lead asked.

"Retired. Wallet's in my jacket pocket, boys."

The pat-down ceased as the second agent found Harry's wallet. He had Harry's private investigation license, his membership to the Benevolent Association, and his union card identifying Harry as a former police officer. The wallet snapped shut and the agent held onto it.

"You want to tell me what you're doing here, Officer DeMarko?"

"Ex," Harry corrected. "Two years now. Wounded in the line."

The lead agent looked at his third guy, who nodded and jumped into the van to make some calls. "Okay, ex-officer. Same question."

"You already know," Harry said. "That's why you stopped me. If you weren't listening, you wouldn't have."

"No," the agent corrected, "we *weren't* listening. Your pal Sal has his place swept for bugs on a daily basis. We haven't gotten anything in there this week. But we have some lovely photos of you in the shop, talking with the boys, and generally inserting your unwanted self into our operation."

"Ah. Okay. A run-down," Harry said, and gave them everything, as word-for-word as he could.

"Hookers?" the second agent said with a sneer. "Who gives a shit about hookers?"

Before Harry could snarl a response, the lead agent said. "Shut your mouth, Dean."

The second agent, Dean, shot a look between his lead and Harry. He scowled but said nothing. The lead agent waited for a long moment. Harry thought he was thinking it over until agent three popped out of the van, and handed Harry the wallet. *Ah,* Harry thought. *Stalling for time.*

"All checks," he said. "It's true, what he said."

The lead agent nodded. "I'm Agent Mills. These are agents Willoughsby and Capretti," he said, pointing to three and Dean in turn.

"Harry DeMarko," Harry said. "I'm not here to step on your toes or jam you up. Just following the leads."

Mills nodded. "I gotcha. Do it elsewhere, though."

"I did what needed to be done," Harry said, bristling. "And if it leads this way again, I'll do it again."

"Obstruction," Agent Dean Capretti offered. "Interfering with a Federal investi-"

"Cram it, Feebie," Harry said with a smile. "I'm not a rookie. But you are, trying out the obstruction line on me."

Harry looked at Mills. "Coulda made it hard for you. Could have gotten a cab and taken a ride out to LaGarbage. Walked the terminals, taken a cab to Grand Central. Maybe toured the subway. Wasted a whole lot of manpower and time on a dead lead. Think I don't know a dozen games to fuck your day? But I waited here in the cold for you to catch up. That's not even vaguely obstruction. Hell, I'm practically gift-wrapping myself. I have intel on the inside of that shop *you* don't have."

Mills scowled at Dean. "Go sit in the van, Junior."

Dean opened his mouth to smart off, but Mills looked at him. Harry saw that Mills didn't have to speak. His agents knew him well enough to know not to argue. Dean bit off his comeback and climbed into the van, slamming the door.

Mills eyed Harry. "What was that about an undercover?"

"Smoke," Harry said. "Just to stir him up."

"And if he finds someone?" Mills asked quietly. "That's on you."

"Come on, Mills," Harry said. "That was just-"

He broke off and stared at Mills with something like horror. He closed his eyes. "Shit. You've *got* an inside man?"

Mills said nothing.

"Okay," Harry said, his voice low and contrite. "That one's on me. Boneheaded. My apologies. It's not personal, it's just street shit."

Mills considered for a moment, and shrugged. "It's probably not a big deal. If they couldn't sniff out any theoretical agents we had inside when we put them there, they won't find them with another sweep. But if they do…"

Harry nodded. "I get you. It's better than a trumped-up obstruction charge to jam me up."

"That it is. And DeMarko?"

"Yeah?"

"I'll let Dean file it," Mills said with a sly look.

Harry grinned. "Every pup's gotta cut teeth, right?"

Mills nodded. "Ain't it the truth. Got a card?"

Harry tugged one out of his wallet that wasn't too badly creased and handed it to Mills. He actually liked the Feeb. For a suit, he wasn't without his charm.

"All right. Get outta here," Mills said. He nodded to Willoughsby and they climbed into the van. With a sardonic, jaunty little wave from the front seat, Dean Capretti bid farewell. His extended middle finger showed a childish tendency toward displays of ego. Harry shrugged and turned away. He grabbed a cab and thought furiously all the way back to the office. He desperately wanted there to be *some* reason, some rational explanation for what had happened to Bebe and Katy, but it was looking more and more like a grudge.

"Hey," he told the cabbie. "Forget Elizabeth street. Take me to 201 West Fourteenth."

The cabbie nodded and they swung abruptly into the far lane instead of the near. Twenty minutes later, Harry climbed the snow-choked steps and knocked on the door of Porter's brownstone. After a couple of seconds the drape was tugged aside, and Francine Rockwell's handsome face peered out. Her eyebrows climbed and she unlocked the door.

"Harry?" she asked. She sounded unsure and Harry didn't blame her. He hadn't been to their place for five years.

"Hey, Francine. Yeah, it's me," he told her with a rueful grin.

"Porter's not here, Harry," she said. She hesitated, and finished, "he moved out a while ago."

"I heard you kicked him out," Harry said.

She put on a guarded look. He smiled at her and showed her empty hands. "Not an accusation. I just wanted to talk for a couple minutes," he said.

"Well, come in, then. Want coffee?"

He followed her into the house, kicking off his snowy shoes on the mat. "Sure."

They sat at the little dinette table sipping strong coffee with lots of sugar. Francine said frostily, "Why are you here, Harry?"

"I don't know. I heard last night that you and Porter split up. I guess I'm being nosy," Harry said with an apologetic smile.

She didn't return it. "It's true. We're getting a divorce."

"I'm sorry," Harry said.

"Why?"

He blinked. "Uh… I don't know. I thought you two were pretty happy. I guess I'm wrong."

"I was. Porter's a different story. I… look Harry, I'm not going to tell stories. I know you're his friend, and-"

"I thought so too," he said. "I think I was wrong. We… we got into it a little last night, and one of our friends mentioned that you and he were split up. I don't know what I'm doing here, really, but I wanted to talk to you. I wouldn't have thought it possible, but Porter was acting like a real jerk, bullying and arguing and just… being a shit, I guess."

She nodded and said with a voice full of regret, "Sounds like Porter."

"I don't know… I thought he and I were friends. And friends try to help."

"There's no help," she said. "He's not coming back. I told him if I saw him again I'd get a restraining order and start to tell his friends what he was *really* like. He packed up his clothes and he was gone that day. I came home and his key was shoved through the mail slot."

Harry nodded. "Did you change the locks?"

Francine smiled bitterly. "I was a cop's wife, Harry. I had them changed the minute I saw his key."

"Good for you. You have my number. You need anything, you call me, okay?" Harry asked. She nodded.

"I can't imagine what that would be, but okay," she said. "The kids and I are good. Mom moved back in for a while, but she went back to Morris and her place over in Queens. Now it's just the kids and I."

"Good deal. You know where he's staying, Frannie?" Harry asked her.

She shook her head. "He didn't tell me. I haven't a clue. I don't care."

Harry shrugged. "Well, I gave it a shot. Can't help if he makes it hard."

She smiled that brittle, bitter smile again. "I wouldn't bother, Harry. You can't help him. It wasn't an accident, and it wasn't a one-time thing. You *know* me, Harry. It isn't easy, being married to a cop. The hours, the fear, the bullshit. And I was married to him for *half my life*. I put up with the cop's shit because I *loved* him. The drinking, the late nights, the nightmares… it was all of a piece. Comes with the badge. But he was fucking around on me, Harry. *For years.*"

Harry blinked, stunned. Finally he shook his head. "Then fuck him."

She laughed, tossing her hair the way she always had when she was really tickled. "That's what I said."

He finished his coffee and set down the mug. "Thanks for the chat, Frannie. And I meant it. You need anything, you call. I'll come running."

"Usually you lose the friends in the divorce," she said, and he tried not to wince at the bitterness. She was only speaking the truth. "I know cops."

"I'm not a cop anymore," he said. "You know that. The blue doesn't own me. No more party lines. Now I *think* about my choices. I'm on your side, for whatever that's worth."

She smiled at him, a genuine smile. "Thank you, Harry."

"The kids doing okay?" he asked.

"They're… coping. Porter was a good dad, but he could be distant. They're okay seeing him on weekends and such," she said. "That should tell you something. He could be hard on them sometimes."

"Imagine that," Harry said. She smiled. He got up and she walked him to the door.

"Good seeing you Frannie," Harry said.

"You too. You've changed, Harry," she said.

He nodded. "Yeah. Not being on the job does that."

"Yeah, but… you're better now. You paid attention while we talked. You never used to be there. You'd talk, but your mind was always elsewhere," Frannie said.

He shrugged. "I have other priorities now."

"It shows," she said. Almost as if on impulse, she stretched up and pecked his cheek. He looked startled. She smiled at him. "What's the matter, Harry? Women don't kiss you when you've been sweet?"

291

"Actually," he said with a blush, "yes. Happens there's a girl. She, uh… we've been kind of living together for a while."

Frannie smiled widely. "Harry! That's amazing! I always figured you for the die-alone bachelor."

He frowned at that. "What?"

"Porter always said that you couldn't see anything that wasn't wearing a uniform," she said.

He nodded. "I was… driven. But since I had to retire…" He shrugged.

She nodded. "I get you. How's the arm?"

"You know. Hurts when it's cold. Largely useless. Same old, same old," he said. "Can't do much with it, but I can hug, so that's something."

Frannie nodded with a huge smile on her face. "That's important. Probably more than holding up a gun."

"I don't know," he said. "I still miss the force, every damned day."

She frowned. "It doesn't miss you. You know that."

Harry said, "Yeah. I know. They tell FBI agents that they'll fall in love with the Bureau, but the Bureau doesn't fall in love with them. Come retirement age, it doesn't matter what you did. You could save the president, stop the Russians, and find Lindberg's baby, and they still chuck you out the door. I think that's true of most any job in law. The wheels roll on. Sometimes they roll right over you."

She nodded and patted his arm. "You were lucky to get away. You've found something more important than wrestling with criminals, I hope."

"I hope so. It's early days, but it feels really good, you know?" he said, and looked guilty. She laughed.

"Harry, don't. It doesn't upset me to see you happy. And yes, I know what it feels like. And I will again, eventually. Porter didn't take away anything I can't find with someone else. But… I'll tell you this: I won't be with a cop again. I'm done with *that* life. I'm like you, I guess."

"What do you mean?"

"I got wounded, but I made it out alive. It's like a new chapter. I get to do something else from now on," she said.

He chuckled. "I like your point of view. At least you don't have a huge scar."

The smile dropped from her face. Harry's smile slowly melted. "Oh, no," he breathed. "No, no, Frannie. He didn't-"

"No," she said with a sigh. "He's never laid a hand on me. But he's a vicious in-fighter. He's said some pretty terrible things, and that hurts. I don't know if you've ever woken up to find someone you rely on has turned on you. But it hurts more than I can explain. I hate him, Harry. I'm disgusted to say that, but I hate him for what he did. I'm not being unreasonable. A one-time affair can be forgiven, I think, if there are circumstances. But he's habitual. There's been *dozens* of girls."

Harry's fist clenched.

"That can't be forgiven, and it can't be healed. That's all I meant by scars. Apparently I wasn't what he wanted. Wasn't what he needed. And that hurts too. It almost feels like my fault, stupid as that is," she said. "It's hard not to feel like I *did* something. Or didn't do something."

He nodded and touched her arm. "I'm sure it wasn't like that."

She looked out the door at the snow. Wistfully, she said, "One can hope. You have a good day, Harry."

"You too, Frannie." They hugged briefly.

"Bring your girl over some night. We'll have dinner. I'll interrogate her. See if she's good enough for you," Francine said.

"Or if I'm good enough for *her*?" Harry added.

"That too. Take care." Harry stepped into the bitter, stinging wind and the door closed behind him. It took him ten minutes to find a cab that would take him home. He relaxed in the oven-like atmosphere of the cab, not minding the overwhelming patchouli smell coming from the front seat. Finally, he was home. He paid and got out. Jasper was back in his usual spot. Harry went inside and found Toni sitting at his desk. Her eyes were huge and solemn. He forgot about the coffee and the pit of his stomach sank.

"Toni? What's wrong?" he asked.

She swallowed a couple of times, and finally said in a small voice, "I called your friend Eugene."

The hairs on the back of his neck rose. "What did he say?"

"He made me go over to the morgue to pick up the files. He wouldn't talk about them," she said. "Not over the phone."

"Okay... so you have them?" he asked.

"Harry... I did as you asked. I asked him for the files on the dead hookers," she said solemnly.

"Yeah?"

She bent over and picked up a stack of folders six inches thick from the floor and dropped them on his desk. There had to be eleven or twelve folders in the pile. He looked at the pile and looked at Toni. He said, "What's this?"

"These are girls going back for three years. He said that you should come see him, but the gist is, he started to think about the stab wounds, and realized he'd seen them before. He went into the unsolved files and started pulling autopsy records. He's found eleven so far, and said he's going to have to go into the archives downtown to find all of them. Harry," she said, and he felt like she sounded: scared and lost. She told him, "he said it's probably the worst serial killer New York's ever seen by a country mile."

Harry stared at the stack of files. He swallowed hard. He couldn't think of much to say except, "Well... shit."

Chapter Twenty-Eight

It took them two hours to go through the files. Harry called Eugene and fed Toni date and places. She scribbled like mad. Harry dug out an old map of New York out of his desk and they started putting circles on the map wherever a woman had been left.

"Harry... I know you're not going to want to hear this," Eugene said, "but I had to kick it upstairs. And I'm going to have to go back and look at *all* stab victims in New York for the past fifty years to see if there are any cases that were closed prematurely. I know you wanted to work this, but I'm betting they won't let you anywhere near it after this gets blown open."

Harry swore. "I wish you could have waited a day or two," he said.

"Harry, come on. You have to be reasonable," Eugene said.

"I don't have to, but I don't see as I have any choice," Harry said. "Let me ask you this: are they going to yank it from Porter?"

"Are you kidding?" Eugene asked. "Once this gets out, he'll be lucky to get a memo about it. This is going to go federal. And you know that means they won't let him near it, they won't let *us* near it, and they certainly won't brook *your* interference."

"Well, fuck, Eugene," Harry said. "How long?"

"They're letting me draft three medical students to finish the search. Say... two days?" Eugene hedged. "Maybe less. If we work from a probable maximum age of sixty from the most recent kills, that's forty years to search. I'm calling for sixty just to be safe, but like I said, we have to go through all the closed cases too, just to be thorough. That's going to take a little time, but not as much as you'd think. Even with solved and unsolved, everything's pretty accessible. We'll be able to pin 'em all down soon."

"All right, all right," Harry said. "Anything you can tell me? I've got the files here, but they're pretty sterile."

"The killer is about five-ten," Eugene said. "Height of the wound is consistent. It's always an upward stab, only varied by the height of the girls. He's right-handed-"

"How do you figure?" Harry asked.

"Grip and blade angle. It's a guess, but educated and backed by sound science. The stabs are too consistent. They come from the front, never from behind, like over the shoulder. Killer always faces the vic. And he uses a straight blade, single-sided, sharp . Most likely a Ka-Bar. It's got the shape. I can't tell if it's the same knife, but if he's smart-"

"He's smart, or he wouldn't be getting away with multiple murders," Harry pointed out. Eugene continued as though Harry hadn't spoken.

"-he'd just dump the knife every time and got buy a new one. They're three a penny at any Army-Navy surplus."

"I don't know," Harry said. "That'd be an easy way to fuck up and get caught. Clerks would notice if the same guy came in and bought a knife every week. Or he could be spreading out the buys. Or maybe he just bought one from each store. I don't know. Have to find out how many stores there are, and who sells what. Going to be a hell of a job."

"Not if the Feds grab it and run," Eugene pointed out. "Which they will."

"Well, we've got a little time yet. Have you called in Porter?" Harry asked.

"Not yet. Uh… Harry… he finds out that you stumbled on this instead of him-"

"I know, I know, Gene. Tell you what, I don't need the credit. It's not like the Big Building's gonna issue me a commendation. Let's leave it down to your persistent nature and unusual insight for details. Maybe you can get a raise out of it."

Eugene laughed. "Right. They're gonna give me a raise for prying into dozens of cases that've been forgotten or closed."

In reality, he was much more likely to garner ill will from a dozen different sources than get a raise. Nothing made a cop look worse than having a closed case reopened because they might have missed something.

"Yeah, well, hope for the best-"

"-plan for the worst," Eugene finished. "I'll go back through the file and see what else I can turn up. I'll call you if I get anything."

"Do that. You need these files back?" Harry asked.

"Nope. Made copies. They officially don't exist. Just… uh… just don't go waving them around, all right?"

"No problem, Eugene. And thanks," Harry said.

"Oh, you're welcome. We're about square, Harry. You'll owe me again, if you ask any more favors."

"Understood," Harry said as he hung up the phone. He stared thoughtfully at Toni.

"What?" she asked.

"You didn't know?" he asked. "I mean you and your... friends? That girls have been getting dead all over?"

Toni shrugged her shoulders. "Harry, these girls are from a dozen spots around the city. I'd be surprised if they knew *each other*, let alone any of us knowing all of them."

"That's true..." Harry said in a thoughtful tone of voice. "The killer's smart. He wouldn't pick from an area that would leave a trace. Hey... did you write down the OIC for each case?"

"The-"

"Officer in Charge," Harry said. "Sorry. Forgot you weren't a cop."

"Oh. Uh, no. Gimme a second." She started opening the files and finding the assigned officers.

"If you count Bebe and Katy," she said, "six of them were to Porter Rockwell. Two of them were further downtown, and one uptown. Three others on the West Village side. So, Porter Rockwell, Haley Simmons, Clinton Barlow, and Miguel Forrento."

She looked at Harry with a question on her lips, but he shrugged. "I know Porter and Haley. Barlow by name. Never heard of Forrento. Cause of death's always a single stab?"

She nodded. "According to the coroner's reports, there was nothing that I could see. Some cuts and scrapes but they were from the body falling. Cause of death was always one single strike to the ex-zeh... zaye?"

He looked at the word. "Yeah. Z-eye-foyd. Just under the ribcage."

"Xiphoid process, then, usually at a left-leaning angle. Always a single strike. What the hell, Harry?" Toni asked. "How's he doing this?"

Harry shrugged. "I don't know. They aren't struggling, they aren't scared, they aren't worried... oh, hell."

Toni cocked her head. "What?"

"Come on, Toni... you used to do this. What didn't *scare* you? What didn't you run from?" Harry asked.

"I don't... oh. Oh my God," she breathed, "he's a *john.*"

"Yeah. He's either posing as a john or he actually *is.* He offers them the money and then he kills them. They're not afraid. They're not *afraid,*" he stared hard at her. "They're not afraid. What johns weren't you afraid of?"

She got it then. "Oh, shit. Repeat customers. Guys I already *knew.*"

He nodded. "Yeah."

He crossed his arms and put his head down. Toni watched him. The look on his face was hard for her to read. He looked intent, and he looked intense. He looked...

He looks like a cop, she thought. *He looked like he used to. Right after he had to stop. He used to get that look. That hard, dangerous, thoughtful look. He'd become someone else. Someone hard. I don't think I'd have liked him when he was a cop. I like him fine now, but that look. That look would scare me if I didn't know how much he liked me.*

On the heels of that thought came one more.

God help whoever he catches doing this.

"Give me the phone," he said in a hard, cold voice. "It's time to call Porter."

Chapter Twenty-Nine

An hour later, Porter sat in the office with them. He leafed through the folders, while Toni sat barely containing herself, and Harry sipped a cup of truly vile, burned, ridiculously strong coffee. He savored the bite, and hoped it would lubricate his synapses into action. Porter hadn't wanted to come down to Harry's office. He seemed embarrassed about the poker night incident, but Harry quickly disabused him of any problems.

"This is *work*," he said. "We can deal with other shit later. You *need* to get down here and see what we have."

Porter had reluctantly agreed to come over. His face had gone from frankly disbelieving to dubious to perplexed stare in a matter of moments, and finally resigned anger.

"How could no one have *seen* this?" he said. "How could *I* have missed this?"

"No one spotted it, Porter," Harry said. "For years. Because no one cares about these victims."

"I know I didn't," Porter said quietly.

"That's his *strength*. Whoever's doing this is counting on no one caring that these women are being hunted. That they're being brutally murdered. Because they're *just hookers*," Harry said. His voice broke at the end, and Porter looked at him curiously.

"Would this mean as much to you if…" Porter trailed off and looked askance at Toni. Toni stared steadily back at him.

301

Harry shrugged. "I don't know. I'd like to think so, but you never know. The girls wouldn't have hired me if I didn't know Toni."

Porter looked confused. Harry said, "You were right last night. The other girls, the hookers. They're my client. The police- no offense- were getting *nowhere*. Toni convinced them I'd have more luck. Or at least, put out more effort."

Porter nodded. "Makes sense. We get reassigned. We get lazy. *I* got lazy. And no one gives a shit when some street chicken gets offed."

Toni inhaled deeply. Porter looked over at her. He saw her eyes and raised his hands. "You know what I mean. It wasn't like a... a declaration. It's just how it is."

She nodded, mollified somewhat.

"I figured it was an exhausted mouse," Porter said. "I tossed it to you to let you bat it around, so you'd feel useful again."

Harry didn't respond.

"Harry," Porter said sincerely, "I'm sorry for that. You didn't deserve to lose your job, but you also didn't deserve pity. That was my mistake."

"Well, it's a good thing you tossed it at me," Harry said. "Otherwise, who knows when someone would have picked up the pattern. The killer's been workin different street crews, different districts... that's why Eugene didn't catch it. Four different coroners were working bodies without knowing what was happening anywhere else."

"What do we do now?" Toni asked.

Porter and Harry looked at each other. Porter said, "Eugene told me he's going to have to send up a flare soon. We *might* have a day or two. What do we do?"

Harry shrugged. "I don't know. I'm not even sure where to start. We really need to start canvassing the working girls near all these kills. We need to start pulling files on guys picked up for solicitation. It's possible the guy is a repeat offender. We think the girls aren't scared because they're familiar with him, they've done him before. We need to find the girls and show them pictures of johns and see who knows whom. Start tracking down the ones busted and find out if they have alibis for the murders. But… that's impossible without an army of uniforms on the streets. That's assuming total cooperation by the girls, and you *know* that ain't happening. And most of the johns don't get picked up anyhow. It's a needle in a stack of needles. I don't see a way to resolve this easily. I mean… each of these women was killed by the same guy. He uses hookers, and they know him. That's the best theory we have. But how many girls compare notes? If this guy's even halfway smart, he goes about it the same way he'd buy his knives- spreading it out so he's never in one place more than once, or at least, never more than once or twice a month. I just don't know. Porter?"

Porter shrugged his massive shoulders. "I've got the same ideas as you. Unless we somehow stake out every hooker in the city and wait, I don't see how this one gets resolved. He's smart, this guy. This is a completely undocumented segment of the street. These girls don't report income, they don't log their johns, they don't do anything. And the pimps keep them from coming forward when they *do* have something out of the ordinary happen."

Toni looked helplessly from one to the other. "So that's it? There's nothing we can do?"

303

"Nothing productive right now. All we have is a half-assed theory so far. No evidence to speak of. The guy is good. He doesn't leave spoor-"

Toni raised her hands in a what-the-hell gesture. Harry explained. "He isn't leaving a trail. Lots of times, the killer leaves a fingerprint, footprint, or *some* kind of trace evidence. Like, dust from his house, or a fiber, or something. He's not leaving any of these things. Or at least, CS isn't *finding* anything. But they're not usually that sloppy. If there were significant clues to find, they'd trip to them. Most of the victims had traces of semen, for instance, inside them, but that's not going to help us except for maybe blood type, and even then... how many clients did these girls have? We could bark after innocent... well, relatively... men all day and never touch the killer."

Harry massaged his shoulder and looked miserable. "Maybe the massive resources of the Feebs will actually do some good this time. They'll have snitches and intel we can't get our hands on. They'll have a thousand agents to draw from and put out on the streets. They'd be able to set up a dozen traps, two dozen even," Harry said. He looked at Porter with his eyebrows raised. "Maybe we should jump it to them now, rather than later?"

Porter considered it. "You might be right. I can't think of anything else we can do. Can't canvass any more than was done at each scene."

"Canvass?" Toni asked.

"Question the people around the scene. 'Did you see anything' kind of stuff," Porter said. "The sites were all done by patrol. Nothing of any consequence, and now the trails're colder than a witch's tit. So no miraculous eye witness to step up and give us the lead we need. No forensic clues that anyone's been able to turn up. A good theory, but no facts to support it. Leaves us high and dry, Harry."

"Yeah. I guess we have to call in the Feebs," Harry said.

A banging on the door startled all of them. Harry went over to look and opened the door. The patrolman assigned to Porter looked at all three of them in turn.

"Detective Rockwell," he said. "They're calling for you."

Porter looked down at his radio. It was off. He cursed. "Forgot to turn the damned thing on."

He tuned it and the static was cut by the dispatcher calling out Porter's sign.

"Detective Rockwell, 2-3-6-2," he said into the radio. "I was 10-7b. I'm back. 10-9, over?"

Toni looked at Harry, who whispered, "He was out of service. Id'd with his badge number. 10-9 is repeat message."

Toni nodded.

The radio crackled. "2-3-6-2, be advised reported 187 at 223 East 2nd street-"

Harry and Porter looked at each other, startled. Toni saw from the looks that whatever it was, it wasn't good.

"Roger that 187. 2-3-6-2 on it. Out." Porter stared at Harry grimly.

"What?" Toni asked.

"187," Harry said thickly, "is a homicide."

"You want to roll with me?" Porter asked him. "In case it's another-"

"Yeah," Harry said. He grabbed his coat and bent down to kiss Toni. "I'll be back."

"Good luck," she said.

"Only if it's him," Harry said.

He followed Porter out the door and slid into the back of the black and white. They sped through the streets with the siren and lights going, and pulled up to the curb where patrolmen were just putting up tape. Porter got out and Harry followed him through the snow. Like the others, this body was in an alley between a restaurant and a bar. They came upon the circle of officers and CS specialists. Eugene looked up.

"Ah, Porter. Harry. It's our guy," he said without preamble. "And this time he's given us something to work with."

Harry went as close as he dared. She was on her back and her chest was covered in blood. Unlike the other girls, this body was different. From the pained grimace on her face to the scratches on her arms to the multiple stab wounds to her chest, this body was different.

Harry motioned to one of the patrolmen. "You got an ID yet?"

The uniform snorted and looked around. "You talking to me, civilian?"

Porter rounded on the officer. "Answer the fucking question and don't take that goddamned tone with him again."

The patrolman gulped. He tugged his pad out and checked it. "Sorry, sir. Uh, the vic's name isn't known at this juncture, but her street name's Timex."

Harry blinked at the man. Porter said waspishly, "What the hell's that mean?"

The patrolman grinned at Porter. "Apparently, she's a specialty girl. She gets paid to get beat up. They call her Timex because, uh, quote, 'she takes a kicking and keeps on licking.'" The patrolman chuckled.

Porter growled. "You think that's goddamned funny?"

The smile vanished. "Uh, no, sir."

"Who's your source?" Harry asked.

The patrolman pointed back at the mouth of the alley. Harry peered at the crowd and realized Cheddar and his boys were standing at the tape. Harry jogged over and motioned him closer.

"Ain't a cop, huh?" Cheddar asked.

"Ain't a cop," Harry said. "But I'm working with them."

"Yeah."

"So, what do you know about this?" Harry asked.

"Same as before," Cheddar said. "Nothing. But I'm pissed off now, I'll tell you that. Whatever you need, I can do."

"Good. I'm done finding bodies. What's her name? The rookie back there said you called her 'Timex'," Harry said.

"Yeah. She's a punching bag. Likes the pain. Guys pay extra to put a hurt on her," Cheddar said. "She's got, like, something wrong with her brain. She don't feel pain, not like we do. Made her laugh. Damndest thing. Never felt a thing when someone'd lump her up. But she could fake it. Guys like to hit, they're looking for a reaction, you know? So she knew how to cry and play it up, but she didn't get hurt. She made more than any girl on the street. Her name's Elaine something. I dunno her last name."

Harry nodded. "She got a record?"

"Yeah, she got a record," Cheddar said. "Hooking, assault, stuff like that. Nothing heavy."

"She'll be in the system then," Harry said. "Stick around. I may need more from you."

He turned to leave and Cheddar grabbed his arm. Harry looked at the hand, and then up at Cheddar's furious face.

"You find out anything, you come to me, you understand?" Cheddar said. "You give me a name, I'll make sure the fucker gets his."

"Why? Because you're losing money?" Harry asked.

"You know, *fuck* you, man. These girls are my livelihood, sure, but they're also my *girls*. They belong to me. I promise them I'll keep 'em safe. That I'll look out for them. Shit like this happens, it makes me look like an asshole. Like I can't protect my own. Think what you want, man, but I don't like being made to look a fool. I *want* this man. You get a name, you give it to me. Fuck the cops, man."

Harry nodded. "All right. I can understand that. But he's ours. Me and the cops. We'll find him. We'll take him out. Bet on it. You know how it happens. Resist arrest, we'll lump you up. Resist enough, you don't wake up. Happens all the time."

Cheddar nodded reluctantly. "Still, though. I'd rather do it myself. Hands-on."

"I completely understand," Harry said. "But it probably won't go that way. Stick around."

Cheddar did something completely unexpected. He offered up a fist. Harry looked at it, looked at him, and bumped it with his own.

"You're still a pig," Cheddar said. "But at least I know you're pissed off about the right things."

"Always was," Harry said. He left Cheddar at the rope and headed back up the alley. Porter had watched the entire exchange. Harry gave them the girl's name and background. When he finished, Porter thanked him.

"They won't talk to me," he said. "Even when they should."

"We have an understanding. It's not like we're pals. But he's pissed. He should be. What do we have?" Harry asked.

"Four stab wounds," Eugene said. "This one fought. I don't see *how*. She should have been incapacitated."

"Cheddar, her pimp, says she had a brain thing. She didn't feel pain," Harry said. "Said she thought it felt good, or something like that."

Eugene's eyes lit up. "Jesus! CIPA!"

"Seep-what?" Porter asked.

Eugene spelled it. "Congenital insensitivity to pain. Her brain couldn't interpret the signals. No wonder she kept fighting! She was probably dead on her feet and didn't know to quit."

"Cheddar said she didn't mind getting beat up," Harry said. "Made her laugh."

"There's blood all over the place," Eugene said. "A lot of splatter. If we're lucky she tagged him, and some of it is his. I'll rush through the blood typing. Might get lucky and he's in the- Jesus, Porter!"

"What?"

Eugene grabbed a pair of gloves and a cotton swab from one of his ubiquitous assistants. He knelt in the snow and grabbed Porter's left shoe. Porter wobbled on his right foot. "What the fuck, Eugene?"

"You stepped in the goddamned evidence, Porter!" Eugene snapped, and swabbed the blood from the side of Porter's shoe. He dropped the swab in the bag his assistant held out. "Be more careful! Shit like that's what'll get this case thrown out!"

Porter put his foot down and nodded. He seemed abashed. "Sorry. Got too close, I guess."

"Watch it!" Gene said. "You keep that shit up, you'll be a fucking meter maid!"

"I got it, I got it," Porter muttered. "I'm sorry."

"I was saying. We might get lucky and he's in the system. We could close this case, *all* the cases, in a week."

Harry nodded. "I like it. All right. Fuck the Feds. This is ours."

Porter looked at the patrolman. "What did the canvass turn up?"

"No one saw anything, Detective," the man said. "We're still looking, but it doesn't seem like it's going to be any good, just like the others."

Porter nodded. He motioned Harry and Eugene off to the side. "So, do we turn it over? Now that we might have more evidence?"

Eugene shook his head. "Let's see where it takes up. Officially, we're still looking at the two we had, plus this one. Let's not kick it up unless we have to."

Harry said, "I'm with Gene. Fuck the feds. We'll give it to them if we have to, but if there's a chance, we take it."

Porter thought about it. "All right. Eugene, get your geeks on it. I'll run Harry home and head to the station. I'm gonna have to argue it with the Captain, and Harry here's about his *least* favorite person."

Eugene turned back to the body, and Porter and Harry headed back to the car. Twenty minutes later, Harry shrugged off his jacket and filled Toni in.

"Jesus, Harry," she said. "Can you catch him, or what?"

"Well, we need to get very, very lucky. Until Gene gets all the evidence sorted, we're at a dead end. It's going to be a balancing act, keeping the case, but not having screwed up enough that Porter gets it in the neck. We can hope. We'll know in a couple days if we can get something from the body."

Toni shook her head. "In the meantime, another girl is dead, and he's out there maybe getting ready to do it again. Harry, we have to *stop* him."

Harry nodded. "I know. We're working on it. I promise we're working on it."

She went to him and hugged him, resting her head on his chest. "I know you are. I just wish it was over."

"Me, too."

"Hungry?" Toni asked. Harry nodded.

"I could eat. What do you want?"

"I think I want a pizza. Want to go over to Ray's?" she asked.

"Good enough. Fix a cup for Jasper while I use the bathroom," he said.

As they locked up and handed Jasper the coffee, the phone on Harry's desk rang. He went back inside to answer it.

"Harry?" an excited, breathless voice called.

"Eugene? What's going on?"

"Harry, we got skin!" the coroner crowed at him. Harry tugged the handset away from his ear, wincing.

"What?"

"Under her nails! She tagged him! We've got good trace under her nails. And I think I found a decent print!"

"You're kidding," Harry said. "I thought he's been wearing gloves?"

"I know. But I got a pretty good impression on her neck. Seven, maybe eight points of comparison!" Gene said. "It won't stand up in court, but God willing it'll give us the lead we need. I'm going to pull down everything, get all the time we need to run it, prioritize it right to the top!"

"Have you told Porter?" Harry asked.

"Right before I called you, sport," Gene said. "Caught him on his way home, I guess. Some kind of urgent thing."

Harry nodded. "All right. Keep me posted."

"Will do, Harry. We're gonna get him! I can feel it!" Gene said.

"I hope so," Harry said. "We could use a win. Later."

He hung up the phone. He started for the door and stopped. He sat down. It was good news. They finally had some good news. A print. Blood spatter. Scratches. Blood. Scratches. Prints. The thoughts whirled around in his head. He sat down to think, and glanced at the floor. A smudge. *Well, it's winter. It's to be-*

His heart stopped. He bent over and rubbed. He leaned back quickly and rubbed his hand on the leg of his jeans. He kept rubbing and rubbing at his fingers. Toni came back in to see what he was doing.

"Harry, what-"

312

"Quiet!" he barked. He sat there, perfectly still. Frozen in place. She didn't even hear him breathing. Toni blinked at his rough tone, but said nothing, standing inside the door, afraid to move.

As if in a daze, Harry picked up the phone and dialed a number. An answer, after a few rings. He asked a couple of questions. Toni cocked her head and looked at him as though he'd gone insane. He asked a few more questions, spoke for a moment, and hung up. He stared into space for a while. He picked up the phone again and called another number. He asked another question. Toni's eyes widened. Her hand went to her mouth. Harry nodded to himself and hung up the phone. He pulled his gun out of his pocket and shook out all five shells onto his desk. He looked up at Toni with *that* look.

"Come here," he said to her in a dead voice. "Pay attention."

Toni joined him at the desk and he ran her through the gun's simple operations three times, from safety to trigger pull. She dry-fired the revolver a dozen times to get the feel for the pull. He nodded. "Good. Now load it."

She pulled the cylinder and began to fill it with shells.

"No, no," he said gently. "Always leave the one under the hammer empty for safety. When you cock it, the cylinder revolves and it brings the first shell into position."

"Okay," she said. She spun the cylinder carefully, the way he'd showed her.

"Good," he said. "Good."

"Harry, do you really think-"

"I don't know," he said. "And I'm not taking any chances. You lock the door behind me when I leave, and you don't open it for anyone that isn't me."

"Harry-"

"You heard me," he said in that no-nonsense voice, and took out his key. He dropped it on the desk. He opened the bottom drawer, pushed papers aside, and drew out a second snub revolver. It was his backup piece, an old Colt Detective Special. He loaded it and slid it into the holster just behind his hip. He tugged on his coat and looked her in the eyes. "When I get back, we'll go for pizza," he said lightly.

She shook her head. "Bullshit. Don't do that."

"Do what?" he said.

"You're not sure you're coming back," she accused.

"I might not. But I might. Call it eighty-twenty for," he said. He went to her and kissed her. "Bet on me."

"I always bet on you, you idiot," she said. She clutched his arm. "But you better come back, or I'll be *pissed*."

He smiled. "Can't have that. I'll see you."

"Be careful, Harry," she said. "You know I-"

"I know," he said. "Don't say it, though. Bad luck."

The furrow between her eyes deepened as she frowned, but she said, "All right. I'll say it when you come back."

"Good enough," he said, and hesitated. Finally, he forced himself to speak, and said, "I will, too."

Her mouth dropped open and he smiled. He poured another cup of coffee for Jasper. He opened the door and closed it behind him, not looking at Toni again.

"Here you go," he said, handing the paper cup to Jasper.

"Thanks, Chief," the bum whispered. His dirty face stretched into a gapped grin. "You're a real humin bein."

"Don't tell anyone," Harry said, repeating his side of the worn ritual absently.

He walked quickly to Houston and grabbed a cab. He gave the cabbie the address. The ride wasn't even five minutes. It was far shorter than Harry would have liked. He wasn't ready for this… but he knew that no amount of time would help him be ready. He paid off the driver, walked up the steps of the run-down building and banged on the door. Footsteps, and a peek out the door through the ratty curtains. A nod. The door opened.

"Come in, Harry," Porter said.

Chapter Thirty

The kitchen was the least messy part of the tiny apartment, and Harry sat carefully in the rickety chair across the scummy table opposite Porter. Porter wore a tee shirt and jeans and his feet were bare. He wasn't carrying anything. He had turned his back on Harry, and Harry had seen all the way around his waist.

"I knew you'd get it eventually," Porter said. His distant eyes were alarming to Harry. He didn't seem upset at all, but he wasn't all the way there. He looked everywhere in the room except at Harry. Harry kept his coat well back from the gun on his hip, and his hand didn't stray far. He examined the scratches across Porter's arms and looked again at his face and those blank eyes.

"Do you want to tell me why, Porter?" Harry asked.

"Not really," Porter said. "How'd you get it so fast? That's what I want to know."

Harry shrugged. "There's a scuff mark on my floor back at the office. I thought it was dirt, but it was blood. Came from your shoe. Gene thought you'd walked in it at the scene, but you already had it on your shoe. Then I called Frannie."

Porter closed his eyes.

Chapter Thirty-One

He said, "Frannie, it's Harry. I have a couple questions for you. They're about Porter."

Her voice was cold. "Harry, I don't know…"

"Frannie, come on. It's important and I don't have time," he insisted.

"Fine," she said. "Ask."

"You said he was cheating on you. A lot of times. Who's the girl?" Harry asked.

"What makes you think there was just one, Harry?" Frannie said bitterly. "And it wasn't *just* a girl."

"What do you mean?"

"I mean, he didn't just find a secretary or some well-stacked fellow cop, Harry. He was screwing *hookers*!" Frannie snapped. "God knows how many street trash whores he was putting it to! He wouldn't even be honest about that! I had to-"

She stopped, disgusted, and finally finished her sentence with a choking, snarling bark. "-I had to get *tested*, Harry. I had to go to my doctor and get tested for VD. Just in *case*. You know how that made me *feel*?"

Harry stared at the top of his desk and tried to think of a response. Finally, he asked, "I… uh… how do you know for sure?"

"He talks in his sleep, Harry," she said.

"Jesus, Frannie," Harry said.

"Now you know," she said in a brittle voice. "Now you know why I threw his ass out and never looked back. He couldn't stop with the hookers. I would… I

317

would have *tried*, Harry, but he wouldn't stop. He… so many names… he'd call out so many names in his sleep."

"Frannie, I'm sorry," he said. His skin crawled at what she had told him. So many names. "I didn't mean to bring up painful shit, but I had to know."

"Yeah, sure."

"Look, I have some things to do, but as soon as I can, I'm going to come around again. I want to introduce you to Toni," Harry said.

"I'd like that," Frannie said.

"Me, too."

They were silent for a moment. Frannie broke it with a question. "What are you going to do, Harry?"

He hesitated, and said, "Frannie, I don't know."

"You sound like you're lying, Harry. But all right. Anything else?"

"No," he said. "Thank you."

"Goodbye, Harry."

"Goodbye, Frannie," Harry said, and hung up the phone. He stared at it for a moment, and then looked up at Toni. She had wide eyes and her mouth was open.

"Harry?"

"Yeah," he said. "Porter."

"Porter… it-it can't be," she said, but she didn't sound convinced.

"Why?" he asked.

"I… because… he and I…"

"I know. You're probably not the only one he… he was with and didn't kill. I don't know why he's doing it. But I know he isn't going to do it anymore."

318

He picked up the phone and called the station. The desk sergeant knew him and verified what Gene had told him; that Porter had left for the day, and was 10-7A, out of service, home.

"I need a favor, Clancy," Harry said. "I need his address."

"Why?"

"I'm throwing him a surprise party," Harry said. "For his birthday."

"Oh," the clerk said. "Okay… uh, hold on."

Harry waited while Clancy looked up the address. It was a tenement a little uptown from Harry. He knew the place.

"Thanks, Clancy," Harry said. "Mum's the word."

"You got it," Clancy said, "long as I get an invite."

"I'll put you down. Later." Harry hung up.

Toni looked into Harry's eyes, and didn't like what she saw. "Harry… what are you going to do? Arrest him?"

"I'm not a cop," he said. "I want answers. Then I'll decide what to do."

"You're going to go after him?"

"Yes."

"What if he's not there?" she asked. "What if he… what if he comes here?"

"Come here," he said to her in a deadly voice. "Pay attention."

She said fearfully, "Why?"

"I need to show you how to use a gun."

Chapter Thirty-Two

Porter nodded. "Smart. Giving her a gun. I wouldn't go after her, of course, but I *could* have. You know, you probably saved her life, Harry."

Harry didn't say anything.

"I don't... I don't pick them," Porter continued. "I mean, I don't set out to just... you know... *kill* someone. Most of the time, it's just a fuck. But sometimes... I just *have* to kill them. I don't know until I see them. And I guess your girl could have gone either way. But you got her off the street. Probably just in time. I think I meant to take her. Instead, I had to get those others."

Porter looked up at Harry. He looked up with a stranger's face. It was a face full of features Harry knew, but they were still wrong. Stranger's eyes.

"It's not personal, you know. I just... just *do* it. Because I can't *not*," Porter said with a helpless little shrug.

"How long?" Harry asked. "How many girls?"

"Oh, not as long as you'd think. You don't need to pull any cases further back than nine years," Porter said. "Nine years almost exactly. My first kill was in December of '71. It was an accident. I didn't *mean* to kill her, but I did. So I panicked and dumped the body. Waited for them to come get me. Instead, they *assigned* me to the case. And I dead-ended it. The only clues I had didn't lead anywhere, because they didn't point to me."

Harry shook his head. "How many cases did you get that you *caused*, Porter?"

"Lot of them. It was easy to derail them. Pimp did it. Homeless junkie did it. Street beefs. Suspects. Interrogations. Lineups. It was like taking candy from a baby," Porter chuckled. Harry's glower killed the chuckle on Porter's lips.

"How many?" Harry demanded. "Total."

"I didn't do it often. Maybe thirty, all told. Most of the time I'm fine. Every once in a while, I need to do the *other*. Sometimes I fuck 'em, sometimes I fuck 'em *up*." Porter shrugged. "It happens."

Harry's mouth dropped open in shock. Porter smiled.

"Come on, Harry. Don't look at me like that. I *know* I'm nuts. I've known my whole life. Frannie... now Frannie almost tumbled. I say their names in my sleep, I guess. She thought they were girls I'd *screwed*. The number of girls I screwed is *way* more than the ones I... you know... did the *other* to."

"Killed, Porter," Harry snapped. "Say it!"

"Okay, okay," Porter said with a charming, remorseless smile. "I killed them. I killed them."

Harry couldn't understand it. He felt as though he were dreaming. Like it was a bad dream, except it wasn't. Not at all. He said, "You really don't feel anything? Remorse? Guilt?"

"Why should I?" Porter asked him. "They weren't anything to me."

Harry started to argue and realized suddenly that it didn't matter. Nothing he said would matter. He shook his head. "I just... I don't understand you. And I'm glad I don't."

Porter smiled. "You know, I thought about pinning it on you."

Harry blinked. "What?"

"Yeah," Porter said. "I was starting to build a case. You were the one. Everyone knew you'd slipped a gear after you couldn't be a real cop any more. So I started planting seeds. I thought I could get it all under the rug, get you taken in, and been home free. No one would have been any the wiser. But you wouldn't take the bait. And then you actually started to *work* on it. Harry, you'd have made a good detective."

Harry couldn't think of anything to say. His mouth went dry as he realized it could have worked.

"What?" Porter asked, sounding concerned. "What's wrong?"

"Porter, you crazy son of a bitch, I thought we were *friends*," Harry said. "I thought we-"

"Are you kidding me?" Porter barked a laugh. "Friends? You're a fucking basket case. You're pathetic. I couldn't *stand* being around you, Harry. You never actually came out and said anything, but you *look* like you're just whining about every goddamned thing in the world! Sitting in your miserable office, finding fucking lost cats and dogs. You're a fucking joke!"

Porter slammed a hand onto the table.

"Fucking joke. And then you got this girl. You started to wake up. You started being a person again. If you'd just fucking stayed dead none of this would have happened. I could have done what I wanted, and then been *done*," Porter snarled.

"Done?" Harry said. "Done? You pin your shit to me, and you're just going to walk away?"

"That was the plan," Porter said. "This was my chance. And then you started poking around. And Gene found his neat little pile of bodies all connected.

And your girl… she… she made you *better*. Better than you were. And this last bitch… she fought me. They never fought before-"

"I'm *glad* she did," Harry snarled.

"Whatever. She had that fucking brain thing, and fought me, scratched me, screwed everything up. You, her, all of it screwed up. It's your fault. Your fault I can't *quit*. You and the last one screwed everything up. So now I can't quit. Now I have to *stop*," Porter said.

"What?" Harry asked, confused.

"I'm not quitting because I *want* to," Porter said reasonably. "I'm being *forced* to quit. It doesn't *mean* anything if I'm forced to do it."

"You've lost your fucking mind, Porter," Harry said. "You're Goddamned crazy."

"Maybe, maybe not. But now…" Porter looked at Harry with genuine worry on his face. "Harry, did… did you call it in?"

Harry drew his gun, like he'd practiced it a thousand times smoothly and cleanly. He leveled it at Porter and hauled back the hammer. "No, I didn't."

Porter's eyes began to tear. "Can I… Can I do it?"

"You want to call yourself in?" Harry asked.

"No," Porter said. "I want to put an end to it. You know what prison is like for a cop, Harry. And you know what it's like when we find out someone's turned against the Blue."

Harry nodded. If Porter was lucky, someone would shank him the first couple of days. If he were unlucky, they'd keep him alive to use as a toilet. Pass him around. He wouldn't wish it on anyone, but Harry wasn't letting him walk, either. Porter has ceased to merit considerations like that.

"What do you have in mind?" he asked Porter.

"My gun's over in my coat," he said, pointing. Harry didn't look away, and the Colt didn't waver from Porter's heart. "I'll do it right."

"How do I know you're not trying to make a play, Porter?"

"I understand how you could not trust me," Porter said, "but I give you my word, Harry. I only need one."

Harry stared at him, considering. It *would* be easier for everyone. Sure, it wouldn't close the cases, but all the people that needed to know would know.

"Please?" Porter asked.

"Slowly."

He tracked Porter as the man went to retrieve his pistol. He did it right, with two fingers on the barrel. He brought it back to the table and set it down and then he took his seat again. His hands were flat on the surface of the table.

Harry cleared his throat. "Porter…"

"Yes, Harry?"

"Do you… do you want me to stay?" Harry asked.

"You'd do that?" Porter asked. "You'd trust me to do it alone?"

"If it came to that, yes," Harry said. "You aren't going anywhere, and I could dime you out in a heartbeat. But if you want privacy, you can have it."

It was tempting, but Porter shook his head. "Why would you stay?"

Harry told him, "Porter, you may not be my friend, but I'm *yours*. I'll stay. But if you make a move-"

"I know, I know. That's okay with me," Porter assured him. He stared at the gun for a long time. Harry steeled himself for the worst. Porter picked up the gun carefully, pointing it away from Harry. Harry's finger tightened on the Colt's trigger.

Porter took a deep, deep breath. "Harry, tell Frannie-"

"I will," Harry lied.

Porter smiled and nodded. One second he was there, and one second later he was gone. The gun went into his mouth smoothly, he pulled the trigger, and his body jumped. The automatic clattered to the floor. Everything Porter Rockwell had been emptied all over the back wall of the dingy kitchen in the shabby tenement apartment. Harry eased his own hammer back down and slid the gun into his holster. He got up and went to the door. He didn't look back. It wasn't a great neighborhood. Someone might call the police, but it could be a couple days. He walked down the street, not hurrying, not dawdling. At the corner he fished a dime out of his pocket, wiped it down, and dropped it. He waited for the answer.

"911, what's your emergency?"

Harry said in a high voice, "Hi, yeah, I just heard a gun go off in my neighbor's place? Like, loud? It was a gun, I think. I mean, loud-"

"What is the address, sir?"

Harry gave them the address.

"Can I get your name, sir?" the operator asked. Harry hung up the handset, and picked it back up. He wiped it carefully and set it back on the cradle. He stuck his hands deeply into the pockets of his overcoat and walked home.

Chapter Thirty-Three

All the way back, he was thinking about Porter, thinking about Toni, thinking about nothing. Everything and nothing at all. When he got to the corner of Elizabeth Street, the flashing lights of the ambulance parked in front of his shop caused him to break into a frantic run. Slipping and sliding precariously, he pelted down the street and skidded to a halt next to the ambulance. Three paramedics worked on Jasper, but they were ceasing their efforts just as he got there. He looked around and saw Toni nearby, his heart trip-hammered and galloped in his chest. The sudden rush of adrenaline made him sick and he ran to her, pulling her into a rough embrace.

"I know you said stay inside, but it was cold," she said. "I t-took him a cup, but he wasn't breathing, Harry."

"It's okay," he said.

"I called the ambulance. I didn't know what else to do, Harry," she stammered. "He wasn't b-breathing."

"It's okay," he said again and hugged her to him. She had no coat and didn't seem to notice the cold, but she shivered all the same. He pulled his around her, and they watched as the medics covered Jasper. They loaded him up, carefully bundling him onto a stretcher and lifting him into the back of the ambulance.

"He was old," the medic said to them apologetically. "His heart probably gave out."

Harry nodded, and felt warmth and damp on his chest as Toni cried.

"Did you know him?" the medic asked.

"He's lived out here for as long as I have," Harry said. "I- we- give him coffee."

The medic smiled. "Good for you. It probably kept him going. He didn't feel anything, I'm positive. He just went to sleep."

They finished their chores and slowly drove away. Harry led Toni inside.

"Harry?" she asked. She didn't ask him the next question because she didn't have to.

"It's done," he said to her. "Taken care of. You can call your girls and tell them. Tell them they're safe. He's dead. Porter's dead."

She nodded solemnly. She bit her lip and said, "I-"

"I love you," he said quickly, beating her to the finish line. "You know that."

She beamed at him through the tears. "I know," she said.

"I just… I don't know what I've been waiting for," he said. "But I'm done. I'm done waiting. I'm done being *asleep*. I want to be awake."

She blinked. "Asleep?"

"Just drifting through my life. I'm not a cop anymore. I'm done with it. I want to have a new life. A better life," he said. "And I want you to be a part of it."

She smiled up at him. "Harry, I always *was*. I've been yours since you saved me."

"Toni, I saved you, and you saved me. We're even," he said.

"I don't owe you anything, and you don't owe me anything," she told him. "I know that. And I also know it's bullshit. I'm always going to owe you. And you're always going to owe me. And that's okay."

He shrugged. "Maybe."

"Anyhow, you promised me pizza," she said, and her voice held a ghost of that old flippant, sassy attitude.

Harry smiled at her and realized he felt lighter than he had in years. So many things he carried with him were gone now, and he felt light as air. Lighter than he might ever have felt. If he hadn't been wounded, he would still be a cop. Probably a detective. And unmarried. Alone. Lonely, although he hadn't realized it then. He was so alone. *Had been*, he corrected. *Until her*. He hadn't always appreciated her, hadn't been nice every time, but she had always been there, joking, laughing, and in his face when he needed it. She'd changed him, had *helped* him change, and he hadn't even realized it. He smiled at her and she smiled back, and realized that the weight on him hadn't just lessened. She'd picked it up and taken it from him.

"Sure," he said. "Pizza. I mean, you can certainly have pizza. That's an option."

"What are the other options?" she asked.

"Well," he temporized. "It's poker night. But we have three or four hours to kill. We could go get pizza *now*, or we could go to bed, and get pizza later for the group."

Her mouth dropped open and her eyebrows climbed. She wanted to shout and dance, but instead she matched his playful tone with her own, licked her lips and said, "Bed? But Harry… I'm not very tired."

He took her hand. "Me either."

She squeezed his hand and they went into the old restaurant that had become their office, that had become their home, and closed the door.

The End

Author's Note

Thank you for reading this far.

The world of Harry and Toni is one that has fascinated me for most of my life. New York City is a distinct personality. It is not a symbiote. The City does not care if you live or die. It does not care if you win or lose. The City is the City not because of the people that live there, but despite them. That personality has changed over the decades, but only in so many ways. New York is a city that merely adds new layers to the overall gestalt.

The original port city still lives. The back streets still carry the faint whiff of the desperation, danger, and brutality of the Depression. The buildings change faces, grow taller, and the bones of the original still show through the new flesh.

The late seventies in New York were a strange blend of old and new. Money began taking over, but the old guard still held sway. Times Square was still a deadly cesspool. Drugs began to wash through the streets like a loathsome high tide.

The streets still belonged to the lifers. The men and women who'd been born, raised, and would die New Yorkers. The cabbies, the street vendors, the hookers. The dockers. The construction workers. The muscle. The pimps. Bus drivers. Cops. The Mafia families were still coming to terms with the changing times, unwilling to believe the City would change.

The beginning of the Eighties were almost a dark before the dawn. Just before the hippies gave way to the yuppies, before Wall Street became the new Mafia, before the gritty, tone-filled streets began to give way to urban renewal... before the City started to accept that it was time to clean up, of course... there was a window of despair, pragmatism, and relentless apathy that signaled the end of a very particular era.

The world Harry and Toni inhabit is similar to the Last Age of many cities long gone. In those dying times, the inhabitants can often sense that something is about to change everything. That the world they understand is about to be replaced with a new beast. Something feral and young, ready to fight to the death over every little thing.

This air, this feeling, is the air that I breathe when I write about the world these two try to survive in. When the words come, and the pages take shape, I can feel that mixture of hope, determination, and desperation that comes with knowing that the ledge upon which you stand has started to grow narrow.

That edge is where they must exist. The fear of falling is why they fight so hard. Even *they* know that you can't hold on forever. When it's gone, so too will they be.

But for now, they live.

Aaron S Gallagher
Visit my website at www.aaronsgallagher.com

Also by the Author

Made in the USA
Las Vegas, NV
09 December 2021

36895860R00187